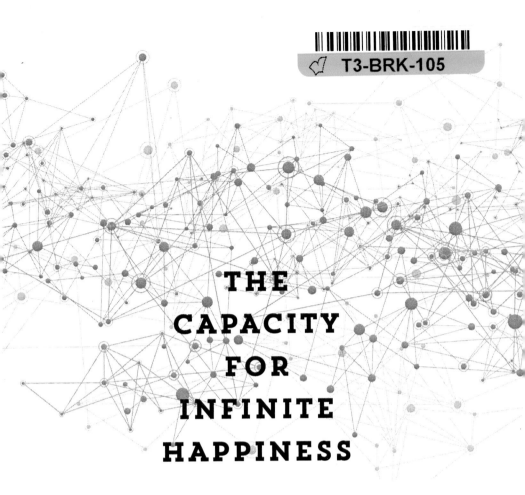

THE
CAPACITY
FOR
INFINITE
HAPPINESS

THE CAPACITY FOR INFINITE HAPPINESS

ALEXIS VON KONIGSLOW

Buckrider Books is an imprint of Wolsak and Wynn Publishers.

Cover image: Mike Kukucska
Cover design: Ingrid Paulson
Interior design: Leigh Kotsilidis
Author photograph: Julia Park Photography
Typeset in Book Antiqua, Trend Slab One, Trend Sans One, Skia
Printed by Ball Media, Brantford, Canada

   Canadian   Patrimoine
Heritage   canadien

The publisher gratefully acknowledges the support of the Canada
Council for the Arts, the Ontario Arts Council and the Canada Book Fund.

Buckrider Books
280 James Street North
Hamilton, ON
Canada L8R 2L3

Disclaimer
This is a work of fiction. Names, characters, places, events and incidents
are either the products of the author's imagination or used in a fictitious
manner.

Library and Archives Canada Cataloguing in Publication

Von Konigslow, Alexis, author
    The capacity for infinite happiness / Alexis Von Konigslow.

ISBN 978-1-894987-97-4 (pbk.)

    I. Title.

PS8643.O535C37 2015   C813'.6   C2015-900833-6

This book is for Oliver and Jake, and my family

It's dedicated to the memory of Margaret and Ruth

BEFORE EVERYTHING

BLIMA, 1928

"Pay attention," said the tall man.

He was so long that he seemed to be folded into the hallway. He was standing close to Blima's mother, his big hands around her smaller ones, pressing papers into her palms. Blima had seen this man before, and she hadn't liked him then either. She backed away, quietly so that they wouldn't know she was there.

"Ayala, I need you to listen to me," the man said again.

Ayala bowed into his chest. Blima shivered.

"I don't want you to panic, or pretend that you're bored. Here's what I want you to do. When the officials ask to see your papers, I need you to pinch the little girl, pinch her hard. Don't tell your husband that you're going to do it. That way, she'll be crying, you'll both be concerned, everyone will want the scene to be over."

Blima crouched down. She was the only little girl in the house.

"Also, make sure that your shirt is unbuttoned," the man said, touching her mother's blouse. "That will help."

"I don't want to do this," said Ayala.

"As a plan, it's perfectly safe. You'll send these back by post. We'll be together again before the end of the year."

"And what about Misha? What about Max, Raisa, Efim?"

"I'll bring them with me."

"I can't just leave."

"I'll find a way to get them out. If anyone can do it, I can. Things will carry on just as they have been. This is a momentary change."

Blima crept away. Sometimes, the tall man kissed her mother. Sometimes the little boy with the ice blue eyes appeared out of nowhere. Blima didn't want any part of it.

When Ayala came to find Blima some time later, she'd been hiding forever, was ready to be found.

"Pay attention," said Ayala.

Blima sat up, and all the dust particles she'd been counting scattered. She crawled out from under the table and scrambled onto the chair across from her mother.

"I want you to practise your spelling," said Ayala. "I want you to write our family name."

Pride welled in Blima. She could do this. She'd known how to write her name for months, forever. She wrote it out in measured letters, careful not to smudge the ink. Then her mother crossed it out and wrote something new beside it.

"I want you to write our name like this."

Blima puzzled over the letters, familiar somehow, but wrong. "That's not our name."

"Do what I ask."

"But that spells something different."

Blima wrote her name again. She turned the paper around, hopeful, but Ayala drew a stroke right through it.

"This isn't fair."

"Who told you that anything would be?" said Ayala.

Blima slid off the chair and inched toward the door, wiping hot tears off her cheek. Nobody had told her things should be fair. It was just something she knew.

"Life will never be fair. And we will never be safe. There

are always people just outside the door. There will always be another threat."

"I know that," said Blima.

"This is how we write our name from now on," said Ayala, writing the word again. "If I ever catch you writing our name in the old way, I'll take out the strap."

Blima rushed back to the table and pushed the paper off. It drifted. For a moment, she and her mother watched it together. Then it touched the floor with a shush.

Ayala stood. "Things in this world are not immutable," she said.

Then Blima watched as she disappeared right out of the room. A few seconds later, a door slammed shut somewhere in the inner house.

IF AN OLD MAN APPEARS, YOU HAVE TO FOLLOW

HARPO MARX, 1933

Harpo felt tugged along, like he was attached to a string and someone at the other end was pulling. He felt like one of those wooden ducks with wheels that tenement families gave their kids instead of pets, and, right now, the string was leading him on a tour of the waterfront.

He slowed, to test it out, and there it was again. So off he went.

His life wasn't working. That was the lesson learned, the great discovery. He was very different from his dad, and his father had been by far the better man. But he couldn't think that much about it right now because he was feeling pulled into the woods.

He hurried along the path, up a gentle incline full of weeds and spots of light like pennies that were less bright now than when he'd started out. It must be getting late. He must be getting hungry. Harpo slowed as he passed the lodge's canoe shed, then tripped over a broken oar, propelled forward again. No water sports. He tried to stop at the equipment shed, but found himself stumbling forward faster instead. No fishing either. That one was okay. He hadn't had the stomach for fishing since that trip to Montauk anyway. Now he could hear the bustling of the people who'd been packed in the lodge last night like saltine crackers in a great tin can. He'd bet they were whooping it up on the waterfront now, with their deck chairs and bathing suits and the little martinis with snaking orange peels. His brothers were probably out there. They might be missing him. He kept moving.

Finally, in a clearing, Harpo stopped and felt no desire to move forward. The rope was slack. So he sat down on a fallen tree. He didn't know what to do next. He needed to change his life. That was clear. But how did you do that? He slapped his pockets, felt for the notepad and pen. There were concrete things he could be doing. He could write to Susan. He'd brought paper after all. He could pretend he was practising his letters, everyone laughed at that line. He could combine the two. Right now L was his favourite letter, L for love, but no, that wasn't enough to justify all that postage. Besides, he'd have to write more than one letter to fix the mess he'd made. Susan was sore. He just hoped she wasn't moving on. Or he could try to write another script instead. Maybe the Marx Brothers weren't as finished as everyone said.

Harpo sighed. His father would have known what to do.

At least he'd finally made it to the lodge that everyone talked about. He was here because this was where he belonged. He was here because he couldn't go anywhere else. He was a Jew. The other resorts wouldn't take him. He was really here because there were beautiful women around. One more wild weekend. One final blowout. One last three-day-long party and he'd consider settling down, finally, just like Frenchie had wanted. And in the meantime he wouldn't have to feel all alone. He'd just have to get himself ready. He'd just have to work himself up to it, if he wanted to go on a proper bender with his brothers.

So he sat back. He could see the lake a little bit, or was that the river, and a sunset, a streak of wicked orange spread over a purple sky, a layer of marmalade over raspberry jam.

He waited for the old magic, the predatory pull. Nothing happened.

When an old man walked out of the forest, Harpo wasn't surprised. He scooted over on his log to give the man room, ready for the company.

"How do you feel?" said the old man as he settled himself beside Harpo.

"Pardon me?"

"What I mean to ask is, how are you holding up?"

"What?" This man couldn't know about Frenchie. It had hit the papers of course, but the papers had all reported that Harpo Marx's father had just died and Harpo looked nothing like the Harpo Marx from the pictures. He hadn't packed the raincoat and fright wig, and without those, he was just a scrawny Jewish man.

"It's okay," said the old man. "You don't have to tell me yet."

"Okay."

"I don't mind." The old man stared. Harpo got lost in his expression. His hair was white and grey and everywhere, and there was something familiar about him, about that face like an old pillow.

"Do I know you?" said Harpo.

"That depends. You'll have to tell me who you are and then I can say if I know you."

"Who am I?" Harpo thought about his name in Cyrillic, how it looked like it spelled something completely different. "I'm Exapno Mapcase," he said.

"Nope."

"Exapno Mapcase, secret agent."

"I don't think so."

He could have been from the tenements of New York, this man. He looked like Uncle Harold a little bit, or Henry, Aunt Hattie's boyfriend, or that other guy who lived in the Bronx. He was taller, and he didn't have that slightly sour smell, but even so. Harpo loved him immediately.

"What's your name, really?" asked the old man.

"Pinky," said Harpo, for his character in *Duck Soup*. "No, Harpo MacMarx."

"That's closer," the old man said. And then he smiled, and Harpo smiled right along with him. There was something about that face, all those wrinkles around eyes blue and bright like a little kid's. "Try again."

"I like you," said Harpo.

"Fine. If that's the best I can get. I see now why you don't talk much."

"Are you staying here too?"

"I'm not staying here." The old man hopped off the log. "I'm going for a walk. You're coming with me. Neither of us is staying here. Why would we when I know a better place to go?"

Harpo couldn't think of an answer, so he slid down too, then followed.

They left the path, then pushed their way into the dark part of the woods, in which direction Harpo couldn't say. He'd guess north, by the way the moss was growing on the trees, or did moss grow facing south, or was that even moss? He kept walking behind the magnetic old man, although he heard a funny kind of rushing sound now.

"Do you hear that?" Harpo stumbled to catch up. "Should we turn back?"

The old man didn't even slow, even though the sounds were getting louder. Harpo pictured wild animals, or maybe marching men, goose-steppers out of rhythm.

Finally, they came to a cascade, and the sound resolved itself into a rush of water, a tiny little waterfall with a roar like Niagara Falls. Imagine that.

Harpo scrambled up the little incline after the old man, who was standing at the top now, staring down. "Can I ask you a question?" he said, reaching the top, no, the *summit*. "I need advice."

"How well do you know the Kogans?" asked the old man.

"Who?"

The old man fixed him with those deep blue eyes. "The people in the Jewish lodge."

"Oh. Of course. I met Sam when I checked in."

"Did you see his wife, Ayala?"

"I saw a picture of her on the desk, and he introduced me to that. He said the real lady probably wouldn't come downstairs much. She's beautiful though. She could be in the pictures."

"That much I know for myself. I have eyes. They have windows. I know what she looks like."

"The rumour is that she doesn't come down from the attic much," said Harpo. "She's been a bit atticky for a while, that's what I heard."

"They have daughters too," said the old man.

"Little ones?" Harpo hadn't seen any little kids. "Do you know them, the Kogans?"

"I like the look of them. I like the way they look as a family."

"Oh," said Harpo. "I like families too. I'm from a big one. Four brothers, two parents."

"Lots of cousins?"

"You could fill up New Jersey."

"I had three brothers and five sisters," said the old man, "but only one daughter." Then he patted Harpo on the back. "I like the look of you too. How are you feeling today? You never said."

"What?"

"I've been thinking about it," said the man, "and you might as well call me William."

YOU HAVE TO FIND TWO KINDS OF LOVE

EMILY, 2003

Emily crept to the kitchen, then up the stairs and through the hallway, then down again toward registration. There must be a vault somewhere with all the family documents. The registration area was too wide open. Nobody would leave birth certificates here. She moved on. The first visit to the lodge that she remembered had been when she was six years old, when she'd visited with her parents. She remembered dragging a towel down this narrow stairway. Corners had been difficult. But still. The lodge had been fun.

She stopped at the shut office door.

On that same trip, she'd visited her grandfather, Papa Moshe, in his office. Every time he'd moved toward her, she'd cried, and her father had had to pick her up. All the adults minus Moshe had laughed. Jonah had been there too, of course, a little boy hovering in the doorway. The door was locked. That boded well. The filing cabinets were locked too, from what she remembered. That was also a good sign, but hard to work around. She'd never figured out how to pick the locks. There might be other hiding places around, however.

Emily crept to the room of windows next, then stopped. Jonah was in there. Jonah, no longer the little sapling of a cousin she'd followed around all the time. He was tall, and his sandy hair was blonder than she'd remembered, and he was tan somehow, even though the season hadn't started yet. Emily felt something, that regular tug toward him, the slight pull of gravity that she must be feeling because objects in space always attract each other. Yesterday, her horoscope had said, "you will soon meet your deity, your perfect power, the person to whom you can tell all your stories." If she could choose the one person she could tell all her problems to, it would be him. So she hid behind the door and searched her thoughts for a way to start: family (no), math (no), ghosts (nope), Harpo (absolutely not). She wanted so badly to tell him everything—that her mother regretted parenthood, that she was MIA from her job—but best not lead with those things. Nobody liked problem enumerators. Nobody liked other people's problems at all, in fact. So she found nothing socially appropriate to say. Then she saw what he was doing, bending over to look at a notebook she'd left open on a table, and so Emily found herself walking right into the room.

Jonah stepped back abruptly, nearly tripping over a rug. "I was just wondering what you're up to."

"Math," she said. If she grabbed the book, he'd notice. She wouldn't have left it open at an inappropriate page. She wouldn't have written his name, say, or a love note in mathematical notation or something equally bizarre, and just walked away. She was more careful than that. "I'm finishing my master's."

"What kind of math is it?" asked Jonah. "Or is math all the same?"

"It's not the same." His eyes were bright blue and shining, and was he teasing her? Emily looked down again. "There's analysis," she said, watching the swirling patterns on the hardwood floor. "Algebra. Topography type of stuff. Classification, I guess." Classification could be considered math, and she'd spent the entire morning at it, quantifying the impropriety of noticing that a cousin was cute. It had to do with the degree of relation, she'd decided, the length of the shortest path that connected them on the family tree. Emily to her mother to her aunt to Jonah would be terrible, but she didn't have an aunt, so that was out. The path had to be longer than four, and since path lengths have to increase by twos, they weren't first cousins. At least she'd established that.

"So which one do you do?" asked Jonah.

"I study connections," said Emily. "It's called graph theory. I'll show you." She grabbed her book. She drew in vertices and edges connecting them, the most basic kind of graph, and felt a hot swell of relief. She had the notebook back at least. "You connect things, then count the degree of the vertices, the number of points they attach to. Then there's calculations, statistics."

"That looks like your family." Jonah pointed to the open page and Emily saw Doran Baruch's name and some half-completed diagrams, nothing incriminating though, that she could see. She'd also been piecing together how he might fit into the family, but he'd stumped her. She couldn't figure out the connection.

"You *can* represent a family tree like a graph," she said. "I'm kind of obsessed with that right now."

"That's a weird obsession."

"Graphs aren't what people say they are," Emily said quickly. "Graphs are really just points and lines, called vertices and edges. You can draw one vertex to show all the members of a family. And then draw edges to show how they're related, count the connections." She drew vertices and connected them. Then she labelled them, with her name, her mother's, her grandmother's, up until her Papa William, because that was all she knew so far. "I want to use the family tree as an illustration for my thesis. But things weren't making sense, so I came here, to figure out what's off in my family representations." She wanted to tell Jonah more than that, why she'd postponed her thesis defence and the start of her Ph.D.

She looked up at him again, hopeful.

"That isn't right," said Jonah.

"What isn't?"

"That line. Edge." Jonah touched the page. "That one." He traced a finger along the Ayala-to-William edge, absently touching the side of Emily's hand. Her fingers tingled.

"William," Jonah said. "He doesn't belong there."

"He's my great-great-grandfather. He was my great-grandma Ayala's father."

"William's related to my family, not yours."

Jonah took the pencil and drew his own graph. "I looked into my own family tree a while back. I wanted to see—I went back to, like, 1888 or something. No, earlier, because William was born in 1860, and I found his parents too. Anyway. William had one daughter, that's my great-grandmother. Then he got a son-in-law. That's all."

"That can't be right." Emily studied the two graphs side by side. "But that's exactly what I kept finding. Connections in the family tree just don't make sense. Nothing was working out. We can't be connected before that, because my side was in Russia then."

"You know William had five brothers and three sisters? No, three brothers and five sisters." He drew vertices but didn't label them. "Anyway, a lot of siblings. They all died before they turned thirty, and their parents died right after that. William was left all alone on the island, except for his wife and kid. It must have been weird to go from a huge family all living together in one house to just a couple people."

"How do you know all this?" asked Emily.

Abruptly, Jonah stepped back. "We're not related," he said. "You do know that, right?"

"Then what connects our families?"

"We're neighbours. That's all. I checked. That's what I was looking into."

"Our connection is geographic?" In her notebook, there were

two separate tree graphs, no vertices touching, no physical connections at all.

"For God's sake," said Jonah. "Don't look so stunned. Sometimes *cousins* is just a thing that people say."

"Oh." They weren't really related. That opened up a new space of possibility.

"So why are you back?" he said.

"Because my mother just told me that she'd never wanted kids, that having me was her great regret."

This time, Jonah looked lost. Why did she always just admit to everything? Other people found graceful ways to segue into conversations.

"I mean I came back for the Seder," she said. "I wanted to be with my family." Then Emily found herself walking again, drifting back to the dining room.

"Don't believe everything your cousin tells you," said Emily's grandmother Blima, as she set the Haggadahs on the central dining-room table. "Relation is much more complicated than just biology."

"I'm only asking about the biology," said Emily.

"You can do the seating for tonight."

"Fine, I can do that. I'll print name cards. But I need information because I want to draw little graphs on them, family trees that represent the biology. You and Auntie Sonja were born to Ayala and Sam Kogan?"

"I'm the older sister," said Blima. "Also wiser. Also, I know more."

"I knew that you're the eldest."

"Old is old to young people. I just want to remind you that there are degrees of it."

"Ayala had four siblings. Max, Robert, Efim and Raisa. You were born in Russia. And Auntie Sonja was born in Kingston?"

"I can vouch for your Auntie Sonja, but for me, I can't remember. I was very young at the time."

"Can you please be serious?" said Emily

And then Blima shuffled back to the table, carrying a big white box. "Blessed are the Pacific Tribes, for they dine with the saints."

"You were born in 1924, and Auntie Sonja was born in 1929."

"It's a family tradition to use your Great-grandma Ayala's good china for Passover's extra setting."

"I know —"

"It's not every family who serves Elijah. You'll find lots of Jews who only pour him a drink. But he needs something to line his stomach. That's what our mother always said."

"When was Great-grandma Ayala born?"

Blima rested the box on the table, then pulled out a big plate, a little plate and a delicate little bowl. "You know, sometimes you called her the old Bubbie. I was the new Bubbie. It's been a long time since I was the new anything." Dark hair, pink cheeks, perfectly put together in slacks and a sweater, she looked exactly the same as she'd always looked, if slightly more compact. She looked delicate now. And maybe she did look a little bit old. Maybe Emily had been away too long.

"I do remember Great-grandma Ayala, you know," said Emily. She used to love to come here to see her. They'd watch Marx Brothers movies together in her bedroom. Harpo was Emily's favourite, so great-grandma Ayala would make up stories about him, like the ones where he got lost in the woods, where he battled the anti-Semites, where he fell in love with the sad lady he saw crying in a dirty window. Emily had brought her Marx Brothers DVDs this visit, to continue the tradition.

"These plates were hers," said Blima. "And now they're mine, and when I die they go to you, so soon they'll be yours."

"Not that soon."

"And they're not for use by just anyone. Especially not guests. They have germs and who knows who raised them. These plates, they're just for prophets and for anyone who isn't corporeal enough to scratch good china. In case I die, now you know how we do things in this family."

Emily fiddled with the cutlery. "Who is this guy who's coming tonight?" she asked innocently, as if she'd just heard that he was coming.

"His name is Doran Baruch."

"Is *he* a relative?" Emily had thought that he was one of Auntie Sonja's old boyfriends, but she might have misread the signs. He might be some long-lost relative, although romance and blood relations might not be mutually exclusive in this place. In all her research into lodge history, his was the name that had come up the most. That's all she really knew. "Would he be included in a family tree?"

"How is your work coming along?" said Blima.

"Fine," said Emily.

"It's your thesis, your mother said. What is it about?"

"I'm studying connectivity."

"That's not what I heard. Your mother said it was about the Internet."

"I did research on the Internet."

"That's fine," said Blima, and then she stared.

Emily didn't know what to say next. Did her grandmother want an explanation? Most people didn't. "I'm looking at the connectivity of people," she said after a moment. "I'm quantifying how people change each other."

"Go on."

"Oh," said Emily. Nobody ever asked her to do that. "Okay. I'm measuring social influence. The Knights of the Round Table were all influenced by King Arthur, and that's why they all went looking for the grail. That's a bad example. I don't know why I even thought of that one." She needed a central analogy for her work, some image that readers could understand, but that was a bad one. She'd been banking on the idea of family trees, of course, or of lodge history, that's the real reason she'd come, but she certainly couldn't tell her grandmother that.

"The writers of the Algonquin Round Table all influenced each other," Emily said suddenly. "That's probably a better illustration of what I'm doing." She might even look into that example more, because non-writers were part of that round table too. Harpo Marx was a part of it, even though he wasn't even thinking of writing at the time. He was only doing crossword puzzles and correspondence then. Maybe Emily could track the development of all the writing, or how Harpo's comedic sensibilities leaked from person to person, or maybe she'd just focus, like her advisor kept begging her to do, on the actual math.

"It's math," said Emily "It's really just math."

"Your mother said it was about social networking," said Blima. "On the Internet."

"That's where I get my data."

"Well you must be almost finished. Your mother said you just needed the quiet, and the lodge is just opening for the season. There aren't even guests yet. There's nothing here but quiet."

"I just got here. But I'm almost done. I'm working some last things out, I just need some help —"

"Maybe my Eliyahu can help you." Blima shuffled around the table again, straightening the napkins one by one. "Except if Elijah's spirit can find his way to our table after all that wine, then it really would be a Passover miracle. You see, lovie, every year, Elijah drinks with the Pacific Ocean Jews, whose geographic location allows them to dine first and be most blessed. Because that's where the sun sets first!"

"Are there even Jews on the Pacific Islands?"

"It's hard to find a safe place, I know. Even here. The Kingston folks are okay, but the people in the townships, well, you know. They're always closer than you think. Anyhow. Soon after the nightfall of the Tasmanian Jewish populations, Elijah gets lost in the region of the Himalayas. Every year, the same. He's *shikkered*, you see, because of all those families and all that wine, and most of it, I hate to tell you, is Manischewitz It reflects badly on our people, but there you have it."

"I like Manischewitz."

"Elijah generally wakes up in late April, in either a cave or in a motel with coin-operated beds."

"Can you please stop being weird?"

"Elijah has to drink with every Jewish family," said Blima, handing Emily the regular plates. "That's a lot of sacramental wine for just one prophet."

"Oh, of course," said Emily, as she snuck one more plate for her cousin Jonah and put it next to hers. She wanted to be close to him, to see what this lack of connection might mean.

"Hang on," said Blima, eyes narrowed. "Are you setting more places now?"

"Can we leave a place setting for any ghost?"

Blima brightened. "Of course we can set places for ghosts."

Emily smiled. Although if she could set a place for a ghost, Emily would invite Harpo Marx. Her thesis advisor might be right about her focus. She had to remember why she was here. "Do we have any old documents? I mean like passports, marriage records, birth certificates, death certificates."

"We might have kept some of those things. If they're important, we would have kept them in a safe place."

"Okay," said Emily. In her family's weird crossword-puzzle world, that probably meant that they were kept in a hidden safe somewhere. Then she felt the need to move well up in her, and then she was walking, and Blima, she saw out of the corner of her eye, was on the move too, creeping right out the door.

As Emily passed through the great hallway a few minutes later, she heard her grandmother again. "But this year *is* different," Blima was saying. "This family is different. Most of our history shouldn't be remembered. Things are hidden here, don't forget, and I don't know why I'd reconsidered that."

Emily stopped. There were hidden things.

"Do you remember when we got death threats?" said Blima "They still throw rocks, paint on the walls. There will always be angry voices right outside the door. Why had I thought the world would be gentler now?"

Emily crept on. If one person hides a thing, it's another person's job to find it. Hadn't that always been the rule?

"Are you still following Jonah around?" Emily's great-aunt Sonja called from inside the bathroom.

"I don't follow him," said Emily.

"You used to."

"Are we related to Papa William?" Emily sat down in Great-aunt Sonja's sitting room, on the overstuffed chair that had always been her favourite in the whole place. Then she shot up again and crept from one glass-topped table to another, from bookshelf to bookshelf. This was a perfect room for hidden things. She picked up a book, flipped through the pages. "Jonah seems to think we're not related."

"Related means a lot of things."

"I'm pretty sure it doesn't."

"Oh but you used to follow Jonah everywhere! Don't you remember? He's a very proficient young man now. Not educated, but he'll do okay in his own sort of way."

"Auntie!"

"We just have to remember not to use our standards when we think about him, that's all." Emily could hear the clink of ice in a highball glass. "Not everyone can aspire to the same things. And he'd be uncomfortable if we made him sit down. Anyhow, why doesn't your mother come to the Seder?"

"She knows she'd drink too much and argue with everyone."

"I wouldn't fight with Rebecca."

"She would probably fight with you." Maybe she regretted the entire family, not just her daughter.

"It's funny to think," said Sonja, "but Jonah used to follow you around too. Do you remember that?"

"Some things are starting to come back, I guess." There were little things that Emily was starting to remember, feelings mostly, colours. Certainly, she remembered *him*.

"Lovie," said Aunt Sonja, "could you help me in here?"

Emily followed the wall into the bathroom, touching the framed etchings lightly. They were too skinny to be safes. But even so. She used to do this a lot. She'd run her fingertips along the walls, to feel the textures and to look absorbed when she didn't want Jonah to know that she was feeling left out.

"I'm all in a state," said Sonja.

Emily blinked into the bright yellow bathroom. There was the powdery smell she remembered, the big oval mirror in its blue and gold mosaic frame. Sonja puttered from the sink to the cabinet to the sink again.

"Doran Baruch is coming tonight," said Sonja.

"Doran Baruch," said Emily. The name that showed up over and over. "Is he Jewish?" Because for some reason she thought that he might not be, yet another detail that had made his file stand out. The whole family was Jewish, obviously. All the old guests had been Jewish too. That had been the point.

"Is who Jewish?"

"Doran Baruch."

"He's close," said Sonja.

"What does that mean?"

"He's a goy with a Jewish last name. That's something that can happen. But you have to remember not to call him goy because we don't say that word in polite company. You can call him a Gentile, I think."

"I'll remember that."

"I haven't seen Doran Baruch in so many years. Maybe I should tidy."

"He's not going to see the inside of your bedroom."

"I don't know if he'll recognize me. Maybe I should put more makeup on my face. I'm feeling atticky, all of a sudden. Maybe I should clean more in here. That might help."

"Why would he see the inside of your bathroom?" Emily looked at her great-aunt's reflection — red cheeks, hair that was still blond, or dyed blond maybe, perfectly pressed jacket sleeve leaning against the gleaming countertop. She remembered sitting on that counter, lifting her arms and Auntie Sonja patting her stomach with a powder puff, the powder filling the air around her like a cloud.

"Well," said Sonja. "Your bubbie, her eyes are going, I think. She wears blue eyeshadow, and I don't think she knows what colour it is. It's blue like bluebells. That is not a colour for a face."

"Blue eyeshadow is in," said Emily.

"Usually, I tell her. But if she wears it tonight, I'm not going to say anything. I'll look better beside her if she looks like a Picasso portrait." Sonja turned back to her own reflection and clucked at it. "Anyhow," she said, "I need all the help I can get. I'm not what I was."

Emily's eyes wandered around the room, at the yellow tiles, the sparkling shower and the bath with clawed feet.

"This is just what happens when you get older," Sonja said. "You stop growing hair on your head, and you start growing a hair on your chin. Not many of them. Just the one. And it's long like a vine. That's what you have to look forward to when you get old."

"I can't wait."

"I don't want Doran to think I didn't take care for his visit."

"I thought he invited himself," Emily muttered.

Sonja smiled at Emily's reflection then cupped her cheek, her hand cool and soft. "That beautiful face," she said, "and those cheeks. I'd give anything for cheeks as red as those. You wouldn't know it now, but your bubbie and I were lookers too, when we were young. We were the legendary Kogan girls. There were songs written about us, but they weren't particularly good ones, so that was that."

"There were songs?"

"Lovie, I was known for dating every handsome young gentleman who came to the lodge."

"No!" said Emily, but of course she remembered. It was a story she loved.

"Oh yes. One man would drop me off at the front door, and then I would have to run to the back door to meet my next date there. And so it went every night until I met your great-uncle."

"What about Doran Baruch?"

"What about him?"

Emily had thought at first that Doran Baruch must have been one of the front-door suitors, a shy young man carrying a single daisy night after night. But he'd invited himself to a Seder, and that was too brazen for a man with a daisy. When she'd tracked him down over the Internet, she'd just asked for an interview, hadn't suggested he invite himself here before the season even started. Maybe he used to bring a rose. Roses were dangerous flowers. Maybe he was one of the back-door boyfriends, who dressed in fancy clothes and was exciting but had no scruples, who Great-aunt Sonja had had to trick and run away from in the night, leave lost in the woods while she giggled about them with her sister, safe in their bedroom. "Did you have a love affair with him too?"

"Who wasn't in love with him?" said Sonja, pulling out a tube of mascara. "It was hard not to be in love with Doran Baruch."

Emily pushed herself off the counter. She'd hoped for a no and a retelling of one of the lodge love stories, she'd wanted her aunt to say that he was certainly in love with her—that was how they all started. "Who is this guy that you put mascara on for him?"

"He's miraculous. He got to Canada first and then to the States from Communist Russia, and he came all alone. I want you to like him, Emily. No matter what else happens in your life, you have to love him." Sonja pressed her mascara pen to her eyelashes.

"He's been missing for so long."

"Where has he been?"

"You know."

"I don't. And anyway that makes no sense. You can't just automatically love someone."

Sonja just blinked at the mirror, her eyes flashing wetly. "The heart has two ventricles," she said, "the left ventricle and the right ventricle. And each of the ventricles holds an equal amount of love."

"The ventricles hold blood," said Emily. "They're part of a pump system."

"We need two ventricles for love, because everyone has at least two kinds of love in their life."

"That's just not true."

"You have your opinion and I have my opinion. We could argue until the end of the night and who would be right?"

"I took human biology courses in university." Emily pushed out of the bathroom. "I would be right."

YOU CAN'T BE SAD ALL THE TIME

HARPO, 1933

William suddenly turned to Harpo. "Did you say how you're feeling?" he asked. "I think I forgot to listen for the answer. How are you?"

"Chilly," said Harpo. He was also a bit sad. But life changed so quickly. One minute you're a scrawny tenement kid and the next you're a movie star. You couldn't be sad every day. Nobody could keep that up. Minnie had told him that, and his mother had known everything.

William looked out at the forest again. He put his hands on his hips like the king of the tenements, like they played when they were kids, when he and his brothers and all the neighbourhood kids all snuck onto rooftops just to see who would end up highest. He seemed very far away. So Harpo searched his thoughts for topics of conversation: beautiful women (probably not), Jews (nope), funerals (definitely not). Then he found something. "Do you know anything about Russia?"

William turned, looked at him with pie-dish eyes. "Why did you ask me that?"

"I'm thinking of going."

William just stared. Well, anyone would be surprised. People weren't exactly lining up to get into that country just now. Soviet Russia wasn't exactly a vacation destination, like, say, Montauk, Long Island.

"I've been asked to work there," said Harpo, when William didn't even blink. "My best friend wants me to." He'd be the first Western performer since Communism. And their last movie hadn't made any money at all, and the MGM contract was up, so no one would hire the brothers anymore, probably. That's what Groucho said. Still, William said nothing.

"I don't know," said Harpo. "It's a gig, I guess. And ever since the crash first and now the Depression, I can't exactly afford to be unemployed. What if I want to get married?"

William massaged his beard. "This sounds just like kismet to me."

"Kiss who?"

"So what's the problem with going?"

"There are Communists there. And they don't have toilet paper, if you believe the rumours." He didn't want to do it alone. That was the real problem.

William nodded as if he'd heard the silent part too. "We'll have to think about this," he said. "We'll talk about it later," and then he turned and disappeared into the trees, moving quickly for an old guy.

Harpo watched him go. He leaned against a tree and absently unrolled a scroll of bark. On closer consideration, maybe that was the wrong question to have asked. If a strange old man appears, then leads you into the forest, maybe the question you should ask is how do you get back to the lodge?

But then Harpo felt that pull again. He followed it away from the waterfall and back into the trees, and he was lucky because the feeling was pulling in the old guy's direction. Hopefully, he was on his way back to the lodgehouse.

That man. William. He really looked like the tenement men from New York, the ones who sat on stoops all day. Except that man wasn't really Harold. He couldn't have been. Since Frenchie was dead and Harold had been older, and oh how it always struck him when he remembered that his father was gone. His grief was a filament and it should light him up like a light bulb, so he was always surprised that everyone couldn't see just by looking at him that he was an orphan now. They should be able to see grief like this all the way back in New York.

The rope felt taut, so he stumbled forward faster. As he moved, a feeling of love came right through him, singing like a rotten mayonnaise sandwich, sweet and bitter, and it made him screw up his face. That love always came eventually, right along with the feeling of loss, so it wasn't the worst thing, remembering Frenchie. He had to remember that.

Harpo tripped and stumbled through the underbrush, but he couldn't find the path again, or the old man. He'd followed a ghost. Blood whooshed dizzyingly in his head. He'd never been lost in a forest before.

"Harpo?" said a voice from inside the mess of branches.

Harpo stopped and held onto a tree branch, relief flooding over him like a wave on the Hudson. That was Chico's voice. This always happened. He was always saved, in the most unlikely way and in the most unlikely place, and usually by one of his brothers.

"Hey, Harpo," said Chico, emerging from the trees. "We were just looking for you. We're going canoeing. Want to come?" Then he grinned, and Harpo remembered seeing that expression before, right before getting thrown in the Hudson, sent flying over cobblestone, pushed out onto a tenement rooftop and locked there. There might not be a canoe involved in this canoe trip at all.

"Did you see an old man just now?" asked Harpo

"No, partner," said Chico in his Italian accent, the one he'd been working on since they were kids. "It's just us in the woods so late. Are you coming?"

"Are we allowed to canoe when the sun's going down?"

"Probably not. Are you interested?"

There *was* a trick in this, of course. "Okay," said Harpo.

"Good," said Chico. Then he turned and hurried into the trees.

Harpo followed. It was a good thing too, it turned out, because that need to move had welled up again. It was a kind of itchy feeling this time, like the rope had pulled taut when he wasn't paying attention. Just like him to forget it like that. He looked up and saw a break in the tree cover, a cloud like a bruised plum.

"Keep up, Harp," and Chico disappeared again.

Harpo hurried after. He burst through the foliage and was surprised to see a clearing, and a tiny little broken-down dock at the end of it, with another of his brothers bouncing on his feet. "Groucho!" he said.

The clearing was pockmarked with dips and shadows, and Harpo stumbled over them like he was a drunk, like he was a toddler just learning to walk. He could hardly see the dock at all. He could just barely make out the canoe bobbing in the water, and Grouch was just a silhouette, a black-on-blue cut-out of a man whose arm was raised in greeting.

Chico reappeared beside him. "We're about fifteen miles from the lodge," he whispered. Harpo turned, but Chico was forcing him out onto the tumbledown dock.

YOU CAN SHATTER LIKE A VASE

EMILY, 2003

Doran Baruch looked like a shadow. That was Emily's first impression. He was a pale shadow. When he'd walked into the lodge, she'd been afraid that he'd tell everyone that she'd been asking all the old guests for interviews, that she'd been tracking everyone down, intruding on their privacy and all that, and so she'd wished for silence. But he'd looked right through her searching for Sonja. He still hadn't so much as looked in her direction. Now Emily wished for anything — a wink, a nod, any acknowledgement at all.

"Lovie," said Auntie Sonja, handing her a glass of wine, "I want you to meet our guest, Mr. Baruch."

"Doran," he said, "please." He was so tall that he seemed to be folded into the room, the goy with the Jewish last name, the miraculous man. Emily couldn't see his face very well because it was darker by the ceiling, but she noticed the gaunt cheeks that shadows cut into, those eyes big like loonies, light blue, the same colour as the shallows in the lake, the same as Sonja's eyes. He might have winked at her, but it might have been the light.

He bowed low. "Blessed are the Pacific tribes," he said. "Because they dine with the prophets."

"*Oy gevalt,*" said Sonja. "Oh for God's sake. Doran, you sound like Blima."

"Did I say something wrong?"

"Blessed are the saints. That's what my sister says when she's acting up."

"I've been saying that to Jewish people on Passover for fifty years."

"That's all right. They probably just thought you were married to a Sephardic. They're strange, those ones. They eat lamb."

Sonja propelled Doran into the room of windows. Emily followed, ducked into the doorway so she could see more closely and not be seen. They were hugging now, her great-aunt and this strange visitor, more than hugging. They were hanging on to each other like drowners clinging to a life raft.

"You wouldn't think it could still hurt," she heard Sonja whisper. "But it does."

"It's physical," and Doran's voice was like a growl. "They always surprise me, these physical manifestations. The heart can break like a vase. We can shatter. But I'm happy to be back again. I needed to be together at least one more time."

YOU CAN FIT INTO THE DARK

HARPO, 1933

"Are you coming or not?" Chico forced Harpo right to the edge of the dock, where everything was in soft focus, purple and black and dangerous.

Harpo hesitated.

"Well?" said Chico.

"I'm going." It was windy now too. And it smelled like seaweed. And it was hard to breathe with all the rushing air. He'd just have to step down, grab the side of the boat, the dock maybe?

"Go on then."

"I am." Harpo shuffled closer to the water. He bent at the waist, but there was nothing to hold onto. His brothers probably had no intention of getting into that canoe anyway. They were probably just going to shove him in and shove him out.

"So get in already, Harpo," said Chico. "Checkout is on Tuesday. We only have a week left." And then he crowded in so close that Harpo had nowhere to go but down.

Harpo stepped into the canoe, but his foot bobbed and moved out from under him, and suddenly he was falling backward, and just as suddenly he wasn't. Chico grabbed him, and then

Harpo was somehow folded into the canoe, holding that funny piece of wood that smelled more like the lake than the lake did. He couldn't see the bottom of the boat, but there had to be water down there, because his knees and shins were suddenly cold. "Is this thing safe?"

"You do know how to swim, don't you?" said Groucho. Then he put an oar across the top of the canoe. Chico did the same, then they settled into the boat without the whole thing sliding out from under them.

They were off, gliding into the dark lake, Harpo bobbing and rocking with the water, his brothers busy with shushing oars. Things changed so fast. One minute he was lost in the trees and the next he was rushing over the water, feeling the air grow warm and close like a hug.

"We have to look out for lights," said Groucho. "We're pretty far away from the lodge now, right in the river. Barges come down here all the time, because it's part of the trade route."

"Okay." Harpo could feel a fine mist on his forehead. He closed his eyes and the gentle little drops touched his eyelids.

Then there was silence. And then, "We're here."

Harpo looked up. The sun had set completely so he couldn't see anything at all. "Where are we?"

"Coronation Island," said Groucho.

Both of his brothers stopped paddling, and for a moment they just bobbed and rocked in silence. There was an occasional crack as something hit against the boat, and Harpo had no idea what that could be. Driftwood? Fishing lines? What did people trade in Kingston, Canada?

Finally, Groucho raised his arm. "See that?"

Harpo saw a line of black on black, and his eyes followed it to the far distance, to pinpricks of light.

"That's the Kingston Penitentiary," said Groucho. "It's like San Quentin in Canadian."

"I'll pay you one hundred dollars if you yell 'jailbreak,'" said Chico.

"Not on your life," said Harpo.

"Get out," whispered Groucho. "We have to show you something. Quick. Climb out. Climb up."

Harpo could now just barely make out that there was a dock in front of him that the canoe was hitting against with every passing wave. That was the cracking sound, the banging feeling. He felt for the slimy wood with careful fingers, then hoisted himself up onto it.

"Where are we again?" He reached a hand out to his brothers, but they were already pushing themselves off the dock with their oars.

"Coronation Island," said Groucho. "This is where the real morons are crowned."

Harpo sat back on his heels. "Mormons?"

"He's had two hours to think about it," said Chico "And that's the best he could come up with. Coronation Island."

"It's been a busy week," said Groucho. "You'll have to forgive me. I've had a lot on my mind."

Harpo lowered his hand. Frenchie's funeral, Groucho meant. And he understood. That had been a hotbed of jokes, just one after another after another in quick succession, just Grouch to him to Chico and back again, then to Zep and Gummo. Then there had been the other people, and that had been the worst. Nobody should be allowed to make eye contact at a funeral. Sympathetic looks should be punishable by prison time. Harpo looked at Groucho's bobbing form, or was that Chico? Because he felt it too. He was wrung out, twisted round, dried up, even here, even though he was in the middle of a lake.

"Well, goodnight, Harp," Chico said as the canoe slid away again, fitting perfectly into the darkness.

"Oh." Harpo saw the joke now. "I get it. You're leaving me here."

"We'll pick you up in the morning," Chico called.

Harpo stumbled from one side of the dock to the other, and felt the cold water lapping up from all directions, the spray cold on his arms and cheeks. Then he walked around the periphery. The dock was a small thing, the size of a king-size bed, and there was no island attached to it at all.

"Hey, Chico," he said. They should be turning around to pick him up again. Any second now.

But there was nothing.

"There isn't even an island here," said Harpo. "It's only just a dock!"

And then he sat. The seat of his pants was cold. It was wet too. There was a wet spot. He sighed, and the night sighed back, the breeze and the water and the strange bird sounds whistling in answer.

Harpo lay down on his back and stared at the stars. He didn't deserve Susan. She was better off without him.

He struggled to his feet. Then he walked.

This was why he didn't like to be trapped out in the middle of lakes. It was because he paced and his thoughts did too, and they always ended up in forbidden areas. Verboten!

Harpo sat down again, chuckling a little at the memory of Frenchie's voice, that fake-o anger. It had never worked. Frenchie couldn't even raise his voice. A few times he'd taken off his belt, pushed Harpo into the hallway and slammed the door shut on the gaping faces inside. But then he'd hit the wall so it only sounded like discipline. His wet black eyes could slay him though, when Harpo knew he'd let him down.

Harpo lay back. He curled in a ball and pain radiated outward in every direction. It always surprised him that it was physical. Missing a person was physical. His chest hurt, but not just that, his head and throat also, they all screamed in bright white agony. Other people should be able to see it. This grief, it should make him bright like a star.

Harpo closed his eyes, remembered standing by Frenchie's bed. It was the last time he'd ever see his father. An earthquake rolled the hospital and suddenly Harpo was in a corner of the room, trapped by his father's bed. His arm was pinched by the headboard, and he had to look at his dad, really look. Frenchie was gone. He'd already checked out. His cheeks were hollow, his skin yellow, his eyes open and vacant. His mouth made a perfect *O*. And oh God. He loved him. Harpo loved Frenchie so much, and he wasn't coming back again so he couldn't even say it. I love you, Frenchie. I love you, Dad. The words burned in his throat. And he couldn't get out of the hospital room because he was stuck between the bed and the wall, and he couldn't call for a nurse because his vocal cords were useless. And they were busy, it sounded like. Something was wrong. Harpo could hear yelling in the hallways, pounding feet, crashing machinery, and he sort of understood what was happening, but sort of didn't. The earthquake meant nothing to him, even as an aftershock shook the room and the bed rolled into Harpo's stomach, so hard he could hardly breathe, so hard his eyes filled.

Now Harpo was back on the dock all alone, eyes watering again, again and always. "I love you, Frenchie," he whispered, his voice cracking, still barely audible.

Just before he'd left for the lodge, Chico's daughter had asked him about Frenchie's last days. Harpo remembered putting his hand on her little head, stroking her dark hair, saying nothing. How could he answer? He'd pictured that gaunt face and the smell, the smell of antiseptics and something else, something sour and terrible, his father's body shutting down. He couldn't tell her that. She was just a little kid. Harpo would wire Maxine in the morning. He'd tell her that Frenchie had bilked money out of the nurses. He'd write, "On his last day on Earth, Frenchie taught the nurses pinochle. He made a four dollar bid and got it." It was time to start taking care of Frenchie's memory. He'd be the grown-up now. When he needed to be, anyway. When it was necessary.

Then Harpo thought he saw movement somewhere, a flash of black on black, and he stood. "Hello?" he called, suddenly cold in all the places he'd been folded up. "Is someone out there?"

There was no response. Where were his brothers?

"Help?"

They should have come back to rescue him by now. Could they have started a card game and forgotten him? He didn't want to be out here forever. He had things to do now. He had purpose. He had to fix his career, be an adult somehow, get Susan back. He didn't want to end up a pile of bones on a dock. One more wild night. But after that…

"Help!"

And then the dock shook violently. Harpo fell to his knees.

The old man climbed up onto the dock, but this time Harpo wasn't ready for him. "Well good evening," said William, the moonlight making him glow, surreal and strange and dry like a bone.

Harpo stood.

"Imagine meeting you here," said William.

Harpo scrambled over to the far side of the dock, to where William had just appeared out of the darkness, but there wasn't a canoe. There were only some ripples in the dark water, and an extra little piece of dock jutting out, a section he hadn't noticed before. He dropped to his knees. He'd already known the old guy might be a ghost, hadn't he thought that when he'd wandered out of the woods? But he hadn't really believed it, it seems, not until now.

"So how are you doing tonight?" asked William.

"How did you get here?" whispered Harpo.

"You're a bit confused. That can happen. Other than that, how do you feel?"

"My brothers left me. And you're not really here."

"I'm not?"

The wind ruffled Harpo's hair. Minnie used to do that. That's how he'd known he'd done something right. Now the Kingston nighttime was telling him well done. So he'd guessed it. He was sitting with a ghost. Now what?

"I've been looking out for you," said William. "And I thought you might want some company this evening. Maybe a rescue too, if you don't get any better offers." Then he seemed to hear something and turned to the shore. "You might get a better offer, however."

Harpo turned to follow his gaze, and saw nothing, an inky lake shimmering with moony reflections. But this wasn't so bad. William seemed friendly enough. And if he was a ghost, then his parents might be ghosts too, and William might even know them. If anyone could fix this problem with Susan and right his tilting career, it was Minnie. Harpo breathed. If they were ghosts, then he might see Minnie and Frenchie again.

"I've been thinking," William said suddenly. "If you do go to Russia, you might meet some friends of the Jewish lodge family, the Kogans."

"That would be a coincidence," said Harpo.

"Maybe it could be the kind of coincidence you arrange before you leave. Sometimes when I listen in the windows, the Kogans are talking about the mitzvah, good deeds. Sometimes, inside the lodge, they're worrying about the people they left behind in Russia. I think it would be considered a good deed if you looked in on those people while you're there."

"I can do that."

"You can?"

Harpo gathered some pebbles and dropped them in the water. They tinkled musically. "Have you ever heard of Minnie Marx?" he asked. "Or Frenchie Marx?"

"Yes," William said softly.

"They were my parents." Harpo felt that same searing hurt in his forehead, burning all the way down his chest. It should be visible. But it wasn't. It was still just as dark out, and nobody could see his grief but him. "I love them, you know."

"It was in all the newspapers," William said.

"It there pinochle in heaven?"

"How could there not be?"

"Then that's okay." Harpo rubbed his eyes. He didn't want the ghost to see him crying. It was vanity, but there it was. "My parents liked playing cards. So it would be nice if they could play together now."

"You're a nice son," whispered William.

"Minnie was never that good. She had five boys, so she always waited for an inside straight." And Harpo took a shuddering breath. "Does Frenchie know how much I love him?" Because he did love him. He loved Susan too. He didn't say it enough to either of them. Was it enough, just to love them, and trust that they know they were loved? Maybe it was that simple, because that's how radios worked after all. You turn a dial and the sound comes. "We always said we were Minnie's boys, but we were Frenchie's boys too. He travelled with us, you know, when we were touring."

"I didn't know that."

"He used to sit in the audience and start all the laughs. That was his job. People are more likely to laugh if someone else laughs first."

"That sounds like the perfect job for a father."

"My brothers and I are performers," said Harpo. "I don't think I told you that. Before he died, I promised my dad I'd stop being so wild, such a hedonist, my brother would say. I said I'd be more like him."

"You were with him at the end," said William. "That's what I seem to remember."

"The last day before Frenchie died, he taught a couple of nurses how to play pinochle. He made a forty dollar bid, and got it."

William nodded, then dipped his fingers into the water. "The lake feels warm now that the night is cold," he said. And then he pointed across the lake. "You're not so far from home, you know."

That was New York he was pointing to, probably. Not the city but the state. But even so. Harpo thought about the tenements, the long days stalking the city, the hot nights on piled mattresses, all the brothers in the same stuffy room, all those times with his brothers and mother and father, and all his dozens and dozens of relatives and kind of relatives, fighting a lot, being wild, laughing like maniacs. Once, he stabbed Groucho with a fork over a dinner roll. "My brothers are at the lodgehouse right now," he said.

Chico and Groucho were probably sitting in the dining room, or in that room that had all the windows, probably pretending to lose at pinochle until the end of the night when they'd throw down and play like the card sharps they really were. Those two boys who looked so much like him even his parents got confused.

Harpo closed his eyes and smelled the soggy air, the cold and the water and all those flowers that didn't open in the daytime. And there were other smells he hadn't known about before. And then, in front of him, the Kingston Penitentiary, all lit up like a birthday cake. And beside him, nothing.

William was gone.

Harpo ran to the other side of the dock. There were definitely ripples in the lake now.

YOU CAN MAKE A NIGHT DIFFERENT FROM ALL OTHER NIGHTS

EMILY, 2003

It was Emily's job to start the Passover ceremony. "Why is this night different from all other nights?" she said, and everyone at the table cooed, and then they all started talking at once. After all that work assigning places, none of them were sitting where they were supposed to, except for Doran, the black cloud at the other end of the table, the threatening weather Emily felt compelled to watch. This man was linked to the family, and in an indelible way, that much was clear, but nobody would explain the nature of the connection.

Finally, Papa Moshe, her grandfather, at the head of the table, stood. "Let's hurry up so we can eat," he said, then sat again.

"We still have blessings to make," said Auntie Mackie, Jonah's grandmother, who must have arrived while Emily had been spying on Sonja and Doran.

"I'd like to bless the candles," said Blima.

"I want to bless the candles," said Sonja.

"I want to bless the wine," said Mackie. "And then we'll see who remembers the most Hebrew. I'm not even Jewish and I can keep up."

"You're not Jewish?" asked Emily. Another broken connection. Her grandfather avoided her questioning look.

He turned to Doran instead. "Have you been to a Seder recently, Doran?"

Emily was aware of movement from the far side of the room, Doran shaking his head. "Not like this," he said after a moment. "I only came when Ayala was around, and this, I imagine, will be different."

"Well, this is an opportunity." Moshe leaned back. "The idea of the Seder is that the community gets together once a year to tell the story of the Exodus. We've all heard the story too many times. It's nice to have someone new to tell it to."

"I like exodus stories," said Doran, and Emily saw shadows contracting along the length of the table, her grandmother and great-aunt sitting up in their chairs.

Emily remembered that he'd had an exodus too. He'd left Russia. She'd love to hear that story now. Because who had *he* been running from? He wasn't a Jew.

"And I like the idea of communal remembering too," said Doran.

"Maybe history is best forgotten," said Blima, "so I say we do the short version. Doran, in the real Seder, we read from the Haggadahs, bless some things, drink some wine, take turns telling the story and we don't eat before ten o'clock. We prefer to get the formalities out of the way as quickly as possible here, this year especially."

"I'll get the story started," said Sonja. "In the Seder, we tell the story of when the Jews passed over."

"You have to say from where to where," said Mackie.

"From Egypt to Israel," said Sonja. "Even the goyim know that part. And it took eight days."

"It took forty years," said Mackie.

"Oh, that's right. And in all that time, Doran, the Jews found the only country in the Middle East that had no oil."

"Mr. Baruch." Jonah bent to fill Doran's wineglass again. He was looking right at Emily, his eyes flashing in the candlelight. "If you ever attend another Seder, please don't tell them what happened at ours."

There was a creak from the head of the table, and eventually, a soft "but this is just fine."

"Let me set the scene for you," said Moshe. "We start in Egypt. The Jews are making the pyramids. They're slaves, and the pharaoh is a terrible master. He tortures them. One day, he goes too far. He says that the first-born Jewish boys will all be killed, for some sort of punishment, I don't remember what." He poured himself another glass of wine, then refilled Emily's glass as well. "Then there's a whole business where a woman has a baby and sends him down the river because he's the first-born son. We all know that part."

Emily heard a moan of wood on wood from the head of the table, Doran shifting in his seat.

"One day when the pharaoh got to be too bad, Moses demanded that he let the Jews go free. The pharaoh said, 'fine then, see if I care.' He said that because God had given Moses certain miracles to play with, and he had already called down plagues on the Egyptians. It was raining fire, so, you know, the pharaoh thought he didn't have that many choices. But now this pharaoh was a mercurial man. As soon as things were back to normal, he went back on his word. He ordered the Egyptian soldiers to go go go and they chased the Jews right to the bank of the Red Sea, where they were trapped. But then, instead of going around, or swimming through, Moses parted the waters. The Jews walked. And where they went, nobody could follow. Because God was watching. He closed up the waters as soon as the tribe was safe, and all the pharaoh's army was drowned."

Nobody said anything. They were left with a silence that settled uncomfortably over the table. Then Emily struggled to sit up. She remembered what this night was for. Passover was about remembering, Doran was right, and she could use the ceremony to get information. There was a secret here. She'd heard her grandmother admit it. "Our family had an exodus too," she said.

"Yes," Blima said softly.

"We came here from Russia."

"My mother and father and I, we crossed the ocean. We had to leave in the middle of the night."

"And so did you, Doran," said Emily.

"Yes," said Doran. "But that was later. And I came alone."

"Maybe we shouldn't talk about the Seder story at all," said Sonja. "Maybe we should talk about our own personal exodus."

Emily sat forward. They'd abandoned the ceremony altogether. Anything could happen now. She could find out anything she wanted. "What was it like coming over?" she asked.

"Well, nobody parted the water for us," said Blima. "It was a difficult crossing."

"Our mother would have expected Dad to part the ocean," Sonja said.

"Our mother went through an ordeal."

"You always stick up for her."

"*Oliv a shulum.* May she rest in peace."

"No. Let's be honest. I'm not going to kid myself. I remember what she was like."

"What was she like?" said Emily.

"She had episodes," said Sonja.

"What?"

"She would go up to live in the attic and Dad would have to take the door off its hinges. With screwdrivers. He had to use tools. Except when she came out, it was worse. In that ratty nightgown, hair everywhere. I was mortified. Everyone was embarrassed. Nobody knew where to look. And when I talk to Blima, it's like it never happened."

"Wait," said Emily. "I'm trying to understand this…" Her great-grandmother had smiled all the time. She'd hummed. She'd hugged people.

"So she retired upstairs sometimes," said Blima. "Nobody minded. Nobody even noticed."

"Retired," said Sonja. "Dad used to have to carry her to the dock. All those nights, like it was the most normal thing in the world. He would take her out in that crazy boat, William's moving dock. She wore the same old see-through nightgown. And she was so pale herself. You could almost see her organs working, her heart beating under her ribs. And sometimes her nose would drip. Everyone could see it. They only pretended not to."

"I never saw this," whispered Doran. "This was Ayala?"

"It always happened right after you left," said Sonja. "But clearly my sister doesn't remember."

"You don't know," said Blima, picking up her glass, spinning it to make spots of light dance. "You don't remember when it was really bad. You were too little then. And you weren't even there for our move. Our father pretended that everything was normal, but she was getting stranger and stranger."

Everyone was quiet now, listening intently but pretending to be absorbed in feeling the cutlery and the napkins and the texture of the tabletop — Moshe, Doran, Mackie, Jonah. And Emily too. She picked up her wineglass. She didn't want to miss a syllable, a nuance. She needed to know everything.

"*I* was with her on the train," Blima was saying, "when a man came into our compartment, when she talked to him in a whisper, then said we had to get off, because that man had been Elijah the Prophet."

Emily sat up in her chair. She remembered that story.

"Our father was asleep, and it was just me and our mother, and her eyes were shining. I was afraid. And that's when she started talking, this whole story about Elijah. He was with us. He'd followed the whole way. From our town to the boat, in the guise of good weather, the wind that blew us to Canada. She saw him when she was on the deck and he was disguised as a cloud, or one time as a breeze that touched her cheek just so. A man in tight pants. And I knew it wasn't true. But I didn't know what to do. I was little and the only one awake."

"I don't understand," said Emily. But of course that story was scary. She'd never thought about it in terms of veracity before, of verifiability. Of sanity. Elijah the Prophet hadn't led her family to Canada. Of course that hadn't happened. Of course it wasn't true.

"You never told me this," said Sonja.

"And then I was the one who had to take care of you, and our father, and listen to her creaks and footsteps in the night. To tell her moods. To make sure she was all right."

Sonja raised her hand. "If she was—"

"If I can forgive her," said Blima, stopping her sister mid-sentence, "then so can you."

"Well," said Sonja. "Do you feel better?"

"Yes," said Blima. "As a matter of fact, I do."

"Well that's the point of Passover," said Sonja raising her glass. "Drink. Get it all out in the open."

"That's not true though," said Emily. "That can't be true. Right?"

"Sure it is, lovie," said Blima. "Why do you think we start drinking at noon, in this family?"

"How about everyone else?" Sonja asked. "Does anyone else feel the need to be unburdened?"

A wave passed over the table, everyone looking to the head. And from the head of the table, nothing, just silence, just crackling air.

"Why did the family come to Canada?" asked Emily. But nobody answered. "I mean, why here? How did they find Treasure Island." Again, no response.

So she'd change tack. She had lots of questions. She could

wear them down, for sure. "Are we related to Papa William?" she asked. "Jonah said we're not, and Mackie just said that they're not even Jewish."

"We're just family friends," Sonja said, playing with the stem of her glass.

"So how did our families connect?" Because if they weren't biologically related, then there had to be a moment of connection. Maybe she could use *that* in her thesis. "How did you meet?"

"We were introduced," said Blima.

"Who introduced you?" Emily sat up, looking for something to write with, because this would be great. A connecting vertex. The dot that connected all the lines.

"It was one of the guests," said Blima. "He went wandering off our property all the time, and Papa William had to rescue him and bring him back to the lodge. The guest introduced us, and we were like family after that."

"Do you remember the person's name?"

But then Blima ended the conversation by standing noisily, helping Jonah to serve the meal. Emily supposed she didn't remember. It had been a long time ago.

FIND A WAY TO STAVE OFF THE LONELINESS

HARPO, 1933

As the canoe creaked and moaned through the water toward him, Harpo was lying on his back, singing "Sweet Adeline." He stopped, but not until the little boat actually hit the dock, and he felt the bump and knew this one was real. A woman crawled up onto the dock. He'd been expecting the ghost, his brothers.

Harpo sat up.

She had dark hair and red cheeks, this strange woman, and shadowy deep-set eyes, and now he recognized her from the portrait on the registration desk. It was the lodge owner's beautiful wife. Ayala. She was wearing a long white nightgown. It was sleek. It looked soft. She was breathtaking. He couldn't have spoken if he'd wanted to.

"Good evening," she said, struggling with something in the darkness, maybe to secure the canoe.

"How did you know to come?" Harpo croaked.

"I had brothers once."

"Did you hear me calling?"

"I sent my little girl to listen."

Ayala crawled toward him, and Harpo could see the material

of that nightgown, translucent almost and clinging to her tightly, and through it he could see her skin as it glowed milky white, as her hips moved and swayed. She was wearing white panties. Ayala stood and Harpo gasped for air. She was wearing a white brassiere too. Ayala took Harpo by the shoulders and eased him to the edge of the dock. He felt the heat radiating off of her, her hot hands pressed to his shoulders.

Harpo dropped into the canoe and felt it bob, with him this time, not out from under him. And this time, the water in the bottom felt warm. It was like William said, exactly. Cold night, warm heart. Or cold water, warm weather. The canoe bobbed again, and abruptly Ayala was sitting across from him. She'd looked out for him. She'd asked her daughter to look out for him also. She was more beautiful now, this apparition, the wind messing her unbrushed hair, her dark watery eyes glittering brilliantly.

"You're facing the wrong way," said Ayala.

"Oh." Harpo looked around. "Sorry."

"That's all right. I didn't bring another oar anyway."

Harpo leaned back. Ayala moved the oar from side to side, paddling slowly, pulling through the water languorously. Languorously! "But wait," he said. "How could your daughter have heard me? The lodge is miles away, on the island."

"You can see the island," said Ayala.

"That's New York," said Harpo. "No, I mean that's Kingston. That's the jail on the shore."

"Your brothers must have played a trick on you. The lodge is right there. You see those lights?"

There were little pricks of prison light in the darkness.

"That's the lodge. They paddled you around the island a bit, that's all."

"Oh," said Harpo.

"I'll take you right home."

Even though the sharp walls of the canoe were poking into his side, he was remarkably comfortable, listening to the breezes skimming the water, smelling the woodsmoke and watching this woman, Ayala, who was grunting adorably as she pulled the oars. Boy, was she beautiful. He'd do anything to see that smile again, to see those almond eyes tilt up. He wanted so badly to give her something back for all this kindness. "I think your family is from Russia," he said.

"Yes," Ayala said after a moment.

"I'm going there. I'm going on tour. I think I've decided. I can do things for you while I'm visiting. If there's anything you need. If there are any people you'd like me to contact." Because that's what William had suggested, wasn't it?

"Could you deliver a letter?" asked Ayala. "Could you bring me back a reply?"

"Sure," said Harpo.

As they walked back through the forest, Harpo heard the lodge before he saw it, heard the gentle wail of the trumpets, not the tinny echo from a radio or record player, but real players, really swinging. He felt his hips swaying, the old forces taking hold. He peeked in the window, to one of the parlours, cleared of card tables now and full of women in beautiful dresses, men in suits and tails, dancing.

Harpo grabbed Ayala and pulled her close. She didn't resist, pressed herself right back, and they began to sway, and he could feel the heat coming off her body. Women always responded to a man with rhythm, with pull. He put a hand on her lower back, then trailed his fingers lower. Then she kissed him. Her mouth was warm and she tasted like baking and he wanted more. They could lie right here by the window. Nobody would think to look out into the night, then look down. But Ayala broke free. She ran up the lodge steps, paused at the door and blew him a kiss. He grinned. Then he ran right after.

Harpo ran into the room of windows. Everyone was dancing, swaying together, and again, the rhythm took hold. His heart was beating faster. He didn't see Ayala. He should find her. If he found someone special, someone he felt connected to, he should stick by her. That's what his father would do. He definitely wanted to be more like his father, but maybe he'd start tomorrow. He grabbed the first girl he saw instead, twirled her, and soon they were pressed together, dancing. There were the musicians, in the corner of the room. He knew it. He knew music that good couldn't be just so much wax and tin. Sounds this good had to be real. No wonder everyone came here. This lodge could swing.

A maid in a tight uniform eased between sweating bodies, and offered him a drink. He took it, and felt champagne bubbles pop straight into his brain. He nuzzled closer to his girl, used his hips to move her to the music. At the opposite corner of the room, he saw Chico pressed tightly against his own girl, caressing her from her head all the way down to her legs. He looked so put together, like a movie star. Chico always looked like he was radiating light. You always expected popping flashbulbs when you were around him.

Now Chico was on the move. He walked closer, edged right past Harpo without seeing him. Harpo's breath caught. Chico looked different close up. His face was pale and yellowish, sweat slicked. He paused and leered at his girl, and he looked frightening and wolfish. He could be her father.

Harpo's finger tingled. What had seemed fun a moment ago looked ghoulish now. Chico had a family at home. He had a wife and child.

Harpo felt a hand on his face, his girl caressing him, kissing his cheek. He pulled away.

"What's wrong, Harpo?" asked the beautiful blond girl, her voice soft, like Susan's.

"How do you know me?" he rasped. "How did you know my name?"

"I go to all the pictures," she whispered in his ear. "And I read all the magazines. I know all the rich movie stars." Harpo stepped back. He might not be a movie star anymore. They probably wouldn't make another picture. And he couldn't live this life forever.

"What's the matter?" said the girl. "Don't I look nice?"

"You look beautiful, sweetheart." And she did. Harpo seemed to be seeing her for the first time. She was beautiful. Her blue silk dress hugged her curves, and she hugged herself against him. He hugged her back, squeezed her tight like she was a life preserver. Another song started, and more bodies pressed in. And in the middle of all these people, Harpo felt unbearably alone. "I have to get some air," he said, pushing her away and sidling out of the room.

Harpo walked out into the hallway, then froze. There, alone in the corridor, was Ayala in her stark white nightgown. She was a knockout. Even in that plain thing, she was more beautiful than anyone at the party. And as soon as she saw him, she smiled mysteriously, then turned and walked up the stairs, hips swaying. But he couldn't move. He just kept thinking about Chico. With that animalistic leer, he'd looked like a bad guy in a silent flick. Harpo closed his eyes and listened to the soft music, to the moans and creaks, house noises. He heard a pop and release, a door opening somewhere. Then he heard a steady groan and shift as Ayala made her way up and up and up. He could go up there. She was beckoning. He knew the signs. That meant her husband wasn't around. But he couldn't move. He didn't know what was wrong with him. He should follow. Wasn't this why he'd really come?

YOU HAVE TO FIND ALL HIDDEN THINGS

EMILY, 2003

Emily couldn't sleep. So she wandered. Nighttime was the worst, when nobody else was awake, when the darkness was smothering. Even here, even at the lodge.

She crept from hallway to hallway, along this path that used to be familiar but wasn't any more.

The lodge used to be a swinging place. They used to have wild parties every night, everyone said. But now it was silent, completely still and unmoving.

Life changed so fast.

This place had been wild, and now it was safe. This had been her home, and then it wasn't. She had a life plan, then she didn't. She had a clue, a hint of a direction. Really, she had some diagrams that she couldn't connect together. That was it.

She sat down on a step. The week before, her mother had told her she'd never wanted kids. She'd wanted to focus on her career, to travel, to live an unencumbered life. It had been her father who'd insisted, who'd wanted a family, and her mother had only changed her mind because she'd thought it would be too difficult to find another partner. When she heard this, Emily had stormed away like a teenager. But it had made her evaluate. She wanted to live an encumbered life, filled with people, a partner, a child. She was on the wrong path for that.

One day ago, her thesis advisor had asked to meet. So she replied that she'd just left for the day, then got into her car and drove right to the lodge. One month ago, she'd had a plan, career goals, a life mapped out. But now she didn't know where she'd be at the end of any day. *This* was a story she wanted to tell. She wanted to talk so badly, and how had that stupid newspaper horoscope known that? She wanted connection.

Emily heard a clatter down the hallway, and started.

She found Blima standing in front of the left fridge, lit by the glow like it was a toxic-yellow-tinged campfire.

"Why are you awake?" whispered Emily. "It's early."

"I didn't sleep much when I was young because I was having too much fun. But now it's too late. When you get past seventy-five, you forget how to sleep." Blima turned, and in the strange light, her face looked old and ghoulish.

"Well, you look great," said Emily, "for so early in the morning."

"I have something to ask you."

"What's that?" asked Emily, excited again: a story was coming. Maybe she'd explain the *real* story of how they'd made their way to Treasure Island. Maybe she'd explain how the family had met Jonah's, or who Doran really was, or why the family tree didn't make sense and the old stories were changing so dramatically.

"What's a ten-letter word for the makeup of a space?"

"What?" Emily saw the folded newspaper. It was a crossword. *Topography*?

"I have something to show you," Blima said before Emily could answer. She opened the fridge wider and yellow light spilled out everywhere. "You have to learn about snacks. I'll teach you. In case I die, you'll know how we do things in this family." She reached inside and pulled out a whole chicken.

"You're not seriously going to cook that."

Blima trundled to the oven. "When our mother used to bake a chicken, she collected the drippings."

"It's four-thirty in the morning."

"She roasted the chicken on a bed of garlic. Just cloves and cloves of it, twenty at least, and what else? Chives. Onions." She padded back to the fridge and rifled. "We spread this thing on toast. I used to make it too, but not for years and years because of this no-fat business. This spread, I hate to tell you this, but it's only fat. But I'm making it again now. It's time. Sit."

Emily sat. She pulled the bar stool closer to the kitchen island. "I'm having trouble understanding the family. Was all that stuff about Great-grandma Ayala true?"

"I'll make coffee. That's also good for mornings. The smell is all you really need."

Emily put her cheek on the cold counter. "Can you please tell me about Grandma Ayala?"

"I don't know what to tell you, lovie. You're the one she used to talk to."

"Me?" She had a vague memory—wood floor panels, table legs, a yellow tablecloth that swayed.

"Oh sure. But here's something I can do. I'll write down her name in Cyrillic. Kogan. It's my maiden name too." Blima fished a pen out of a drawer and wrote on a napkin. And then she was off again, puttering by the oven, doing something, Emily didn't know what.

Emily took the napkin, traced her fingertips over the word. "Do we really have a big family secret?"

"Yes," said Blima.

"Will you tell me? Just give me a hint. Anything."

"I have a question for you." Blima cleared her throat. "I was thrilled to hear you were coming for Passover. But I have to ask you. Where is your mother?"

Emily just shrugged. How do you answer that? Her mother clearly didn't care about any of the family. Now they both had secrets.

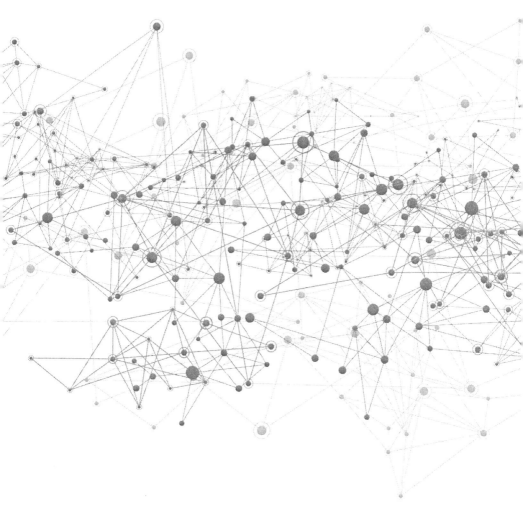

THE SECOND DAY (OR THE FIRST DAY OF PASSOVER)

FIND THE RELATIONSHIP BETWEEN FOOD AND MEMORY

EMILY, 2003

The sun was just starting to rise, blazing over the horizon, and Mackie was razing a path from across the street. She might know about how the families had met. Emily leaned her head against the lodge's front door and hoped, fervently, that the story that she dug up would be a good one. Because otherwise she was going to be fired. Nobody was allowed to up and leave their job like this. She'd brought the papers she had to mark, but hadn't even unpacked them. They had to be due some time. Someone was bound to complain. And of course, she only had seven days left to hand in a completed thesis draft to her committee.

Suddenly, Mackie was at the door, pushing her way inside, and Emily was stumbling backward. "Thanks for coming over," she said. "I wanted to ask if you remember the first time you met the family. Do you remember who introduced you?"

Mackie thrust a letter toward her. "I found something for you."

"Do you remember any guests?"

"The lodge has lots of guests, dear."

"I mean, from when you were very little."

But then Aunt Sonja appeared beside Emily. Obviously, she'd appear. Why had Emily thought that she could get up before the old people?

"Jonah seems to think she's working on a family tree," Mackie told Sonja.

"Jonah told you that?" said Emily.

"Anyhow," said Mackie. "Blima was looking for letters, like the old game, so I looked in my place too, and wouldn't you know it, I found one."

"Why is Bubbie Blima looking for a letter?"

Mackie held out the letter, but Sonja grabbed it. "Emily, this is from your great-grandma Ayala. She wrote letters to my mother, every time they went away travelling."

"What else did Jonah say about me?"

"People sent letters in their day. That's what was done, darling."

Darling. As her Aunt Sonja frowned at the envelope, Emily tried to determine, from Mackie's expressive face, what Jonah might have said to her. It was Mackie who, at some Hanukkah years before, third glass of Manischewitz in hand, had waved Emily over and whispered with sweet breath, "Darling, my Jonah loves you." But maybe she'd said it out of pity. Maybe Jonah didn't like her anymore at all, and Mackie was trying to make her feel better. That tended to happen in this family. People tended to say exactly the opposite of what they were thinking.

"We were just talking about the old times," said Sonja. "The old times and the old letters too, I think. Didn't we talk about old letters last night?"

"I don't think so," said Emily.

"Isn't it funny how everything happens all at once," said Sonja. "These things are never coincidences, these moments of confluence. It's not nothing."

"Well, ladies." Mackie kissed Emily's cheek. "I have to get back. I'm making a strudel with matzo. I don't know. We'll see."

Emily watched her toddle back out again, then turned to her

aunt. "Can I see the letter?"

"Soon." Sonja didn't look up as she pulled a crinkling paper out of the envelope. "Later."

"Do we still have things left from when the family was in Russia?"

"Sure," and Sonja waved vaguely. "There are boxes in the cellar."

"The basement?" Emily crept around the door frame and smelled the garlic spread from earlier that morning. "Are there papers anywhere else?"

"The final ones are in the office."

"Final?" First, she'd go to the office. She'd search for those files, to find out what final meant. Plus, she could use the computer to send an email. She'd tell her advisor that she'd just come by his office and hadn't found him, and that would buy her at least a bit more time. It would work too. Russell was always late.

Some time later, minutes, hours, Emily opened her eyes and Jonah's head was on the dining-room table, looming beside her like a plate. He slid a mug of coffee in front of her, and it clanked against the other mug, and Emily willed him not to speak, not to move, not to do anything. But not to leave.

She held her breath. There was a new smell in the room now, a smell like licorice. She closed her eyes and tried to follow from image to image like before.

"Are you okay?" he asked.

Emily put her head in her arms. "My family has a secret." But she was fine. She was great. She was right on the verge of remembering something, and, whatever it was, it would blow the day right open, would crack the secret open like a coconut and fix her thesis too, she could feel it. She'd come in here to work, and that's when she'd been accosted — by the smell first, and then by the memories.

"Did you sleep at all?"

Emily shifted to answer, but she smelled her matzo instead, and it happened again, her head buzzed with images, memories of things and caffeine. Jonah would love the connection between food and memory, but how could she explain it?

"I thought I heard you get up last night," he said. "What have you been doing?"

"I've resorted to unconventional research methods."

"What?"

"Hard copies." Emily sat up, and revealed the mess of papers on the dining-room table: obits, death certificates, cemetery papers and funeral programs. But now the images she'd been remembering were gone. The feelings too. Her mind was filled with white and grey like a Kingston sky.

"Yeah, right," said Jonah. "Everything must be on computers for you." He picked up her matzo and sniffed, just like she'd done, and Emily felt herself nodding and nodding. Jonah must understand. The tangy smell, that's what had done it, that's what had made her remember. There was something else now too, something on the periphery, her great-grandmother holding long strips of Scotch tape. Suddenly, Emily could feel the tacky things stuck to her fingertips, little jolts as they were pulled off again, the feeling of thrilling complicity. She couldn't have been more than six.

"Are you still working on that family tree?" asked Jonah. "I've been thinking about that. We could look up your family on the Mormon website."

"We're not Mormons."

"The Mormons help with genealogy. It's a thing they do."

She should have looked this up before coming. She'd just noticed incongruities in her genealogy, vertices that didn't connect and orphans on the peripheries, and had come right here. "How do you know so much?"

There was a silence. Then, "You know, Blima's got a registration outside."

"What?" Emily stood, and the morning changed again. She

held the back of the chair to steady herself. There was sunlight streaming in from outside, like a flood, like a torrent. "I promised I'd help her with those. I said I'd be more helpful. I forgot." She'd promised herself she'd have a new thesis draft finished by noon. When she'd come here, the light had been going the other way, from inside to out. And the sky had been a dusty purple. What time was it?

Emily picked up her cup of coffee. Which would be more serious? Girl with mug, girl with arms crossed, girl with hands on hips. "Blima was supposed to get me. Show me how we do things in this family and all that."

"They get this way. They get into their pranks and they forget."

"I should have been listening." Leave the coffee. Take a pen. That would look good. "I want to help. I want to work."

"You shouldn't work here," said Jonah.

Emily bristled. "Why not?" He didn't want her here, that's what he meant.

"This place isn't what it was."

"Maybe it can be." Maybe it had to be. What if she got busted for her disappearing act, and got fired? Where else would she go?

Emily hurried to the desk where Aunt Blima stood facing a young man and woman in Queen's University jackets. She edged away from the desk, closer to the back cubbies. She'd always wanted to be the one behind the counter, but now felt unaccountably shy.

"You kept separate last names then?" Blima was saying.

"We're not married," said the young man.

"Oh. So then you want two rooms?"

The young man hesitated, and the young woman said, "Just the one."

Emily grabbed a room key and the registration book. When she straightened, Jonah was weaving his way behind her. His shoulders were shaking. Was he laughing? This didn't make sense. Blima and Sonja had always been too open about sex. They've been around a while, that's what they always said. They made condom balloons sometimes when they filled the guest room dressers.

"What about meals?" said Blima.

"We're just going to sleep here." The young man handed Emily a Visa. His name was Ryan. "I mean, we're just going to sleep," he said. "We'll be in the city. We're just graduating."

"We're having a special dinner tonight," said Blima. "It's a Seder. That's a special evening in the Jewish culture. And it's become our family's tradition to make sure that everyone has a place at a special meal, even if they're not Jewish. It's not everyone who does this. You'll find most Jews don't even worry about whether their Gentile friends eat a good gefilte fish."

"Wait," said Emily. "Other Jews don't do this?"

"We already have plans," said the pretty girl.

"We appreciate the offer," said Ryan, " but we've got plans in the city every night."

Then Emily took the boxy machine from her grandmother's outstretched hand.

"You have a nice *night*," said Blima.

Emily turned to face the office, then the students. She felt her blush like a fever. "I'll show you to your room." She could be scalded by shame like that.

When Emily came to the lodge as a little girl, she and Blima used to swim together, and Blima would always carefully wet her armpits before traipsing into the water. That's what Emily told the students, Ryan and Amy, as she stood in front of their door.

"Seriously," said Ryan, lingering after Amy had already disappeared inside. "You don't have to apologize."

"Blima's not actually offended that you're not married," said Emily.

"You really don't have to worry," said Ryan. "This is a nice place."

Emily followed his gaze down the hallway, at the unevenly

faded wallpaper, the worn carpets, the light that seemed to hover in slanted columns of dust.

"It feels like history here," he said.

"Great."

"I was in this other inn, in Pennsylvania, this one time. It had old pictures on all the walls. Oh and it showed the family trees of all the famous people who had stayed there. I like things that are old."

Emily balanced on the top step so she could see the window, the tops of the trees and the sky. Things just kept coming up. How many people had talked about family trees since she got here? Two. No. Three. Jonah and Mackie. And now this Ryan. Grandma Ayala would have said that it's *besheret*, meant to be. It should be in her thesis after all. This was proof.

She hopped down a step.

This could be her unifying vision, her thought experiment somehow, and she felt closer than ever to figuring out why she'd been so obsessed with genealogy, because this would do more than give background and history for her thesis. She could make the claim that the family tree was the first instance of a social network, graphed, and she could graph them as social networks. She could show the community of Treasure Island as a concrete example, a graph whose vertices could be tracked and analyzed. They'd show more than the obvious connections too, much more than only birth and marriage. What if she could use the family tree to do stuff? She could use the graphs to map the passage of oddities, like Blima's story about Elijah in cheap motels. Emily had heard that one before, from Great-grandma Ayala. So she could track it down the generations, all the way from Russia to Kingston. No. Farther than that. All the way to Brooklyn or Boston or wherever Doran was from. Maybe she could show how the stories changed. What if she could show how these pathologically strange people had affected each other all these years and use the family tree to map traits, like biologists did, and determine the origins of quirks, senses of humour and things. She could make lists of personality flaws and treat them like genes. This island was isolated like the Galapagos.

At the bottom of the stairwell, she heard voices, so Emily stopped at the entrance to the room of windows and hid behind the door frame.

"What's a nine-letter word for lie?" asked Sonja.

"*Obfuscation*," Blima said absently.

"'To lie,'" said Sonja, "'a verb.'"

"*Disseminate*," said Blima. "No. The other one."

"*Dissemble*."

"That's it."

"We could go on *Jeopardy!*, you know," said Sonja. "If they ever allow two halfwits to make up one whole person."

Emily sat down on the step. Dissemble. Disassemble. She opened her notebook because whenever you're starting something new, you should always go back to first principles, and what did she really know? She had two graphs, no, three. She had her family, Jonah's and Doran's, and they were all connected somehow, by influence if not by blood. She made a list of all the names she knew, then organized them by line, first her family, then Jonah's. Then she moved on to Doran's family. She wrote in Doran's name, and that was all, a little orphaned vertex in the corner of the page. Where was everyone else?

"I found the letters, you know," Sonja said suddenly.

Blima gasped. Emily could hear her all the way in the other room. She looked up from her diagrams, scooted forward on the stair.

"Oh," said Blima, "the love letters. Our collection. I'd forgotten all about those."

"So now do you feel better?"

"That's not the package that I've been looking for."

So Blima was looking for a package. Well, Emily would find it, and she'd find it first. She'd look through the place methodically. It really just came down to science.

Jonah appeared in the hallway. "Hey," he whispered, nudging her with his toe. "I just thought of something. Have you checked the guest files?"

"I'm more interested in family information now," said Emily. "I'm giving up on old guests."

"They might keep family information in there." He shrugged. "Technically, all family members were also guests. Trust me — their filing system is that bizarre."

"But anyway," said Emily, "they're in a filing cabinet. It's locked"

"I have a key." He gestured for her to follow.

Everything came down to science, if you thought about it. She was having trouble reconnecting with Jonah. She could use science to solve that too. There had been old psych experiments on friendship formation, how to force people to fall in love with you, she'd read them as an undergrad. She'd just have to look those up again, she realized as she hurried after him.

FIND ALL THE HIDDEN MAIL

HARPO, 1933

Harpo thrust his legs into the lake. It was frigid. The sun was just starting to rise, and it looked like a bloody eye, and it wasn't doing anything to warm anything, so what was the point? The whole thing was stupid anyway, because he'd come out to see a ghost, and William wasn't here. This morning, he'd woken up alone, had forgotten that he hadn't brought a girl back to his room last night, and when he'd stretched out his fingers and toes and felt that expanse of soft white sheets, he hadn't even felt the thrill of the chase. He'd just felt lonely.

The lapping water wet his bunched up pants to the knees and he was taking a perverse pleasure in letting them get wet higher and higher. He'd catch a chill. He might get pneumonia. People died of that. He might die of it. Then his brothers would be sad. Minnie might say that he was feeling sorry for himself, but Minnie would be wrong. He was feeling sorry for his brothers. They'd have a sorry time without him when he was dead. Who would Chico play cards with? Who would fling pennies into their cups and water glasses? Groucho? That was a laugh. He always missed.

Harpo arched his back and felt slimy little rocks with his toes.

"Did you forget something out there?" said a familiar female voice.

Harpo fell right off the dock. The water only went up to his thighs, but he looked down and noticed that he was wet to his waist.

"Or do you want me to rescue you again?" said Ayala, pointing toward the dock on which Harpo had been stranded last night. He could just make it out in the blinking water. "If you're going for a swim, that's fine. I might not want to rescue you later, so if you could do it soon, that would be best."

Harpo nodded, and Ayala smiled. Then Harpo danced in a circle, and she laughed outright. It was a pleasant sound, kind of like the twittering of a bird, so he danced more and more wildly, like those funny Russian dancers, crossing his arms, kneeling and kicking. He could do it now. The water let him float. And she liked it, it seemed. She was Russian after all.

"Stop," Ayala said after a few minutes of this. "It's enough now. That's too much laughing."

Harpo jumped up onto the dock beside her and shook himself off.

"Stop it," she said. "I can't laugh anymore."

"That's your quota for the day?" he said, putting his hand on her knee.

"Yes," and she fixed him with her strange dark eyes, serious now, all the hints of laughter gone. "Precisely."

Harpo waited, but she didn't say anything more. He was imagining what he wanted to say to *her*, when abruptly he pictured William, red cheeked in the breath-white night. If there was a ghost on the premises, she might want to charge him to stay. "You know what I discovered?" he asked.

"A letter?"

"No," he said. "Wait. What? I like letters." He wished he'd found one of those. "I like ripping them up. That's my specialty." The first time he'd ripped a letter onstage, they'd been in that little theatre in Queens—Groucho playing a teacher, he and Chico, students. Professor Groucho had been sitting at his desk, sorting through his personal letters, and Harpo had come over and taken one, just grabbed it and ripped. And then a second passed, then two, then the audience's laughter had surged like a wave. Then Groucho waited a beat and said, "He gets angry because he can't read." God, he loved his brothers.

Harpo walked his fingers up her thigh. "Have you met Chico and Groucho yet?"

"If you didn't see my letter," said Ayala, "then it must have been a dream."

"Wait," said Harpo. "You dreamt about a letter?"

"Did you say something about Russia? I think that really happened, at least."

"I told you I'm going there." Harpo squeezed her leg. The rumours were true then. She did have a mind like the attic of a house, or a frame of mind like a house frame, all scaffolding, all layered ideas and ladders in between. She was beautiful though, more so even, since he felt a bit protective now. "You asked me to deliver a letter for you. But you didn't have it with you."

"I had a dream last night that I wrote the letter," said Ayala. "I brought it back to the dock, but I couldn't find you. There were just some saplings instead, waving in the wind like skinny ghosts. And in the lake the water was clear, and there were some underwater lightning rod plants, I could see them distinctly. I remember addressing that letter and everything. I remember writing Simon's name."

"Simon?"

"I felt better. It's been so long since I wrote it."

"Who's Simon?"

"Then I put the letter back on my drafting table, and I was going to ask Blima to take it to the postman. But when I got up in the morning, the letter was gone. It's funny because I remember the feeling of the ink on my hands. My fingertips were slick." Then she held up her wrist and hand, and they glowed, unmarked and moony white in the pale sunlight.

"Did you check your pockets?" asked Harpo. "You were wearing a nightgown last night. And I seem to remember pockets." And how they held tight to her thighs as she moved toward him. Harpo felt that familiar movement, the tickle and stir. He crossed his legs. There might be people around. He didn't know where this girl's husband was. "Maybe you just misplaced it."

"It's not the sort of letter that I would misplace," she said, watching him with that strange intensity.

"Do you often write to Simon in your dreams?" But that sounded too incongruous. Incongruous! Why would she dream about a letter when she could so easily dream about the man himself instead? That's what Harpo would do. "Maybe your husband took the letter. Maybe he wanted to say hello too."

"No." Suddenly, Ayala's cheeks were pink like they were windburned, and her lips were red, and Harpo was very aware of his hand, lying on the soft skin of her leg. It tingled. Ayala had had an affair with this man. Suddenly, it was in the realm of things he knew.

And just as suddenly, Ayala stood. "I think I saw the postman," she muttered, turning away. "I think I saw him leave."

"The mailman?"

"I have to see after the mail," and she walked quickly into the woods.

Harpo stumbled after her, quickly, to keep up. Maybe she'd lead him up to her bedroom again. This time he'd definitely follow. Maybe it wasn't such a coincidence that both he and Ayala liked the mail. Who didn't like letters? But he didn't dream about them. That was new. She probably didn't tear them up like he did, so they were even. Harpo imagined a conspiracy in the post office — himself, as a postie, tearing up all the letters as they came. Harpo the Postman.

Wait.

This could be something.

It could be a movie. It could be the movie that saved the Marx Brothers.

Harpo saw that he'd fallen behind, so he galloped forward faster. He could play a postman. He could rip up letters for a whole entire picture. Maybe he could tear up only all the letters mailed to one person. Find someone mean, or someone to tease. Good old Maggie Dumont and her broken-down smile. Or maybe he could redirect the mail and help the people who needed help. What if girls needed help finding the right man? Harpo the Postman could cut up letters, tape together the wrong halves. Jokes. Pranks. Sometimes finish the letters the writers had meant to send. He could start romances, he'd bet on that. He could start nonsense, that was for absolutely certain. This could be perfect. It could be the movie that redeemed them from *Duck Soup*. And it was Ayala who'd given it to him. Like a gift. Like she knew he needed an idea just like this one.

Harpo took a deep breath. It felt like there was more oxygen in the world somehow. He could breathe easier. And it was all because of her. Wherever she was.

Harpo stopped, looked all around him. Ayala was gone. She'd disappeared, and he was all alone in the woods again. He took a few halting steps forward and abruptly the trees thinned, and there was the lodgehouse. The newly risen sun was hitting it straight on and making the windows shine like copper pennies. Somehow, he'd wandered right back again. At least there was that.

He trudged up the path. Something always happened. People were always ditching him.

Except Ayala was probably being coy, was all. He galloped up the stairs.

Harpo pressed his face against the crack between the kitchen door and the wall. Then he looked in the dining room, then in the long hallway. No Ayala in sight. He ran through the stuffy room with all the doors in it, and then, in the room filled with windows, he found Chico. He was sitting at a coffee table, practising his shuffle and deal, with a heaping plate of food in front of him, with Groucho eating across from him, shovelling up forkfuls of eggs and meat and were those croissants?

Chico put down his cards. "Where were you last night?"

"Where was *I*?" said Harpo, picking up a hot cross bun. "I was on a raft."

"We went back for you," said Groucho. "Where did you go? How did you get back here? I even saved the crossword." He put his hands on the table, then hit his pockets. "It's around here somewhere."

Harpo sat. He wasn't ready to talk about last night yet, about the ghost and the beautiful woman, the strange loneliness of the morning, any of it. After a moment, Groucho gave up and lifted his fork. And Harpo was hungry, he realized. Where was the buffet? But then Chico started shuffling again, and Harpo just watched him. Why did he bother practising? There wasn't another person who could play with such panache. Chico grinned at him, as if he knew what Harpo was thinking.

"Pinchie Winchie?" said Chico. "I found a piece of coal this morning."

"Maybe later."

"I was thinking of finding a fourth after dinner. You in?"

"I'm thinking of going to Russia."

"Not tonight."

"September."

"I heard that. Someone already told me." Chico scratched his chin with a card. "I have a gig too. I'm going to Vegas. None of this has anything to do with pinochle."

Harpo looked out the window. The sky was still bright and blue and dazzling. He wished for thunderclouds. He wanted hail, sheeting sleet, Noah-style rain. Of course Chico was going to Vegas. "You're going on tour without me?"

"It's a piano tour, partner. You don't play the piano."

"Yes I do."

"'Love Me and the World is Mine' isn't enough for a whole tour."

"I can play it in four different keys."

"I don't think an audience would like that. Especially the Vegas crowd."

"Yeah." Harpo turned away. "They have discerning tastes there in Vegas."

He'd said *discerning*. Groucho was intent on his food, so he hadn't heard. Harpo would tell him later. No. He wouldn't. He'd never tell him at all. He'd never tell Groucho anything ever again. So they were going their separate ways. Somehow, it had already been decided.

"I'm taking Maxie with me to Vegas," Chico was saying. "She'll love it there. It's nice for a kid, lots of colours, and it'll be nice to spend some time with family."

Harpo nodded, even though he was their family too. And he'd been their family first. Stupid tied down brothers.

"I just thought of another game," said Chico.

"I don't want to play." It had been comforting to know that he wasn't all alone. But maybe he was. Maybe his brothers were moving on. They had separate families, and they even had separate jobs now, it was only Harpo who was nothing without them. *Duck Soup* had been a great movie. Why had nobody liked it?

"Okay." Chico dealt, pushed Harpo his hand. "So it starts a bit like Pinchie Winchie."

Harpo stood. He'd come here to be with his family, not to be the only one who was sad and lonely, all lit up by grief. "What happened to being a string of Christmas lights?" he asked.

"We're Jewish, Harp," said Chico.

"What was that?" said Groucho.

"I didn't want to be the one to tell you," said Chico, "but there it is. We're Jews."

Harpo turned to the door. Ayala would know what he meant. She seemed to know what grief was. He didn't know how he knew that, but he did.

"What did you say about light?" said Groucho.

Harpo turned to answer Groucho, but just then Ayala walked up to the table. "And how is your stay?" she asked. "How was your night last night?"

"What do you mean, how was my night?" said Harpo.

Ayala didn't acknowledge him, instead turned and engaged Chico in conversation. She didn't wink, didn't smile, didn't look at him at all. After a moment Harpo stalked away. He didn't care where.

Harpo was a lone wolf. He was alone anyway, and he felt like prowling.

He walked laps around his room. He felt like mauling something. Not one of his things. Chico's. Groucho's. And wouldn't that make Chico all superior like he was right, and Harpo was still a little kid. But he was, kind of, and wasn't that the point? Chico was still his big brother.

Harpo sat down heavily in front of his suitcase. He hadn't unpacked it yet. He opened it and threw a shirt at the wall. That felt nice, so he took out another one and threw that too. Then he threw some socks. Then he threw a pair of pants. The buckle crashed noisily against the wall, so Harpo looked through his suitcase for more trousers. He found a pair and threw them, hard. Then he threw pajamas.

Here he was, in a fancy resort, a movie star now, for the moment anyway, and still he was alone. He was still that scrawny little boy, that dropout, that fall-out, that thing that attached himself to people he thought would be his friends for life, when none of them ever were. Still none of them were his friends. Maybe not even his brothers, now that Minnie and Frenchie weren't around to tell Chico to include him. He missed Minnie and Frenchie so much. He missed making movies with his brothers. He missed Susan too. He didn't want to be alone. He threw three shirts at once. They didn't hit the wall at all. One of them fell in a heap right at his feet.

Harpo took a deep breath. He didn't even feel better, and now he was out of clothes to throw. He opened his suitcase wide. Inside it, under a flap of material, he found a sewing kit, and inside that was a pair of scissors. He put on a tie, then cut it in two. There. He'd dressed for dinner. When they were booking their stay, Groucho said you have to wear a tie here, but he'd forgotten to specify what you *weren't* allowed to do after you put it on.

He loped out of his room.

Harpo walked from hallway to stairs to hallway again. He wanted to find that secret staircase, Ayala's sexy attic room, to find the Ayala he'd had such a strong connection to. Maybe it would be different if he got her alone again. But he couldn't find her. He wanted so badly just to find her, or to be found himself, or caught, or pulled by that string again, but nothing happened, he still felt all alone. He'd just keep walking then, that's what he'd do. He'd walk until he got back to New York, then give up and be a tenement man himself, live the rest of his life on a stoop. He wouldn't bring his coat and fright wig and nobody would be able to find him. Even if they wanted to. But what if they didn't want to? What if they didn't even notice he was gone?

Harpo rounded a corner, and saw the desk at which he'd registered, and there was Ayala, standing at the very end of it. He crept forward. The scene changed. Ayala's cheeks were red. She was holding back tears. She was holding onto envelopes, tight like they were the sides of a sinking canoe.

Harpo took another step. But this time he stepped on a loose floorboard. He felt the creak before he heard it, and he wanted to stop the next few seconds from happening. But he couldn't. The floor creaked. Ayala turned. She saw him and fled.

Then Harpo had it—he figured out what the postman movie would be about. The movie would be about a sad woman that the Marx Brothers had to save using the mail.

Harpo walked through the door and into yet another long corridor. He nearly bowled right over a little girl. He stopped. Their eyes met, and Harpo felt a shock, like his blood was suddenly carbonated. The little girl's eyes were like Ayala's. She had the same shiny dark hair, and her face was like Ayala's too, heart shaped and red cheeked and serious, but smaller, as if made on a tiny, perfect scale. This must be Blima, the little girl who'd heard him shouting from the lake.

She looked at Harpo's chest, and he remembered the cut-up tie. He waved the stump sheepishly, and, suddenly, the little girl's face brightened. And then she laughed. And the day changed, the whole world was transformed. The little girl had a laugh like pennies falling into a glass, like when he flung one in and got it. It was the cutest laugh he'd ever heard. Harpo felt a pull of protective feeling, and it was so visceral that he stepped toward her. Visceral!

Blima ran away. She hurried around a bend in the corridor, and Harpo froze. But then her face appeared again from behind the wall, smiling impishly. She was playing! For real this time! She was undoubtedly playing, and not just excluding him. Harpo loved playing with little kids. Susan said it was because he was still a little kid himself. Maybe. Maybe he wanted kids. And wasn't that a shocking thought. He'd never really thought seriously about it before.

Then they both heard her mother calling her, calling out "Blima!" Blima's smile disappeared, and, seconds later, so did she.

Harpo walked from hallway to hallway, from room to room, touching the walls to feel their texture. He used to do this in the tenement buildings. He'd thought, then, that nobody would think he was lonely if he looked busy, so he'd gone up and down the hallways and stairwells and fire escapes, seeing how they all felt.

He'd lost everyone now, both the girl and the little kid.

He stopped in a big room and looked at the window, waiting for Ayala. She had to come now. The coy act wouldn't work if he couldn't find her, and he absolutely couldn't find her, he'd looked everywhere. So he just stood there, waited for her image to appear in the streaky window, but only his own face looked back, pale and soup-bowl eyed. Boy, he could look stupid.

He made a face, a Gookie, just like Mr. Gookie the cigar maker on lower 82nd.

There were moments in his life that had changed everything, not just after, but before too. Like the first time he'd imitated Mr. Gookie rolling a cigar, cheeks puffed out in concentration, eyes crossed, and the kids on the stoops had laughed so hard they'd had to hold the railings, the first time ever they weren't laughing at him. The world had changed. Just like that. Then he'd run upstairs to do his impression, and Minnie had screamed with laughter too, and after that it was like he'd always been funny. Then there was that card game in twenty-two when they got their nicknames. He'd turned into Harpo forever after, but before that also. Now, when they talked about the tenements, they talked about little Harpo who was on his way to Broadway and then the pictures. All the loose moments in his life, running away from gangs, getting into scraps, getting scraped, running through the streets like a marble in a box maze, all those things were just the necessary steps on his way to becoming Harpo Marx, the Marx Brother. But that other boy, that scared little kid, he was still there. Harpo could see him now in the stupid window, little Ahdie, who played all by himself and stuck by all the wrong people because he didn't want to end up alone.

Life always changed so quickly. So why wouldn't it change now?

Harpo flopped down on the overstuffed chair that faced the window. Fine particles of dust alighted and lit the dreary room, flying all around him like it was snowing upside down. He settled in to watch them.

NOBODY KNOWS EVERYTHING ABOUT FAMILY

EMILY, 2003

Emily and Jonah crept into Moshe's office, then Jonah eased the door shut behind them.

"We just need trench coats," said Emily.

"I was thinking that," Jonah said seriously. He unlocked the filing cabinet.

Emily knelt and thumbed through the dusty files. She looked through the Ks first, for Kogan, but didn't find anything. "Are they alphabetical?"

"Some might be chronological. I haven't totally figured out the record keeping."

Emily found a file marked Ayala. In it were registration forms for Doran Kogan, sheet after sheet of room bookings, starting in 1933. She'd known he was a frequent visitor. But then she ran out of forms. They just ended. And she hadn't found any registrations for his parents. She lifted the papers. "I found Doran's forms. They're in a file marked 'Ayala.'"

"I'm convinced there's a logic to all this," said Jonah.

"I can't find his parents though."

"Check P for parents."

Emily flipped through all the *P* folders. "Nothing."

"That doesn't make sense," said Jonah. "This wasn't a summer camp. Kids didn't come by themselves."

There was a sound outside. Jonah stood, and peeked out the door.

Emily reached back into the Ayala folder to see if she'd missed anything, and found something smaller, hidden at the very bottom. She pulled it out. It was a postcard, two postcards. She pried them apart. They had cute greetings written in childish letters, signed with love from Doran. She flipped over the cards. The first showed the Marx Brothers, all the boys in the midst of some frenetic movement. She and Grandma Ayala used to watch all the Marx Brothers movies; it was their ritual, an indelible part of visiting the lodge. Grandma Ayala used to talk about them too, Harpo in particular. Harpo was a good man, that's what she'd always said, he was a good father. She'd been wistful when she said it, every single time. He'd gotten married late, by the standards then, had adopted four children and had loved them more than anything. The next postcard showed Harpo alone, out of costume. Without the coat and fright wig, he looked strange. He looked like he could be just any normal person. He was staring into the camera, strangely serene, clutching at the strings of his harp. He did look like he could be a good father, and, incongruously, he wore Grandma Ayala's wistful expression, had the exact same earnest, watery-eyed stare. Emily slipped the postcards into her jacket pocket.

"Do you know anything about Doran's family?" Emily asked, finding her grandmother in the dining room. "Where did he come from?"

"That was a long time ago," said Blima. "A lot of years have passed."

"Who were his parents?"

"You never met them."

"Did they ever come to the lodge?"

"Doran was a guest of the family. We did that sometimes, took on guests for the children. It wasn't unusual way back then."

Emily sighed. Blima handed her the extra plate, the one she'd set that morning for Jonah. "Put that back, lovie," she said. "Your cousin needs to serve."

"Oh," said Emily. "That's not for him," because a lie in kindness could still be considered a mitzvah, and she really wanted Jonah to sit beside her at dinner. "It's for someone else."

"Not another one of your Auntie's boyfriends," said Blima. "I didn't even hear the phone ring."

"One is for Elijah. But you said ghosts were okay, so I put an extra one out for Harpo Marx."

Blima stopped. "Harpo," she said. "Why?"

"I don't know." She had those postcards that she was unaccountably reluctant to show. Plus, she'd been thinking about Harpo since she got back here.

"You like the Marx Brothers?" asked Blima.

"Harpo was my favourite. He was a good man. And a good father. Well, that's what Grandma Ayala always said."

"That's right." Blima's eyes flashed like lightning on the lake. "He was a man you could really love."

"Grandma Ayala used to say that too."

Blima didn't respond. Silence seemed to be coursing toward her somehow, like she was a black hole at the centre of the room. Then suddenly, she looked up again. "Harpo came to the lodge, you know."

"He came here?"

"Oh sure." Blima straightened, on the move, again the normal chattery grandmother with a story on hand, Emily was sure. "He nearly drowned once." And there it was. "He got stuck at the little floating dock and it was dark out. He yelled and yelled. I'd followed him outside, so that's how I knew."

"You actually heard his voice?"

"He wasn't really a mute. He just played one in the movies."

"What did he say?"

"What do you think he said? He said, 'help.'"

"Does that mean that Grandma Ayala met him too?"

"Sure she knew him."

Knew him.

"I knew him too," said Blima. "He protected me from anti-Semites in the woods, angry men from the townships."

"I want to know more about him," Emily said, suddenly knowing exactly what to do. She'd include Harpo in her thesis too. He'd influenced everyone — writers, artists, moviemakers, lodge guests who might have met him. She could track his family, the people he'd known, find a way to measure changes in their lives. "What years was he here?" She'd interview everyone, track down more names from her list.

"Your grandfather would know which years."

"Papa Moshe knew him too?"

"Oh sure," said Blima. "They were the best of friends."

"Why did nobody tell me this?" Harpo Marx came to the lodge. He'd interacted with her family. They were part of his history. They might even be in the books. She'd never seen mention before, but, then again, she hadn't known to look.

Emily ran to her room, threw her car keys in her purse, then rushed outside to her car. The Kingston public library had books about him. She even knew exactly where to find them, if they hadn't reorganized too much.

AND NOW GO THROUGH LIFE THIS WAY

HARPO, 1933

Harpo woke, and then he saw he was in a chair, and then remembered where he was. Lodgehouse. Treasure Island. Canada. He looked up to the window and saw the back of someone in reflection, so he quietly lifted the blanket over his head and made himself look like a cushion. From now on, he wouldn't be heard or seen any more either, and he'd go through life this way, watching it in the reflection of dirty windows.

But then, "Blima," said that familiar female voice.

Harpo peeked out through a corner of the blanket. It was Ayala in the entrance of the room, her pretty reflection in the glass just like he'd hoped for, but something about her voice made him huddle deeper into the chair.

"Yes, I said," came the chirpy reply.

"Blima, you look at me when I'm talking to you."

Harpo lowered the blanket a bit more. Now he could see Blima's sweet little face, those teardrop-shaped eyes. They met his in the window, and Harpo felt an immediate chill. But the little girl didn't say anything. She didn't give him away. She just looked back to her mother.

Now Harpo had no choice but to hide in earnest. Ayala couldn't know he was here. She'd be furious, think he'd been eavesdropping. Besides, she had his mother's fiery look, that Minnie expression. And maybe it had been her Minnie tone of voice that had made him hide under a blanket in the first place.

"You can't talk back to me that way," Ayala was saying to Blima.

"I'm sorry, I said."

"And when I say you have to take your sister to talk to the guests, I mean it."

"Except Sonja was feeling shy, so I can do it by myself, I don't mind."

"When I tell you to do something, you do it. Sonja is cuter. Guests like her more. And a child's duty is to say goodnight to everyone. You have to do it by name. And you have to curtsy. Both of you, and it's *your* responsibility to make sure that it gets done properly. This is the only place that Jews are allowed to be, so we have to make it proper."

"Okay!"

"You know what you're doing?" said Ayala. "You're making my heart shrink. You make my heart shrink every time you misbehave."

There was a silence, and suddenly Harpo was worried that his stomach would growl and give him away. If it wasn't his stomach, it would be his heart. It would break right apart. It would sound like a zipper. Harpo peeked. Blima was opening and closing her little jacket.

"Do you want me to be able to love anyone at all?" asked Ayala.

Blima looked up, not at her mother but at Harpo.

"Yes," said Blima. "I want you to love me and Sonja and Daddy."

"Then you can't make my heart shrink anymore," said Ayala. "If you do, then there won't be room for any love at all. I'll live in the attic forever, and lock the door behind me."

Harpo's fingers tingled. He thought—he didn't know what

to think. He knew he wanted to hug that little girl. She wasn't a heart shrinker. She was a love conductor. He'd thought the word *conductor*. He'd have to tell Groucho. He would. He'd tell him. He loved his family.

Harpo shrank deeper into the chair, grimacing at the groan of leather, but the Ayala in reflection seemed not to notice. She turned and left the room, tugging at Blima's arm like she was an old toy she wouldn't mind if she broke.

Harpo sat back, let all his muscles relax. He'd tensed everything up, even his jaw, so had to work now, massage his face with his fingers, to get the muscles to release. Poor little Blima. If she was his daughter, he'd never let her feel sad like that. No daughter of his would ever be broken-hearted.

He stood. He needed to find that little girl. He needed to talk to her, to explain what mothers could be like, to comfort her. For once in his life, he'd be something other than a playmate to a little kid.

"Your name is Blima," said Harpo, creeping into the garage where Blima was threading binder twine around a tin can. The little girl didn't look up. "Is this a game? Like when you ran around the corridors?"

"No," said Blima. "That one was called Wall Mouse. This is something different."

"I see." Harpo crept forward slowly. He could feel his connection to the little girl, and it was tenuous like worn-out twine. And this moment was fragile too, one wrong move and it would pop like a soap bubble. What kind of husband would he be, what kind of father would he make, if he couldn't even help a little kid? He sat down on a stool near the door. "You look sad," he said. He wanted to tell her that he didn't want her to be, that if she was his daughter, she'd never be sad again. Susan always said she wanted kids. Harpo saw it now. Maybe he wanted a family too.

Blima unwrapped the can and spun the chord around her wrist. "Jews are allowed here, you know."

"I know."

"They're not allowed to go anywhere else. This is the only place that's safe."

"Boy," said Harpo. "Don't I know that one, kid."

Then there was a silence. Finally, Blima unwrapped her can again. "I did something terrible," she said.

"What did you do?" But Harpo knew already. She hadn't asked her sister to greet the guests by name. "Whatever it was, it can't be that bad. Your mother just gets into funny moods sometimes." And didn't he know all about that as well. "Your mom told me that you're very smart."

Blima looked away. "My mother wouldn't say a thing like that."

Harpo pulled his stool forward, to look closer at that cute little face he liked so much. But the base of the stool was caught in the twine, and it toppled a bit. Harpo grabbed it, and walked it backward a little, to where it would stand up again. "Your mother trusts you to look after the guests," he said. "Especially when their brothers leave them outside on docks."

"I did that by myself because I wanted to."

"Your mother didn't tell you to go outside and listen for me?" Harpo picked up a piece of twine that was coiled up by his feet. There was string everywhere. He wrapped it around his fingers, and a can on Blima's workbench twitched.

"I saw you go outside, and then I saw the two men laughing. I wanted to make sure you were okay."

"You're a good girl." Harpo tugged on the twine around his fingers and saw that it came from a length of it. "You have a good spirit." He tugged it higher, and saw that it came right from Blima's spool. He must have the other end. He let the twine out, so that he would have a lot of slack. Then he stood slowly, slowly led the twine closer to Blima, winding it around stools and tables as he went. She was fiddling with a hammer now, and didn't look up, and so Harpo crept closer still.

"Whatever you did, it probably wasn't that bad."

"I hid something," Blima whispered, "something that didn't belong to me."

And abruptly Harpo remembered the letter. What if it hadn't been a dream after all? What if Ayala really had written something for him to deliver? "Did it belong to your mom?" he asked. "This thing you hid?"

Blima hammered her can. "Maybe."

"Did she give it to you, to put in the post, this something?"

Blima hammered harder.

Harpo wound the twine around two more stools, some hammers and an instrument he didn't even recognize. "I like to hide things from my brothers," he said.

Blima looked up. "What do you hide?"

"Crosswords. Cards. Coffee mugs, books. Once, I hid my brother Chico's pants."

"How did you hide pants?"

"We were sharing a room in a hotel." Harpo pulled tight on the twine, holding his breath, but Blima didn't seem to notice that they were connected to everything in the place. "We were in a play. So we were travelling from one theatre to another. One morning, my brother slept late, so I got up quietly, and I took away all his clothes."

Blima hid her face. Harpo crept around and around so that all the tools were caught now.

"Then Chico had to come down to the registration desk wearing his pajamas."

"Oh," Blima cooed. "We have a registration desk. I like mischief stories."

"I've done loads of mischief," said Harpo. "You know that I used to jump out the window in school? I'd jump right out of Miss Flatto's second grade class, and walk back in through the front door." Really, he'd been thrown. Two bigger boys hauled him up by the armpits, pitched him right out.

"I like your stories," said Blima. "I like you, Mister Harpo."

"So that makes us friends." And then Harpo spun around and around so he would be caught by the twine too, they would have everything strung up between them.

"I want to be your friend," Blima said.

Harpo felt that light-bulb feeling again, lit right up, looking at poor little Blima's stricken brown eyes. So he shrugged, big, raising his rope-caught arms. The twine pulled taut, and the stools lifted right off the ground.

Blima, who had jumped off her chair as all the tools in the room were rising, bubbled over with laughter. She jumped up and down, and Harpo jumped too, and everything in the shed clattered and banged. It took them half an hour to get Harpo unstuck again, another hour to tidy, Blima chattering away like a little bird, Harpo not feeling like a playmate this time. He felt different. He felt like he could be different now. He wanted a family. His family would have to include kids.

EVERYONE COMES FROM SOMEWHERE

EMILY, 2003

Emily hovered outside the dining room, just around the door. She could see that everyone was inside already, all the old folks ready to start the Second Seder — Mackie, Blima and Moshe, all together, and then, off to one side, Sonja and Doran, standing close again. They looked the same, Emily thought vaguely, but it must just be the way the candlelight was flicking shadows in their hair. They were keeping secrets from her, all of them, it seemed. She'd find it out though, whatever was hidden.

"I noticed this before," said Blima. "It's a name at my spot at the table, but it's not my name."

Emily moved to walk inside, to correct her grandmother, explain the name cards, but Jonah touched her arm and she was moving behind the door. "I'm not ready to go in yet," he said.

"This is a new game," said Blima. "That must be what Emily intended when she made these cards."

"I think this means that I have to pretend to be my sister," said Sonja.

Jonah put his hand in the crook of her arm. "They know what the name tags mean." He stepped closer, and suddenly Emily could feel his breath on her neck. It teased all the little hairs into standing.

"I sat down where I saw my name," said Doran.

"That means that you play you," said Blima. "That's fine. There's less research involved."

"They're killing me," whispered Emily.

"That's probably the point," said Jonah.

"Now I have to think of what Blima would say," Sonja said loudly, from the other room. "I think she would say, 'I want to tell a story about the sister of Moses. She was a famous vaudeville star.'"

"I have to think of what Sonja would say," said Blima.

"No," said Sonja, "because you have the Moshe ticket."

"Well," said Moshe, "Moshunya would say, 'let's eat.'"

"Moshunya would say, 'let me tell you the story of a cellar,'" said Sonja. "You're every bit as bad as Blima. You always were, you know. I didn't want to be the one to say it, but there it is."

"I could tell the story of a cellar," said Moshe. "That's not a bad idea. It's a story about my father."

"It's *my* story," said Blima. "It's about *my* father."

"No it isn't," said Moshe. "I remember distinctly."

Someone picked up a drink. Emily could hear the clinking of ice cubes. She didn't know this one, couldn't have said whose story it was.

"Where did you go, before?" Jonah whispered with sweet orange breath. "I heard you leave."

"Harpo used to come here," Emily breathed.

"Harpo Marx?"

"Why didn't they say anything before? All my life, I've loved him."

Jonah straightened. "I remember that," he said, turning his head. "You were always in love with Harpo Marx."

"No, you're right," said Moshe. "It's Blima's story. I know because it happened in Treasure Island when I was very young, but I grew up in Toronto, and my father didn't own the Treasure Island Lodge, come to think of it. Oh well, I'll tell it anyway. We just have to find Emily, because she's been asking about the family, and I think she'd like this one."

Emily shifted a little, to hear better, and abruptly Jonah was off, walking away, and she was stumbling, watching him disappear wordlessly into the kitchen. She'd been comfortable suddenly, and just as suddenly, she was shivering a little, walking into the dining room all alone. The world changed so fast.

"Let me tell the story," said Moshe as Emily took her seat beside him. He filled Emily's wineglass. "Emily, this isn't my story. It's your Bubbie Blima's story, but I tell it better."

"I tell it better than any of you," said Sonja.

"I'm the one who was there!" said Blima.

"Nevertheless," said Sonja.

"This is the story about the Treasure Island cellar," said Moshe.

"I want to hear about Harpo Marx," said Emily. "Did he really come here?"

"Harpo's in this one, don't you worry."

"Seriously?"

"Emily, when your great-grandmother Ayala and your great-grandfather, Papa Sam, moved to Treasure Island, the lodgehouse wasn't a lodge at all. It was a more like a shed. Even after they opened it to the public. They had very few rooms. Now, your Papa Sam had already added extensions to the house."

"Wait," said Emily. "Papa Sam did that himself?"

"Oh sure," said Blima. "Your Papa Sam had never even been trained. He just got up one morning, and decided to teach himself. People did that sort of thing in those days."

"That's true," said Sonja, "you could teach yourself anything back then. Want to be an architector? Well, sure. Get some books from the library and off you go."

Emily shifted in her chair, and felt a slight give in the floorboards. Had that always been there? "Is this place even safe?"

"Sure," said Blima. "We've had inspectors in and they all say the same thing. The lodge is flawlessly built."

"So Papa Sam had already added extensions so that more guests could stay," said Moshe, "but what Ayala really wanted was a cellar. She wanted to store things, like in the old country, and make root beer and sauerkraut. So Sam, and Papa William and Harpo Marx, they all got together one morning, and went out and bought some dynamite."

"Harpo?" asked Emily.

"Although Harpo was nervous," said Sonja.

"You were too young to remember any of this," said Blima.

"Oh, I remember *that*," said Sonja. "Harpo kept asking me whether this was a good idea. Me. I was four years old. Nobody has to remind me of that. He made his brother take me for a walk. He wanted the kids nowhere near the lodge when it happened."

"Wait," said Emily. "Which of Harpo's brothers? I didn't know his brothers were here."

"We should make sauerkraut again," said Blima.

"We couldn't do it like our mother," said Sonja. "Although how she ever did it is still a mystery to me. She refused to walk into the cellar. That sauerkraut is yet another miracle of childhood."

"I thought she wanted the cellar," said Emily.

"She did," said Sonja, "but she thought your Papa Sam was stupid to dynamite on his own. She wanted him to bring in a professional."

"Did he clear the house at least?" asked Emily.

"God no," said Blima. "All of the things were still inside, probably the guests too, I don't remember. Dad dug a hole in the ground in the back and filled it with gunpowder. Then he and Papa William sat on lawn chairs and watched the whole thing happen. Harpo didn't sit with them. He paced and paced and made me promise not to let him tell Dad another single idea. Then there was the explosion. And then there was dust everywhere and we were weak in the knees and thought for a moment that the island might sink. But it didn't, so that was that."

"They did other things too," said Sonja. "They broke open the room of doors. They put holes in the walls, that later become windows. They did it so that you could see windows in the next room over. They unclogged the pipes with boric acid that Papa Sam sucked through a hose."

"Boric acid?" asked Emily

"The cellar, though," said Sonja, "that was the best. Our mother was so mad."

"No," said Blima. "Our mother wasn't angry, not then. She laughed. I remember distinctly. That was one of the moments when I thought this is what I want to be. I want to be the kind of lady who can laugh as the whole world is exploding out from under me. After, though. I'll admit. That night, she got mad. I heard it all the way in our bedroom."

"I didn't even know that Great-grandma Ayala and Papa Sam fought," said Emily.

"Only very rarely," said Blima.

"Oh, all the time," said Sonja, at the same time.

Then Doran's were the only eyes that would meet hers. "Doran," said Emily, "do you remember anything from your childhood?"

"Yes." Doran nodded slowly. "I remember everything."

Blima held up her glass. "I think we should skip the ceremony tonight," she said. "I think we've remembered quite enough."

"Tell me more about Harpo," said Emily. "Please. I need to know. What did he do on his next visit?"

"That was the last one," said Blima.

"What?" Everyone always came back. That was the point. "How many times did he come?"

"Twice," said Blima. "Once in the summer, then once the next fall. Never again."

Emily sat back. Something was wrong. Harpo Marx had visited the lodge. But he'd come twice and then never again and that wasn't normal: the lodge prided itself on lifelong guests. Some visitors even mentioned this place in their obits. The old folks didn't tell the story of his coming here when they told stories about everything else, when most of the stories they told weren't even true? Why hadn't they mentioned this before? What had happened in the time of Harpo's visit that they didn't want to talk about?

But nobody would make eye contact with her, not even Doran.

THE GODS OF *THE NEW YORK TIMES*

HARPO, 1933

Harpo tiptoed back to his room and sat down with his back pressed up against the door, in a nest of thrown clothes. He loved this place. He'd protect it. He loved that little girl too, and he'd protect her from anything. He'd find a way. Susan wanted kids. He thought, for the first time in his life, that it might not be a bad idea. For the first time ever, he imagined himself as a daddy. And all because of Blima. She needed help with her mom, and Harpo had a lot of experience with this sort of thing. He knew what Ayala was trying to say. He'd just have to mitigate the rest of it. Mitigate!

Mitigate, four across, from the crossword with Groucho the morning after Frenchie's funeral—it occurred to Harpo, and not for the first time, that it must be some higher power that set the crosswords, not some dime-a-day employee. The words Groucho taught him were always immediately useful. What other words had he learned lately? Filament. Incongruous, tenuous, discerning. Orchestra, no orchestrate. Immutable maybe? Every time Grouch taught him a word, he always heard it again the next day or the day after, or he used it himself to explain something that would have been unexplainable before. Well now he'd put the words to use, some of them at least.

Blima was afraid that her mom didn't really love her. Harpo had a secret fear too. What if he hadn't settled down because he was incapable of settling down? What if he moved from woman to woman because he secretly knew that no woman would love him for the rest of his life? What if he hadn't had a kid yet because he secretly knew he'd be a lousy father?

Well, he'd just have to see, one way or the other. Maybe he and Blima could help each other.

Harpo would fix Blima's relationship with her mom. Everyone needed to be loved by their mother, and nobody was more lovable than that little girl. And if he could be a father figure to her, then maybe he'd be good enough at it to start his own family.

He'd consider finding the secret attic staircase too, maybe, but not until later. He wouldn't seduce Ayala until she'd made up with her daughter. It was only right.

ALL THINGS LOST

EMILY, 2003

When dinner was finished, and the plates had been cleared, Emily hesitated in the doorway, and Jonah came out to see her. Then Sonja sidled up to Emily, and Jonah slipped away again, back into the kitchen.

"You know, lovie," said Sonja. "When your Bubbie Blima and I were young, we thought it was our job to visit every person who came to the lodge and ask them if they were having a good time. 'Has your stay been marvellous?' and 'We hope that your stay has been just marvellous,' that sort of thing. That's what we said. That's what was done then. We started when I was just three years old."

"That's cute."

"I think it's nice for people in the family to visit."

"Oh," said Emily. She folded herself in the little space where the two walls met, exactly where she'd stood with Jonah. Only, it wasn't warm now. It wasn't cozy like it had been, didn't smell sweet like coconuts.

"You could make up for your mother who never comes, who never helped."

"Right." She wouldn't be like her mother. If her mother hadn't helped, then she would. She'd be good to her family.

"Especially if you're thinking of helping out in the lodge, lovie," Sonja was saying. "I think it's nice for the people who want to help out here to make sure that everyone's having a nice time. Especially if she's a beautiful girl like you."

"I guess I should mingle."

"You go check on all those guests."

"You mean Mackie and Mr. Baruch."

"That's a good girl."

Emily found Doran Baruch on the veranda. He fit into the shadows, or the shadows fit him, and he looked like a misshapen leather glove. "Mr. Baruch," she said quickly, before she could talk herself out of it.

"Doran," he said simply, and, suddenly, Emily had no idea what to say next. "How has your stay been?" she asked. "I hope it's been just marvellous."

"Of course." He sat down on the steps.

Emily sat beside him. She felt the wet seeping through her pants, through her underwear, right into her skin. Had it rained? "Do you really remember everything?"

"I used to remember nothing," he said slowly.

"Yeah." She could probably warm to a guy who liked to wind up her family. "That makes sense. Blima doesn't really remember anything either. I used to bug her about it."

"About Russia?"

"All she could remember was a white room, with a cupboard that she crawled into one time."

"A cupboard?"

"She remembers being yanked away from it. But she grabbed onto a drawer handle and it opened as she was pulled. There were glass bottles in it and she burst into tears."

Doran nodded slowly. "You remember what she told you."

"I've been interested. I've been kind of interested in your family history also."

Doran lapsed into a sort of heavy silence, and Emily became intensely aware of the sound of her own breathing. He wasn't answering, but she hadn't really asked the question either. How could she ask? Do you know anything about your family? That sounded crass, mean, in fact, if the answer was no. Some people knew about their parents and that was it, and he'd had to escape from Russia. That would make genealogy rough. Wait. Hadn't he come by himself? Where had his parents been then?

"The last time I came here, it was in this time of year," Doran said suddenly. "But it was different. There was snow, the first few days. But that was years ago. Decades." He exhaled, and his breath lit up the night all around them. "It snowed more then, I suppose. I thought, if one thing would stay the same, that would be the weather. But things in this world are not immutable."

Then he pointed. Emily saw a band of darker black and followed it to the swing set. It was lit by moonlight, the bars winking dully.

"Those were there, then," said Doran. "There was snow from the ground to the rubber seats. Then on them too. It looked like there were dead bodies slumped on the swings. There weren't bodies though. It was just snow, and it wasn't covering anything. I checked, of course."

Emily still didn't know how to ask. Had he come to Canada alone? He would have been young. That must have been terrifying.

Doran shook his head. He looked like a weird, ambulatory shadow. "I don't know why I said that I remember everything. My first memory used to be at the lodgehouse. I was lying on the floor under the dining-room table, looking out the window. There were adults in the room. I could hear them whispering. I knew that they were talking about me, but I didn't care to listen. I covered my ears."

Emily put her head on the banister. "My first memory," she said, and she thought about a hill, a lampstand, a bookshelf. "I'm drunk again." She always drank too much when she visited the lodge. These dinners were insidious, everyone always filling glasses.

"But since I turned seventy," said Doran, "I *have* been remembering things. Before the lodgehouse. Before this country. There's a memory that I have. I'm inside a room. It's a hidden church. There's a very tall man in front of me. He shows me a wafer and says, 'This is the body of Christ.' I'm terrified that Jesus will come. I got it the wrong way around. I pictured the wafers making up the man."

"Oh." Emily pictured a monster made of crackers. "Where was this?"

"Russia," said Doran. "Or what was Russia then." And then, "You have a friend here."

"What?" said Emily, still picturing twitching sacks in the pantry, monstrous things crawling out of cupboards.

"You and Jonah are close."

"Oh," said Emily. "Yes. We used to be. It's sort of a work in progress now."

Doran nodded and nodded. "It's difficult," he said, nodding still.

"I want to be his friend. There has to be a way to go about it, to make someone like you. There have to have been experiments. Research. Someone must have developed methods."

Doran was nodding still.

Emily felt herself blushing. Other people, she reminded herself, didn't look to science to solve every single problem. "Well at least there are no more Seders," she said.

"These ceremonies only come in twos. It always felt like there were more—"

"Because we celebrate for eight days."

"—a calendar year maybe. Three-hundred-and-fifty-seven days of remembering, and then you can take eight days off. It always seemed to me that the Jewish culture had the better idea on the subject of how to grieve. You never say goodbye. You always remember."

Then he stood, and bowed, and walked toward the lake, a monstrous stain leaking across the landscape. Emily hadn't asked the question, but she had twenty-four hours respite, to rephrase, to think more about it. At least there was that. She'd established that he came from Russia, originally. That was something too.

Emily lay down on her back, then closed her eyes. Do you have any family? No, she couldn't say that. Of course he had family, everyone came from somewhere. Do you know names, dates, do you have death certificates? This was stupid. Mathematicians should never have to deal with people directly.

She heard the door creak open, then footsteps and an expectant sort of silence, someone hovering in the doorway. She didn't have to sit up to know that it was Jonah. "It's nice out," he said after a minute, and Emily felt the night open up a crack. Maybe he had been looking out for her all along. She heard a series of creaks as he sat down beside her.

"Is there something you wanted to talk to me about?" she asked.

"Sure," he said, and she heard the crackle of paper. She stretched her neck and saw the outline of his nose. He was beautiful, but far away. "What's a four-letter word that means audible bounce back?"

Luckily she knew that one. "*Echo,*" she said. She waited, but Jonah said nothing more.

There were things he could say. Why he was outside. Why he still worked at the lodge and didn't want her to work here too. If he'd missed her. She didn't even know if he had been looking out for her all these years, or if she'd been following him. It could be that she'd just sort of anticipated his trajectory, put herself in all the places he was going to be, a mathematician's version of love, maybe, or of stalking. "I've never understood the expression 'companionable silence,' Jonah."

She listened to his slightly arrhythmic breathing, the sharp exhalations that might have been a laugh. She sighed loudly. "Are you even a bit happy to see me?"

"I do plan to go to college," he said.

"Oh," said Emily. "And study what?"

"Management. Culinary science—it is a science, you know."

"Like chemistry."

"I'm not in a rut."

Emily struggled to sit up. "I didn't think you were."

"Do you know where Doran is all the time?"

"What?" said Emily. "With Sonja?"

"Upstairs mostly, in the attic. If you listen, you can hear him creeping around like a cockroach. He's going up now, I think."

Emily closed her eyes, and she heard it, a creaking without a source, round and round it sounded like, sometimes cracking dully where Emily could swear there weren't even floors, just sky. He must have gone back in the front. Then Emily heard another set of footsteps. She turned to look at Jonah. "Does Sonja go up there with him?"

"Sometimes I catch her looking through the keyhole."

"They don't talk," whispered Emily. Sonja couldn't connect either. And Sonja was so much more charming than she was. She always knew what to say, how to make people like her.

"Hey, are you holding your breath?" asked Jonah. "I'm the one who used to hold my breath. I used to pretend that you'd killed me. Remember? You used to get the mirror and hold it in front of my nose? You were pretty easy to mess with back then."

Emily turned her head. She wasn't the little girl who would cry all alone in dark rooms anymore. She wasn't easy to mess with, she'd grown up. She was an adult, a scientist. Also, there were ways to make someone interested in you, she remembered with a start. There *was* research. It was all physiognomy, science. You could manipulate causality. All you needed to do was simulate the experience of falling in love, present yourself to the subject and presto chango, the brain mistook the cues and induced a love reaction. Scientists had pulled it off with a shaky suspension bridge, hundreds of feet above rapids. They'd put men on it, one by one, shaking it with invisible chords to make the subjects think they might fall into the churning water below. Then as soon as the men stepped off the bridge, safe, they made a pretty girl walk by. Ninety percent of the test subjects asked her for her phone number.

Emily could take Jonah down to the lake and push him in. She could jump into the bushes. Or she could arrange to meet him later, then jump *out* of the bushes to scare him, that would make him love her. She sat up on her elbows. But Jonah was gone. She hadn't even heard him get up.

Emily crept to her room and checked her email. Russell was getting irritated. That wasn't surprising. So she sent a reply: the reason he hadn't found her was that she'd had a headache and gone home early. If he thought he could pin her down, he had another thing coming. She could keep this up forever.

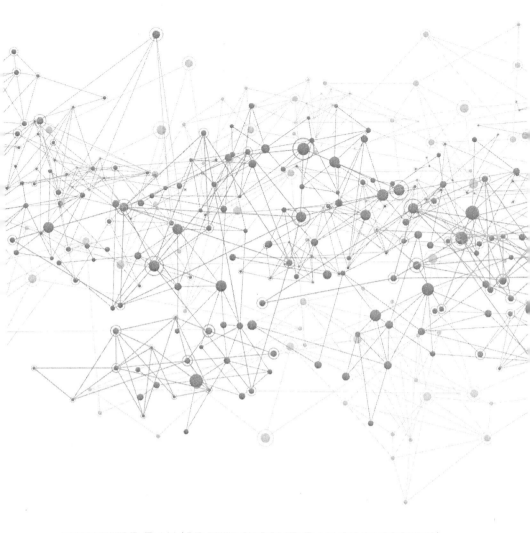

THE THIRD DAY (OR THE SECOND DAY OF PASSOVER)

PRETEND TO BE THE DRESSMAKER'S DUMMY

HARPO, 1933

The water was sparkling and pale blue and should have been warm, but wasn't. And there were footsteps approaching. It was Ayala. It had to be. So Harpo kicked, and water flew everywhere. She might get wet, but that was a risk he was willing to take. He had work to do. He had to fix her relationship with her daughter.

"That's the splashing of a man who has something on his mind," said Ayala as she sat beside him.

Harpo was thinking about her wonderful little girl. He started to tell her that, but then noticed that Ayala was all made up, looked entirely different from the straggly thing who'd crawled out of a canoe the night they'd met. She could be a different person altogether. His mother could transform herself like that. Minnie also knew how to use makeup like it was armour. Harpo edged farther away on the dock.

"I recognize the look because I have things on my mind too," Ayala said, smoothing her fancy skirt and starchy blouse.

Harpo missed the nightgown. He had an atticky feeling for that thing. And her clothes hadn't gotten wet, so he kicked again, and this time they definitely did. He could see through the blouse, right to the brassiere beneath it. He ogled, but his heart wasn't in it. She reminded him a little of Minnie right now. He looked away.

"I've been thinking about the letter that I want to send with you," said Ayala.

"Did you find it?" asked Harpo.

"I need to enclose something in it. But how does love move from person to person? That's what I need to know first, before anything. How does love travel?"

"By mail?" said Harpo.

"Love might be like the smell of baking."

"Yeah." Harpo shifted, moved a rock out from under him. "I like food."

"I think it might travel through the air like a gas. I think that might be where it comes from."

Harpo looked at the surface of the water. He remembered seeing Minnie standing under a broken light in an empty dressing room and thinking, 'I can make her happy.' He'd grabbed the dressmaker's dummy and waltzed with it, and just as quickly, he was on the ground. She'd lashed out with the measuring stick, he realized as a strip of pain opened up across his back and legs.

"If I want to give love away," Ayala was saying, "then how do I do it? How does love go?"

"That's easy." In Harpo's memory, he was crouched on the dusty floor, picking up the sewing pins Minnie had knocked down, tipping them up so the pointy ends stuck his fingertips. Love was a desperate feeling inside his stomach, like the need to find a bathroom. "It just does. It just goes."

"How? You love and the other person is loved? That's too simple. There must be more to it."

Harpo nodded vaguely, but then realized that Ayala wasn't right, so he stopped. But it was too late. Ayala was smiling like he was in full agreement, and smart people always did this, they made easy things seem so complicated. They lost track of the point.

"Could there be a time difference?" said Ayala. "It can't be true that as soon as I love someone, they know it already. I've hardly had time to make up my mind at all. It seems to me that it would be a bit presumptuous of love."

"If I love someone when I'm on a train, would the love move faster, do you think?"

"Probably," said Ayala. "Yes. Of course it would."

"Good then." He'd loved Susan on the way here, as the train had pulled away from the station. He'd thought about her very tenderly, like he'd never really thought about any girl before. His Susan. That's what he'd thought. His Susan who'd asked if she could bring her mother on a date. She'd been teasing him. That was funny. "So if I think a nice thought about a girl when I'm on a train, then it'll find her and just sock her."

"Unless the train was moving away from her. If the train was moving in the opposite direction, then she might not even know about it yet, this nice thought. It's going to take some time, just to get to her."

Harpo sighed. This was all too much for a boy who'd fallen out of school in the second grade.

"Love is not easy to think about," said Ayala, nodding. "It's complicated. It's like with time zones and clocks."

"Clocks?"

"That's my new theory. I'll work at loving now, and hopefully everyone will find out about it sometime later."

Harpo nodded, but couldn't begin to fathom what he was nodding at. This woman was coming unhinged. Susan would never do that. Susan was stable, but managed her stability in the classiest of ways, wasn't boring or uninteresting because of it. God, he missed her.

"Because otherwise," Ayala was saying, "something about the way I love is broken. I love my girls, and I don't think they know it. It's not a working transaction. That's why I prefer that guests pay with cash."

"Oh," said Harpo. "You're worried about your girls." So

maybe this wouldn't be too difficult. Maybe he could solve their problems.

"When you write a letter, your words should go, but your love should go with it. The Canadian postal service doesn't charge a tariff for that, so I'm concerned that they're not taking it seriously."

"Wait. You're worried about your letter?" Could this be the thing that Blima was so worried about? The thing that she'd hidden? "Ayala, *was* that a dream? Did you actually write a letter?"

Ayala was looking out at the islands. "Maybe it was a long time ago that I wrote it," she said. "It could be that it was a *memory* and not a dream at all, and that particular letter was sent years ago. Maybe all this time I've been waiting for an answer."

"Did you send this letter yourself, or did you give it to someone else to send for you?" Harpo remembered Blima's stricken expression. She hadn't sent it. She'd hidden it instead. "What was in it?"

But Ayala had disappeared inside herself.

"Ayala?" Harpo waited, but her eyes still had that dull cast. She'd found a new way to ditch him. But it was fine. He had a place to start. If he could find the letter and return it, then Blima would have one less worry, and maybe they could make up. He stood, and dusted himself off. Besides, he had a movie to write, a comeback to orchestrate. Orchestrate! Thank you, *New York Times*.

The first five minutes of the picture show how the world was before the Marx Brothers upend it, so here's how it was. There's the peaceful neighbourhood (little houses, winding lanes), and there's the postal service (shiny hallways, uniforms, letters in big canvas bags), and there's the star of the show, a beautiful lady with a sad smile, timidly walking in through the post-office door. And now there are the Marxes: Groucho behind the counter with a shy young man, the romantic lead, Chico sorting, Harpo with mailbag, Harpo escaping out the back way, pulling bones from his mailbag and feeding all the neighbourhood dogs.

Then there would have to be a little kid too. Harpo pictured a little girl who looked just like Blima. She was sitting on a stoop, reading a letter and crying. Then Harpo the Postman appeared. He took the letter away and ripped it to pieces. He could be a reverse mailman sometimes too. That would play. There was nothing more powerful in this world than comedy that sort of hurt.

What kind of a letter would make a little girl cry though? That's what he needed to figure out first.

He found himself at the stairs to the lodgehouse and ran inside.

Harpo crept into the room of doors. His brothers were in there in a big knot of people, laughing and playing cards. They didn't notice him, didn't even look up. It was their loss. They didn't even know that there was a new movie being written or a mystery to be solved. He stumbled out again.

Where would a kid hide a letter?

In the hallway, there was a couch, and Harpo sat on it nonchalantly. At least, he hoped he was being nonchalant. He picked up a book from the bookshelf beside him, flipped through it, and when he was sure nobody would walk in on him, he reached under the couch's bottom cushion. Nothing. Wood. He flopped onto his side and slid his hand farther, and still nothing. A penny. That was it. He sat up and saw people outside the window, and they were looking at him. He waved. They turned and walked off again, and Harpo continued feeling up the couch like he was a particularly methodical lover. Methodical. That had been in a crossword recently too. The gods of *The New York Times* were showing him the way.

Harpo crept to the next couch. Nothing under the seat. He turned and felt under the topmost cushion, the one against the back. Nothing. He slumped and felt under his own bottom. The letters had to be in a couch. They couldn't be near the floor because that Ayala was a compulsive mopper, Harpo knew the type, and Blima was too smart a girl.

Then he saw the picture on the wall, and he felt behind it, along the very edge of the frame, but didn't find anything. That was probably too high for little Blima to reach anyway. She was just eight or nine. Ten tops. Short. Harpo checked the rest of the frames anyway, just in case. Maybe Harpo the Postman could be a part-time detective too, but what would he detect? Mail theft. Fraudulent letter writing, insincere use of the postal system. No. He'd break into people's homes and find all their unsent letters, the ones they didn't have the courage to mail, and he'd deliver them. Harpo, the real one and not the fictional postman one, had started a letter to Susan, but he'd never got past the first two words: he'd written "Dear Susan," and that was it.

What if Harpo the Postman had to finish the letters? What if Harpo the Postman couldn't write, and had to get that little girl to help him? She could do the spelling. She could do the cursive too, come to think of it. He'd mime the words and she'd write it all down, because she was smart like that, she could do it.

Harpo reached the end of the row of pictures and found himself at the entrance of the room full of windows. He snuck in, and went right to the couch. Under a blanket, he found a miniature saltine tin. Cute. He carefully replaced it and ran his hand along the pillows. He felt paper, and pulled out an envelope, triumphant. A letter! He extricated the folded paper. A love letter, but written by a Malka something, and not by Ayala. He thrust his hand back in the sofa. He must be close. He was still busy checking under the bottom cushions when people came in, a man and a woman, and they sat on one of the sofas. They looked at him suspiciously, then turned away. Then the woman shifted and sat on the man's lap.

Harpo considered finding another room to snoop around in. But this room had lots of overstuffed chairs and sofas, and where better to hide a letter? Harpo's instincts had to be right. He remembered from the tenements. Chairs and table bottoms were the two things nobody ever tried to clean, so any time he found a penny, he taped it away, under the clawed foot of the dining-room table, on the underside of a chair. They might even still be there, his secret stashes. That furniture might be worth twice as much as its new owners thought.

Harpo reached his hand between the chair and the cushion, and those other guests turned to watch him again, so he froze. He closed his eyes. He'd wait them out, pretend to be napping. Then he'd search again as soon as they left. And so Harpo let his thoughts drift away on the churning sounds of muffled laughter.

THE VERY LAST VAUDEVILLE SHOW

EMILY, 2003

Emily turned on her computer. Six days before she had to submit
her thesis. And there they were, two new messages from Russell.
She closed them without reading. Then she found her horoscope.
"You can succeed right now, the stars are with you, but here's a
cosmic tip: your success will mean more if you use it to help other
people too."

She put her face on the cold countertop.

When she was ready to get back to work, Emily opened her thesis
document. She wrote, "Abstract," underlined it, then closed the
document again. Then she thought about Jonah. She should go back
to first principles for that problem as well. She wanted Jonah to be
her friend again, and there had to be research to explain how to go
about that. There had to be scientific principles at work. The bridge
experiment had been conducted at the turn of the century, and there
had to be some more recent work than that.

She opened a search engine, wrote the question and immediately found an interesting theory. You're more likely to hear a
confidence if you offer one first. It had been proven. It was in

common usage too, it seemed. Charities used the principle to solicit donations. They offered small gifts like postage stickers or postcards, because that made it more likely that people would offer a gift in return.

Emily turned off her computer and went to find Jonah.

But she lost her courage, her immediate resolve anyway. She couldn't think of what to offer. Anyhow, she had more pressing work to do, thesis work. Emily stopped at her grandfather's office door. It opened. Papa Moshe's smiling face appeared in the crack, and Emily cupped the soft wrinkles, kissed both cheeks, then followed him inside. She loved her grandfather. And maybe he could help her.

Moshe showed her to the couch. "Can you tell me about Harpo Marx?" she asked. "When did he come here? What years?"

Moshe sat behind his big oak desk, paused, then cleared his throat. "It's early in the Marx Brothers' careers. Harpo and his brothers have just been kicked out of what might be their last vaudeville theatre." Her grandfather had never been one for preambles.

Emily stood. "Who did he used to talk to?" Then she noticed that the office was full of hiding spots. She needed family documents. Also, Blima had mentioned that something was hidden. Everyone was looking for that package.

"They were kicked out for some sort of misbehaviour, I don't know what, and the manager said he'd have them blacklisted."

"Yeah," Emily said vaguely, creeping from one bookshelf to the next, touching the spines of all the books, looking for the telltale tip of a hidden letter. Anyway, she knew this story. She couldn't remember why the Marx Brothers had been kicked out of vaudeville either.

"This could be the end of their careers. The theatre manager said they would never book another vaudeville theatre, he'd make sure of that."

Emily tipped back the tallest book on the shelf, and felt the gold-edged pages. Books were sometimes hollowed out. Her family might have hidden valuable things inside empty ones. They'd escaped from Russia after all, and they must have hidden their stuff somewhere. She pulled out one book, then another. She flipped through the pages. Nothing. Just books.

"They all know that it might be the end of their act," Moshe was saying. "Nobody says it, but as they all squish into their train compartment going home, they're all thinking it. Ironically, Harpo is the only one to say anything. He says, 'nuts,' and walks out again, then wanders through the empty corridors."

Emily straightened all the books.

"Anyhow. When the train ride is coming to an end, that's when Harpo joins his brothers. He walks into the compartment and they're all in there, excited and talking. They have ideas about their next gig. It's a play this time, not just a show. So they've been kicked out of vaudeville, so what? They'll shoot for Broadway. They'll make their act bigger. So Harpo, he sits down, and he makes up ideas too. But before that, in the train hallway, that was the only time Harpo ever felt sorry for himself. That's what he wrote in his book, and I believe it."

"I'm not feeling sorry for myself, Papa."

"You seem a little lost, that's all I'm saying."

"I'm not lost," said Emily. "There's just something I need to find."

"That's something that can happen." Moshe brightened. "Oh!" he said. "Second Present? No, it's Passover, of course, we need to hide the afikomen."

"I'm too old for that," said Emily, "that's a child's game. Is there a package everyone's trying to find?"

Moshe rifled through his papers, not making eye contact. Then he picked up a carved statue from his desk, a nude woman carved out of some dark wood. "Was she perkier when we first bought her?" he muttered.

"Do you know what years Harpo came here?"

"Well, that's easy," said Moshe. "1933."

"Right before *A Night at the Opera*."

"That's right," said Moshe. "I heard them talking about it. They were planning out bits, thinking about the story."

"That's my favourite movie."

"I always thought it was funny that you loved them."

"Ayala and I talked about them all the time," Emily said. "They wrote the movie here?"

"And then Doran showed up, of course, and everything changed."

"Doran knew him?"

"Maybe." Moshe wouldn't look her in the eyes. "I don't know. It was so long ago."

Emily stood. This place was maddening. It was the opposite of university, like nobody wanted anyone to know anything, and was it any wonder that she'd left for so long?

"Just don't tell your grandmother that you're looking for things," said Moshe.

"Oh." Emily stopped in the doorway. "Why not?"

"She might not like people poking around just now." Moshe patted a pile of papers on his desk. "There are secrets she used to protect, I think is her concern."

"I thought the family rule is that we have to find all the secrets."

"Not the big one."

"What big one?"

Papa Moshe was studiously examining his mail. But Emily knew the rule. You have to find all things that are hidden.

Emily stood very still in the kitchen. She'd set the table, then rifled through all the cutlery drawers, ostensibly organizing. She'd vacuumed this morning, searched under all the rugs, and everyone had commented on her helping spirit and dedication to cleanliness, so she couldn't vacuum again.

She could go through desk drawers, pretend that she was dusting, but that still might look a lot like snooping. Of course she could start writing up her thesis, all these new ideas. Or she could start a crossword puzzle, then everyone would come to her. She could clean out the kitchen. The lodge had two fridges. Emily opened one. Then she opened the other. Then she closed them both. And then she felt a flush of heat despite the breath of cold air. There were places she hadn't explored yet. She knew where she should go next.

Emily crept past registration, past the guest rooms, right to the basement door.

Cellars weren't actually scary places.

She opened the door quickly and ran down the stairs before she could rethink her decision, then quickly found the lights. The basement wasn't as eerie as she'd remembered. It felt smaller now. Compact. An ordinary room. There were the barrels, formerly for sauerkraut and root beer. And there were the stacks of old boxes. The top box gave up with a cough of dust and dried glue to reveal a tangle of old things inside, telephone cords and gadgets. And an envelope labelled 'old.' Emily carefully picked it out.

She sat back on her heels. She'd accomplished things. She'd overcome her fear of the cellar, and found stuff here. Second Present! She'd been brave just like Grandma Ayala had been brave when she moved here, in a smaller sort of way, granted, but even so. She wondered if she could turn this moment into a graph. Maybe she could graph all the family traits, and once they were all written down, choose which ones she wanted to inherit. Imagine if her thesis could be one half Milgram and one half Mendel, if it could mess around with personality traits the way scientists messed around with plant genetics. Maybe the whole thing was working already. She was in the cellar. She'd done it. She'd let Papa Moshe tell his weird meandering story too, and hadn't gotten exasperated. It seemed to Emily that you could be a Harpo, or you could be a

Groucho—you could be weirdly funny and random, or you could be witty, but harsh. Those seemed to be two orthogonal ways in which to approach the world, the axes with which you could measure personality. She could graph that too.

Emily opened the envelope. It was full of pictures, and they were old, the label was right. They weren't black and white even, but beige and sepia, and they were cut in all different sizes and shapes. There was her great-grandfather, Papa Sam, but young, standing stiffly beside two other men who looked just like him. They were holding one hand behind their backs. Emily flipped the card. Bobby, Sam and Dima, 1907. Those must be Papa Sam's brothers. The picture must have been taken in Russia. Then there was another one, a cute little boy in a sailor suit. She flipped the card—Blima, port of France. She flipped the photo back over. It *was* a little girl. Blima. Emily could see it now. She had her hair cut pixie short.

Emily flipped through more images of men and women in stiff poses—Max, Raisa, Efim, the labels said. It was strange to think that they were all long dead now. She put the pictures back in the envelope and slid her fingers under the flap to seal it. It made an eerie crinkling sound, and that's when she made the mistake of looking up. There were the shadows and bumpy walls that she remembered. This was how she'd pictured jail cells before she ever saw a real one on television. She used to expect murderers down here, and once, when she'd been alone, she'd heard ragged breathing that wasn't hers, and she'd felt a cold air that seemed to seep up right from the soil—or had that been a dream?

Emily settled in at the registration desk, fanned out the pictures from the envelope and waited for her pulse to return to normal.

She turned on her computer and looked up the Mormons, like Jonah had said. She typed in Ayala Kogan, Russia. Why had the Mormons put so much effort into this? Why had she started her project though, chronicling a little known university social networking site, drawing diagrams, linking people who contacted each other, read the same articles, touched the same links? The FamilySearch website, at least, provided information interesting to more people than just the information collectors themselves.

She found nothing for Ayala, so moved on to her great-grandfather Sam Kogan, and the website found no results for him either. She tried births, then marriages. Nothing. Then she tried the other names: Bobby and Dima—Robert and Vladimir. Max, Raisa, Efim. Nothing.

Emily heard a creak, and looked up, heart racing again, but it was just Jonah. "I can't find my family anywhere," she said as he peeked over her shoulder.

"They die all the time," said Jonah, "but they're never born."

"And that's not weird?" said Emily.

"Is that what you're doing with your math?"

"Checking whether people were born?"

"I just always wonder what math is for."

"I'm trying to see how people change each other," said Emily. "I'm trying to figure out the effect of people on each other, on the ideas we have."

Jonah was already off at the back, puttering in the cubbyholes.

Emily went back to her computer. Examining changes did need math. Idea formation was a science for sure. Who you are was a direct result of who you knew, and what you thought about depended on what they talked about every day.

Emily looked up Harpo Marx in FamilySearch. The family was called Marx in the States, but Marrix in Alsace, she remembered that from his autobiography, and it always astonished her how much names could change. She liked to think about Harpo, how he might have been outside the movies. She used to do that a lot when she was a kid here, especially in all those quiet summers. She used to read about him, from all these same books from the Kingston public library: Groucho's short stories, Chico's daughter's memoirs, Arthur Marx's autobiography. She'd scan them for references to Harpo and would pour over those sections, read them over and over. She quickly wrote down a family tree for Harpo Marx.

Then she checked her email. Three new messages from Russell.

"Is that math too?" asked Jonah.

"Just sending my prof an email," she said. She saw her chance. She had to offer a confidence, a vulnerability, if she wanted to get one in return. "My boss said that he knocked on my door twice today. I replied that I knocked on his door twice too, it must have been at the exact same time."

"He doesn't know you're here?"

"Nope."

Silence followed. Jonah didn't offer a confidence of his own. It hadn't worked. Clearly she hadn't done it right. So Emily turned back to FamilySearch. She looked for Doran Baruch in Russia. Nothing. Then she searched for him in the States, then in Canada, and found no birth certificate in either location. If it weren't for the awkward conversations they'd had, she'd assume that he'd never been born. "I have a question about your project," said Jonah. Emily looked up. She'd been doing it again. She wanted to connect with people, but she was focusing on the dead ones. "Why are you so obsessed with family?" he asked.

"Because I want to have my own," said Emily, surprising even herself.

"Excuse me?"

Emily stood up so quickly that she knocked over her stool.

"Ma'am?" Ryan was standing at the other side of the registration desk. Emily had never been called ma'am before. She wasn't sure she liked it.

"I seem to have had an accident." Ryan shifted on his feet. "We did. Amy and me."

"Are you all right?"

"The lamp."

Emily looked down. Indeed, he was holding a lamp, one of the little ones that were mounted on the desks in each of the rooms. Jonah moved toward the office.

"I don't think it's going to work anymore," said Ryan. "I'd be happy to pay for a replacement."

Emily looked to Jonah, who shook his head. "That won't be necessary," she said.

"You had an accident?" asked Jonah.

Ryan didn't look hurt. He was sweating though. He thrust the lamp at her and ran back up the stairs.

Emily held the lamp to Jonah. "What do you think is wrong with it?"

Jonah plugged it in. "Flick it on."

Emily touched the button, and it shot out one spark, then nothing.

Jonah stood, then took her shoulders and squeezed a little. "Don't touch it," he said, then moved past her, to the desk.

She still had colours dancing in her peripheral vision, thin little lightning streaks, lights and shadows and the outline of a thin filament. "What did he do to it?" Emily gingerly touched the bulb's glass cover. It was warm, but not very.

"It smells like flowers," said Jonah. "Can you smell that? I think we should call it Jasmine."

"The lamp?"

"It could be Jazzy for short."

"You need a nickname for the lamp."

"When you were a kid, you always had weird pets. Do you remember your pet rock? It was quartz, I think. His name was Aleck."

"That's right," said Emily. "I remember that." Then she decided to try again. She'd find a new confidence, one that she wasn't ready to share with anyone else. "I don't think that I'm good enough at my job," she blurted out.

"What's your job?"

"Math student."

"Oh, of course," said Jonah. "Why don't you think that you're good enough?"

"All the other students in the department can see above the math. I feel like I'm only good at solving the problems that other people give me."

Jonah took a deep breath. "There are things I've wanted to do my whole life, but I don't know whether I'm good enough. So I haven't even tried. I just stay here. And wait."

Emily struggled to stop herself from smiling, from grinning. It had worked. He'd confided in her. "What are you waiting for?" she asked.

"Just a sign, I guess." And then Jonah stood, reached for Emily's hand. "I think we should find Jazzy a cookie."

"It has to be a kosher one, though. You know how she is."

"Is she very religious?"

"I caught her davening, swaying back and forth while praying. I thought she was going to put herself into a trance."

"That makes sense," said Jonah. "We have a toaster who I swear is a holy roller."

Emily let herself smile for real, and enjoy walking beside him, feeling the heat that radiated off his skin. Maybe it could work. Maybe all her half thought through plans would lead to something, anything, other than loneliness.

MAKE YOUR OWN MIRACLES

HARPO, 1933

When Harpo woke up some time later, he wasn't sure where he was, but he wasn't worried either. This wasn't an unusual state. Sleeping was his favourite pastime. He often drifted off during the day, and always in the strangest places. He looked around, saw the owner of the lodge sitting across from him. Sam. Harpo remembered him from behind the desk when he'd checked in. Sam, the husband of the woman that he'd been chasing for days.

Harpo realized that his arm was still under the cushion, under his bottom. He must have left it in there and fallen asleep. Now he couldn't feel it at all. He couldn't move it either. He yanked it out with his other hand, and it weighed more than a house, and you couldn't get gangrene from this, Minnie had told him once, or else all the restless sleepers in New York would be walking around limbless. Abruptly, he remembered why his arm had been there in the first place. He'd been searching for Ayala's letter. The strange love note was stuck behind the cushion, where he must have dropped it. Harpo shifted to sit on top of it.

Sam looked up.

Harpo wiggled his fingers, and it was a good thing he could

do it now too, because he didn't know what to say. Usually, he just said whatever popped into his head, but he couldn't say what he was thinking now. Sam couldn't know about his wife's affair, about the letter probably addressed to that other man. What had he been called? Simon? Oh, and Harpo had been thinking about Ayala's hips as well. Not now. But earlier. He'd planned to find Ayala's room, had thought about finding a bed or some quiet spot, lying down with her, and—he certainly couldn't say that. Harpo raised his tingly arm again, supporting it with the other hand.

Sam nodded, so Harpo smiled and raised his hand again. Sam smiled and put down his newspaper. Harpo smiled and Sam smiled, and Harpo felt like bounding over to Sam's newspaper and ripping it to shreds. He might do it too, if they did this smile routine one more time. He'd rip up the paper, then dive behind the sofa and catapult the balled up pieces right into Sam's coffee mug.

"I'm going to Russia," Harpo said quickly.

"Are you?" This time, Sam folded the newspaper neatly and put in on the table. Harpo made himself nod and think some more normal thoughts. He pictured a ship.

"Well, you'll probably go on a passenger boat," said Sam, and Harpo looked up, his mental picture of a boat rocking. "Frankly, I think that you should. Travel in a bit of comfort. You won't regret it."

"You swam?" said Harpo.

"We came over on a boat carrying coal dust. The captain was the second cousin of a partner of mine and he got us passage on board without too much fuss about papers and exit visas. We had some, but maybe not very good ones. It was a rough crossing."

"Do you have any advice about visiting Russia?"

Sam scratched his beard. "Eat borscht," he said. "It's not the same here. And find someone who bakes. That's my advice. I think you should eat."

Harpo leaned forward. "Tell me more."

"You like food?"

"I love food," said Harpo. "My father—his name was

Frenchie—he cooked. It was great. He was the greatest. I don't know how he did it. We were poor. But still. He managed. I used to stab my brothers with forks over his dinner rolls."

"Just my kind of man," said Sam. "I'd stab a man for a piece of mandelbrot. It's a hard fact to face, but I believe I would. Do you like coffee? Have some. My Ayala makes it herself. She roasts the chicory, or whatever it is she can get her hands on these days, and whatever she finds, she makes it taste good."

"That's like Frenchie," said Harpo, and it felt good to tell someone about him, to say his name out loud again. "Frenchie was a magician."

"I think I read that in the newspaper." Sam's expression wasn't pitying. It was something else. Wistful maybe. Wistful! "They wrote many wonderful things about him."

"You read about my father?"

"I would have liked to have met him."

Harpo liked this man. He liked Sam a lot. "Frenchie would have loved meeting you too."

He wouldn't sleep with Ayala. That was out of the question. What had he even been thinking? He reached under the cushion again and crumpled the love note he'd found. Maybe he could find the letter, make amends for his intentions, for every time he'd gone through with it in the past. And if he did, then maybe that would prove something. Maybe he could show himself that he was capable of having a family. He'd run straight home to Susan.

Sam started to say something else when there was a noise outside, and two little girls scrambled into the room, Blima and another one, a smaller kid, three or four years old at the most, a streak of shiny blond hair and gleaming black shoes. She tore through the room, put her head in Sam's lap, and he hoisted her up by the hips until she was upside down and her legs were dangling.

"These are my girls," said Sam. "Blima and Sonja."

The upside-down girl wriggled, and her father set her down

and patted her backside, and she disappeared behind the chair with Blima. Sam was beaming.

"And what are you two up to?" asked Harpo.

Blima climbed onto the back of the easy chair, like a monkey. "We hid our toys. So that way, when we find them again, it's like we're getting a present all over again."

"That's clever."

"It's called Second Present."

"And where do you have these treasure hunts? In this room?"

"Not only here." Blima brushed her father's hair around her finger, made a little ringlet. Then the little one popped up beside her. They made a lovely picture. They had such different complexions. One was light, the other dark, but both had those beautiful red cheeks.

"Other places?"

"Yeah," said Blima. "We hide stuff other places too."

"Where else?" Harpo remembered the cozy little room where they played cards in great blue clouds of cigar smoke. He squished his love note again. "In that room with all the doors?"

Blima ducked behind the chair.

That room wasn't used that often during the daytime. She'd have lots of privacy to hide things there. And it had lots of chairs and hiding spaces too. He'd look there next. "I like that room," he said. "It's a great place to hide things, I think. It's like it's the centre of a maze."

"That's because Dad built things all around it," came a reply from behind the easy chair. Blima. Blima the monkey.

"It's peaceful in there," said Harpo.

"I don't go in that room," said Blima.

"Never?" asked Harpo.

"Blima's right," said Sam. "I hate that room."

"Why?" asked Harpo, but the girls didn't wait for an answer. They ran out, Blima first, then the smaller kid tearing right after her. They must know this one. They must have heard it before.

"There are no windows," said Sam. "I built rooms on all sides of it, and I forgot windows. So it's stuffy. You could suffocate in there."

"Have you considered punching holes in the walls?" asked Harpo.

"That's brilliant," said Sam. "Except instead of punching, how about we saw? Girls? Blima? Sonja? Where are my helpers? Where did they go? Come, girls, we're going to redecorate."

"Right now?" Harpo quickly stuffed the crumpled love note into his pocket.

Sam stood. "If I can get my girls to hold the wall straight, then why not right now?"

"I'll help," said Harpo.

"You will?" Sam clapped Harpo on the back and ushered him out of the room. "This is perfect, because I've been looking for something to do with my hands."

"This is an important project," said Sam, as he led Harpo and the girls into the garage where Harpo had found Blima last night. "Here's why. The room of doors has one important piece in it. It looks just like a vegetable cart. In fact, it is a vegetable cart."

Sam was assembling tools, and the girls were circling around them, like Blima was a tetherball and just didn't want to get too close. Sonja just stuck by Blima, her little shadow.

"This is the cart that we pushed from Russia to France," said Sam, "and we even smuggled it on the boat to Canada. I've always wanted guests to gather around it, so that we can talk about it, and tell them about our journey, the good parts anyway, the exciting things. But nobody goes in that room except to smoke or suffocate or gamble so it's just ended up pressed against the wall, behind a folding chair."

Blima opened a tool case and took out a hammer. It looked absurdly oversized in her little hands.

"Blima," said Sam. "Blima was there. We had to leave in the middle of the night. Remember, Blima? A man came and pounded on the door. He said it wasn't safe anymore. The Jews had to get out. We'd been found out, us and some others, maybe. He gave us some things and told us to leave quickly."

Blima pounded at the sand.

"We went straight to Avi the fishman and stole his cart. We pretended to be vegetable vendors, travelling from town to town. Gypsies, Jews, we're all the same to them. So we got away, a great adventure."

At this, Blima crept to the tool case again, a tiny little 83rd streeter casing the joint. She took a pair of pliers and shoved them inside her sleeve. Crab claws. Adorable. Blima the monkey was now a crab.

"We stole vegetables from the fields as we were walking," Sam was saying. "But that was only part of the disguise. Inside the cart, that's where we'd put our valuable things. I'd built in a secret compartment. You can still see it if you really look."

Harpo sat heavily on the tool box. Sam had everything. He had a vegetable cart. A tool kit. Saws, a work table, work benches, a whole exodus story of his very own. But that story was a scary one, Harpo realized with a start. Sam was telling it like an adventure, but he remembered creeping through empty corridors in the middle of the night. Harpo's family had to do that too, bundled in clothes, carrying all the family's possessions as they slipped down the echoey stairwells. And they'd just had eviction notices. He wouldn't have wanted to hear pounding in the middle of the night. "Did you get much out of Russia?" he asked.

Blima came so close now that Sam was able to hook her around the waist. He pulled her into his arms and kissed the top of her head. "It should have been more difficult," he said, "but we got lucky. It all seems a bit miraculous to me now."

Blima wriggled away. Her expression made Harpo pause, desolate like it had been in the window, despite the monstrous snapping fingers. Harpo watched her sadly put the pliers back in the box.

Sam caught him watching her. "Do you think you want a family?"

"I do want my family back," said Harpo. "Our movie was a bust, and my brothers are moving on. If my parents were around, they'd say you can't break up the team."

"I meant children," said Sam. "Your own family."

"Oh." Harpo did want that. For the first time, he realized that this was the thing he really wanted — to be a family man just like Frenchie. But what if he couldn't pull it off? Well, that's what this experiment was for — if he could help this family, that would mean he was mature enough to have his own.

"I suggest you try it. Rent a wife and some children for a while. See how the whole thing strikes you."

"I like your family."

"I wouldn't part with them." Sam was looking through his tool bag, and Sonja was helping by sprinkling sand and pebbles on his shoes. She had a very serious expression. "I've regretted a lot of things in my life, but never that. I've never regretted one second with my Blima or my Sonja."

"Do you think I should have kids?" he asked Blima, and that did it, that got her attention.

"Of course you should," she said. "Also, you should get married."

"It's shocking that you're not married yet," said the little one.

"Okay." Sam flung his tool bag across his shoulder. "We're off. I need my helpers."

Blima scurried out of the room.

"You're not helping, Blima?" asked Sam.

"I'm very busy today," came the careful reply from just outside. "I just don't have time. If you'd have given me some advance notice, then I might have made arrangements."

"And what about my Sonja?"

But Sonja had already run after her sister. "You have to give us notice," she called behind her.

Harpo scrambled to meet Blima in the doorway. He knelt.

"We have a very busy day today," she whispered.

"Second Present?"

"Also, Finding Stuff. It's our job to go into the rooms when guests check out. If there's anything left to collect, we have to show our parents, and sometimes we get to keep it if nobody wires to get it back."

"That's a lot of responsibility."

"We also have to mail away for samples, watch for the ice truck, and across the street, there's a little girl whose face is white like the moon. I didn't talk to her yet, but sometimes I wave."

Harpo held the wall that was moving back and forth as Sam pulled on the saw. Would the whole thing just crumble? The entire lodgehouse might fall right down on top of them. He shouldn't have suggested this. In his defense, people usually knew better than to listen to his ideas.

Sam pulled the saw out of the wall and inspected his work. "This was a great idea, Harpo."

"I was just thinking the opposite."

"This should be good enough."

"What should?"

But it was too late. Sam had already turned back to the wall. He gave it a punch, and the whole thing cracked inward, jaggedly. Then he pushed. Then he turned and leaned all his weight against it. Then the wall gave a cough of sawdust and gave up, and a chunk the size of an oven fell into the next room over. Harpo caught Sam before he could fall after it.

"Well," said Sam.

Harpo didn't know what to say.

The dust was clearing and revealing an uneven hole, one of those irregular shapes he could never identify in Miss Flatto's second grade class. Harpo leaned closer, and hooked his fingers through to feel the edges, all the revealed strata of wall stuff — plaster, wood, some other things he couldn't even guess at. *Strata,* meaning layers, seven down the Tuesday before last. This was uncanny. Also, this wall was thick. Walls couldn't be this thick everywhere. He could swear that he and his brothers had punched through a bunch of them racing around the tenements back in New York. They'd run right through them, hit a wall and continued into the next room over, the next apartment over sometimes, having left vaguely person-shaped holes in clapboard roughly the width of paper.

"Well," Sam said again.

"This place is well built," said Harpo.

Sam picked his way through the wreckage. "That's funny. I built this wall. I did it myself when we first moved in. But for the life of me, I don't remember using anything except a couple planks of wood."

"You built this wall?"

"I know that I had nails and glue maybe?" Sam ran his hands down the jagged edge. "I don't remember any of this other stuff. Well. Miracles happen all the time."

"Miracles?" said Harpo, not understanding, not seeing how a wall can grow inwardly. "The miracle of clapboard and insulation?"

"I think that's my favourite thing about Canada. Miracles happen far more often here than they did in the old country, and it's funny too because the old country was the place of prophets and golems and saints. But I guess everyone has to move on sometime."

Harpo stepped back and looked at the window. His fingers and toes tingled. It didn't look miraculous to him. It also didn't look like a window. It looked like a hole in the wall. This wasn't how he imagined it would go, but then what had he thought would happen? They hadn't even brought a ruler.

"We just have to make it look a touch more presentable." Sam rubbed his hands on his pants. "That should be easy enough. We can do it later. After lunch maybe."

"We just had lunch," said Harpo.

"Let's have another one," said Sam. "Suddenly, I feel like a bologna sandwich. Then we'll just have to wait for another miracle. I'm telling you—they happen all the time."

Harpo found Blima hovering near the room of doors. "I don't think that my mother is going to like that window," she said.

"I'll fix it." Harpo sat right in the doorway. "Don't you worry about a thing." Blima scrambled over to sit beside him, and Harpo offered her half the sandwich Sam had given him. She pulled out a slice of bologna, then handed the rest back.

"I like it though." She cuddled into his side, rolled her bologna into a cigar shape, then pretended to smoke it like Groucho.

"Hey," he whispered. "I found a letter." He pried the sofa note out of his pocket. "It was in the room with all the windows."

Blima carefully flattened it out. "A love letter!" she said. "Sonja must have put it there for Second Present."

"It's not your mother's letter, though," said Harpo. "Is it? Could that have belonged to your mother?"

"No," said Blima, and she tucked the letter inside her waistband, hid it under a shirt. "It's from a guest. Her name was Malka, it says."

"Did you hide one of your mother's letters two nights ago?"

Blima's eyes widened. They were big like dish plates, bigger. "How did you know that? Except it wasn't two nights ago. It was, maybe, two hundred nights ago. Or one thousand."

"You're sure it wasn't just the other day?"

"I thought that I'd forget the whole thing happened, but I didn't. I just feel worse every single day."

"Oh." Harpo leaned his head back against the wall. Suddenly, he didn't know what was happening here at all. "Do you remember anything from when you were little? From back in Russia?"

Blima nodded gravely. "I remember everything."

THINGS THAT ARE HIDDEN

EMILY, 2003

"So how is your stay?" Emily sat awkwardly beside Doran, who was sitting on the veranda stair once again. She hugged herself tightly. She was cold, because it was cold at night here, but she could still feel a bead of sweat dripping down her back. Tonight was the night. She'd figure out where he'd come from.

The more she thought about it, the less his connection to the family made sense. His family wasn't Jewish. They weren't from the same little town in Russia, couldn't be, she'd checked the website. So how had he wound up here?

"My stay continues to be wonderful."

As Emily contemplated the swaying grasses and the sliver of moon, deciding how to start, her stomach made a sound like a whale's song. She clutched her hands over her midsection.

He stood. "I should let you warm up."

Emily stood quickly. "How did you meet Sonja?"

Doran took her hand. His were hot. He towered over her. "You're cold," he said finally. "You should go inside."

"Okay," said Emily. "Well, have a good night then."

"Yes," but Doran didn't let go. "Thank you." He seemed to

be watching her, but she couldn't see his face properly, couldn't read his expression. "I didn't know anything, couldn't remember anything about my biological family."

"You were adopted?"

"But I have some memories now. They've been coming back faster since I've been here. Now I can remember a place."

"The church."

"Ayala was there."

"But Ayala was Jewish."

"Religion wasn't allowed. The church was hidden. You had to walk through an office, a shiny white room with a cabinet, what looked like a cupboard inside was really a door that led to a secret chamber."

"You remember Ayala from Russia?"

"I'm on a bench," Doran said, tightening his grip on her fingers. "No. A pew. It smells like chalk. I liked to curl up like a worm or a larva so I wouldn't be noticed. I saw Ayala come in. And then my father. They whispered together, and I wanted them to stop so I dropped a book. It echoed. I think they were holding hands. The little girl was watching them too, was angry, was clearly very angry."

Emily shifted and looked at the door.

"I think she's the one who saved me in the end," said Doran.

"Who?" asked Emily. "What?"

"Ayala. Your family. That's what I think must have happened."

"I don't know what you mean."

"She hovered around me," Doran said, squeezing Emily's fingers again. "She was always around, sometimes crouching down, touching my face with the tips of her fingers. Maybe that was why. She wanted to memorize everything about me so that she could find me later. She was planning to save me in the end."

"That could make sense," said Emily, but it didn't. It didn't make sense at all. Save him from what? He wasn't Jewish. Things were different for the Gentiles, that's what she'd always thought anyway, and why would Blima, who loved telling stories, loved the mystical journey from Russia to here, have kept something like that to herself?

"So have you made any progress with Jonah?" Doran's tone was different, lighter now.

"What?" said Emily. "Oh. No. I try, I keep trying."

"Have you found any scientific principles?"

Doran's face was obscured by shadows, but he didn't sound like he was making fun.

"I remembered something else for you," said Doran. "I remember coming over. On a boat. There was a man with me. For a long time, I hadn't been safe, but then, with that man, I felt like I was."

"That's good." Emily didn't know what to say. "That you're remembering now."

"During the morning, the man slept. I stalked the engine room. It was three storeys high. Inside it, there were noises. Yawns. Grunts like an animal. But it was machinery that made them. I checked. One time, there was a giant inside the shadows in the corner of the room. I felt his breath on my shoulder. But that might have been a dream."

"What did he look like, the man who brought you back from Russia? Did he have grey hair, even in his ears?"

"He had short dark hair. It was wispy."

"It could have been my Papa Sam."

"No," said Doran. "I knew Sam. This was a different man. But he was like Sam. Both those men, they radiated love."

Emily looked up. *Radiated.* That was a good word for that, for love.

Doran cleared his throat. "We steered the boat together, the other man and I. Until there was a storm. Then the wind was driving the raindrops so hard they stung my face. I couldn't breathe. They were coming at me so fast, the water, the wind, there wasn't time to find air. I pressed my face against the man's slicker, and he picked me up and carried me inside. They had to turn the ship around so it faced the waves. I wasn't allowed to do it."

"Do you still speak Russian?"

"Russian was always spoken in the house where I grew up, in Manhattan. It was the language of secrets. My new parents used it when they didn't want me to understand. Of course I still speak."

Emily looked down. He'd offered so many stories, so much vulnerability. Maybe he hadn't been making fun of her. Maybe he was struggling to connect with people. She could understand that.

"I've found some experiments that deal with making people like you," she said. "One is the bridge experiment."

"Where the men walk across a shaky bridge, and are presented with a woman. When their pulses are high already. When they're already experiencing the symptoms of love."

"Yes!" said Emily. "That's the one."

"I've read it," said Doran. "I found it last night. On my computer. And I've been trying to startle Sonja. I've been walking around corners quickly. But no luck so far. She's never on the other side of the wall."

"I keep trying to find a reason to go down to the lake at night."

"The planning is difficult."

"Yes!"

"Coincidences are hard to come by. They're hard to manufacture."

"I know," said Emily. "I found another one too. People are more willing to give something, when they've been given something first. That's why charities give out address stickers, then ask for money. So I'm trying to confide in Jonah."

"To get a confidence in return." Doran nodded. "Yes. That one sounds easier to engineer."

"Yes." And then there was a silence again. And then. "How did she do it?" whispered Emily. "How did my great-grandmother save you? What did she save you from?"

Doran let go of Emily, and abruptly her hand was freezing, like it had been thrust into cold water. "Well," he said.

Emily didn't know what to do. She needed more information, had to keep the conversation going. "Do you know the last name you were born with?" she asked.

"I never changed it. I didn't take my adoptive parents' name. They never asked me to."

"Then why can't I find you?"

"Well," said Doran, letting her hand go. "Well. What a night. I think I may go for a walk by the lake."

Emily watched him walk down the stone path toward the dock, a swaying behemoth casting a thick shadow on the moving grass, and then he moved into the black of the forest. And just like that he was gone.

ALL THE WORLD'S HIDDEN RESERVES

HARPO, 1933

Harpo was cold, and the dark forest smelled smoky, and he couldn't find the ghost anywhere. He'd been wandering for what felt like hours when he found the pale little oak trees that meant the lodgehouse was near. And there it was, the big sprawling house lit and glinting like a diamond tiara.

He walked closer and saw a man bent at the waist, peering in a window. Harpo crept closer. Then he recognized William. He was standing beside the window, next to a shining thing, a bucket, it looked like. Why did he have a bucket filled with water?

Harpo ran toward him. "I've been looking for you," he said.

"I've been looking for you too." William pulled him into a hug. "How are you feeling?"

"What?"

"Have you been a help to our Ayala?"

"I tried to make a passageway in their house, so the room of doors could have windows." Harpo sighed and, for a moment, they watched his breath light up the air between them. "I think I'm explaining this wrong."

"You're doing just fine," said William. "Did your window work out?"

"No," said Harpo. "We fell right through the wall. It looks terrible."

"I can help," said William. "I'm an architect. I fix things for them all the time. Will you open the door for me tomorrow night? I'd prefer to come after they're sleeping. I'm too shy to say hello."

"A shy ghost," breathed Harpo.

"That's right," William said. "That's me. I'm shy like a ghost. Tomorrow night. You open the door and I'll have my tools ready." Then he turned and clapped Harpo on the back. His palm, Harpo saw, was streaked with a spooky green. Ghostly colours. "So are you going to Russia? Have you decided?"

"Yes," said Harpo, still riding the high of having found his friend again, exulting in that he was here, he was real, after a fashion. "I'm going."

Harpo crept to the desk. Sam was staring vacantly at the back cubbies, holding a hammer, and there was no reason to be shy. He and Sam were friends. They'd talked already, about food and fathers, and Harpo had vowed to himself not to seduce his wife, and what were stronger bonds than those things?

Sam looked up. "Harpo!" His face lit right up, and he grabbed for Harpo's hand and shook it. "Would you like to have a drink?"

"Can I please send a wire?" asked Harpo.

Sam turned to the back cubbies. He reached into a hidden compartment and came back again with a pen and paper, the form. "You tell me what to say and I'll take it to the post office when I go into the city. Or maybe I'll just send Blima tomorrow morning. That's what we usually do."

"The wire should say this," said Harpo. "Aleck. Stop. I'm in. Stop. Get the visa."

"This is interesting," Sam said sadly. "Is this top secret?"

"I think that as my next career, I'm going to be a spy." Exapno Mapcase, secret agent. He looked up at his friend. Sam looked sad.

Harpo couldn't look at his face. He'd nearly hurt Sam in the worst way, he realized. He'd nearly slept with his wife. Just like he'd slept with the wives of many men before. He had to change his life. He wanted to be a family man, just like Sam, just like Frenchie.

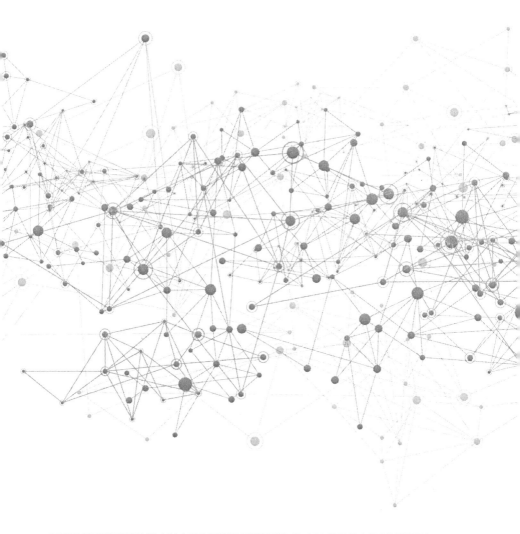

THE FOURTH DAY (OR THE THIRD DAY OF PASSOVER)

YOU SHOULD ONLY BE ON ONE SIDE AT A TIME

HARPO, 1933

Harpo crept from the trees to the shrubs. Ayala was sitting on the dock, kicking like a kid in a bathtub. Her eyes were bright, and her cheeks were red, and she looked softer this morning. He stepped lightly onto the dock. To talk only. No funny stuff. He was here to find a love letter, that was all, find it and get rid of it to protect Sam, and Ayala would forget about this other man given time, just like he'd forget about his feelings for Ayala.

Abruptly, Ayala stopped splashing. "Of all the prophets," she said, "Elijah is my favourite."

Harpo froze. Had she heard him? She couldn't have. He hadn't made a sound. There was that old fear, though, the insecurity that comes from sharing a room with four brothers, that people could read his thoughts. "I'm sorry I broke your house," he said. Since he'd left the lodge what had he been thinking about? Breakfast: eggs, rogalah, buns. Coffee. Coffee was safe. Harpo sat.

"Elijah doesn't come from anywhere," said Ayala, "he appears out of whirlwinds and storm clouds. That's why he's always welcome at the lodge. Do you know my favourite story?"

"I don't—"

"Once he visited an old man and woman," she said, "and he asked the angel of death to take the cow they loved. The cow died and they were devastated. The angel of death was already on his way, that's what nobody realized, was already coming for the old man's wife. One tragedy to protect from a greater one."

"I understand," said Harpo, but he didn't really. He struggled to formulate a question, but then they both heard a sound, a crunching in the driveway, and Ayala froze, fist clenched.

"What did you hear?"

Ayala didn't answer. Harpo uncurled her fingers and pried away a stone, and he turned it over in his hand. It was quartz, and had a little ribbon of pink winding through it. It was round like Aleck. Rotund. Rotund! And then there was the sound again, a person on the gravel drive, the postman probably, Harpo realized. "That's right," he said, rubbing Ayala's palm. "You watch for the mail." She'd love Harpo the Postman, he thought vaguely, wondering if he could start trying out bits right here, wondering how he could find himself a uniform. "Wasn't that the postman? Shouldn't we run and greet him?"

"Oh no," said Ayala. "I don't see him. I see the mail. I come here to compose myself."

"Like a letter!" said Harpo.

"What?"

"You compose letters. Groucho says, 'I have to retire to my chambers so I can compose a letter,' ever since they were the answers in a crossword this one time." They'd all been answers that day: *retire, chambers, compose* and *ritual* too, oddly. Ritual had been four across in the same puzzle, and it occurred to Harpo that Ayala had a ritual when it came to mornings, to getting the mail. That's why she was out here. She stayed away when the mail was delivered and went to look only when she knew she'd be alone. In the movie, all the girls in the little town would have their own rituals. The sad girl would light a candle on the mail mantle and wish for a love letter to appear. Then Harpo would knock and she'd open the door. Harpo would shrug sadly. He had nothing for her. The girl would cry a few prettily placed tears, lean her head on his shoulder and he'd fiddle with his mailbag.

"Does sitting out here help?" he asked.

"There are ways to charm a day," said Ayala, "to wring just a little luck out. The morning you came, I was sitting here as the sun came up. Then later, you came to the door. My husband ran upstairs to tell me."

Harpo looked up. She thought of him as a portent of good luck. But why? But that didn't make sense. It had been a long time since he'd been good luck for anyone. "This is the Russian man you're waiting for," he said. "You're waiting for a letter from Simon."

There they were, sparkling in Ayala's dark eyes, the prettily placed tears. How could he help her too? How could he make her feel better without breaking Sam's heart? This wasn't right. You were only ever supposed to be on one side at a time. You were only supposed to have one love of your life. "Is all this because you want to see him again?" he asked.

"I want to know that he doesn't regret what he did."

"What?" The morning changed.

"I want to know that he doesn't regret what he gave me."

"He gave you something," Harpo whispered. "What did he give you?"

Ayala didn't answer. Harpo sat back. The sky was pink, but it wasn't soothing anymore. It threatened. The clouds loomed. He'd thought Ayala was waiting for a love letter.

"I shouldn't have let him help us," whispered Ayala. "But the truth is that I couldn't say no. I had children. And I love Sam. Maybe not as nicely as I should, but I love him all the same."

"You love both of them."

"I thought we're not built for so much love. But Simon always says the heart has two ventricles. We have hidden reserves everywhere. I just need to know that Simon's safe." Then their eyes met, and they had another of those moments of tacit understanding (tacit!). The man, the one who'd had a secret affair with Ayala, he'd helped her family get out of Russia.

"I'm sorry," Harpo whispered.

Ayala stood. "You should be sorry." She smoothed her skirt, then wiped her eyes. "You broke a hole in the house."

"I'll fix it," said Harpo.

"You'll fix everything, I know." She seemed to hesitate, then crouched and kissed him lightly on the top of his head. "I've been waiting for you for a long time."

Ayala was off, jumping off the dock, then disappearing into the woods. In the movie, the pretty girl's worries would be easy, completely resolved in just over an hour, no, under an hour if you include the chases and musical numbers.

Harpo ran back to the lodgehouse. He had to get that love letter. *Was* it a love letter? It was important now, not just to read it, then get rid of it, but to figure out what had happened too.

He stomped up the wooden steps. He also needed the envelope, he realized. That would have an address on it. If he got an address, or some kind of last name or identification, then he could write to Simon himself. Then he could tell Ayala that Simon was safe and didn't regret what he'd done. Then the whole thing would be over. The Kogan family would be saved.

Harpo crept to the little chairs that faced the big registration desk and sat down in one. He reached his hand into the cushions and pulled out a soft grey glove. A treasure. A present, rather. He pressed it against his face, then put it back where he'd found it. He hopped onto the next chair, and there he found a little bear tucked just under the arm. This was definitely Second Present. He must be getting close. He put the bear back and reached into his pocket. All he had was a piece of tie and a rock. He hid them on the other side of the cushion, then sat still and listened for footsteps. Nothing. So he sidled close to registration. The mailman must have come and gone by now. Sam would already have looked through the mail. He'd probably just sort and run.

Harpo leaned against the desk. No mail there. No letters or papers on it, nothing of interest at all. Just a mug. He sniffed at it.

Coffee and something sweet and strong, rum probably. He'd seen a maid walking around with that earlier, before the sun had even risen, and she'd been weavy a bit, even then. Everyone was playing at something here. He hoisted himself up and peeked behind the desk. There were loads of drawers back there. And cubbyholes against the back wall. Mail must go over there somewhere. Mail and other things too, Second Letters maybe? Missing Mail?

He crept to the windowed hallway again to check for people. He needed a lookout.

He looked at the photographs framed on the walls. They were of people he didn't know, standing straight-backed and serious. He tried out the pose, put one hand behind his back and scowled. He should do that in the pictures. He'd have to find a reason. Then he saw a picture of a little boy. He leaned forward and saw that it wasn't a little boy after all. It was a little girl dressed in a boy's sailor suit. She was all crouched down, smiling slyly, ready to jump at the camera, unmistakably Blima. In the background was a dreary brick building on a cobblestone street. Harpo touched Blima's cute little head, put his finger right on the glass.

He heard footsteps, so he ran to the doorway behind the registration desk, and eased himself inside the leathery room. He let the door shut on his foot. Those were the footsteps of a girl trying not to be heard, Ayala tiptoeing nearer. And there she was, a sliver of her framed in his field of vision, stepping behind the desk. Harpo held his breath. He shouldn't be here. He was suddenly sure of it. He'd made a mistake. This was private.

Ayala eased a drawer open very slowly. She took out a handful of letters and sat down behind the desk. This must be part of the ritual.

Harpo felt a tickle on his back, so he shifted, and Ayala froze. Had she seen him? She'd be really mad. But this was research for a movie, he could say. This *was* research. He'd write a scene just like this one. He'd write himself in it, though. He'd scoop the poor sad girl into his arms and kiss her all over her face. Although that wasn't really his role. It was the romantic lead who did that. So he'd lead the romantic lead right to her.

Ayala bent over the letters again, and Harpo let out a very quiet breath. She was sorting with slow fingers. He slipped into the office completely and leaned his head against the shut door. No letter had come for Ayala. No letter had come for Susan today either, no love letter, anyway. He should know because he hadn't written one. Suddenly, Harpo thought of Susan on their last date, sitting on his rug, looking at him sadly with those big eyes. They'd had a hell of a time together, but things had just turned sour — she'd gotten close, and Harpo had lashed out, teased her. He'd been rough. Then she'd said, "You're not going to marry me, are you," her voice catching, "you're not the marrying type." Then he'd looked around, and that's when he'd seen his apartment for what it must be to her: a bachelor pad. He saw himself for what he was: not ready. He was a bachelor, a cad, really, a bad idea for any good girl, and Susan was definitely a good girl. And he loved her. He'd love her forever if he thought that she would have him still.

Harpo peeked through the door. Ayala was gone. He'd missed the end of the ritual.

The whole morning, he'd thought about Susan only. He'd sat with a beautiful woman and hadn't pictured her without clothes, hadn't even imagined undressing her once. He'd passed many beautiful women wearing bathing suits on the beach too, he must have, but he hadn't even thought about it, hadn't noticed. That had to mean something.

Harpo walked to the room of doors, his mangled window, and crept inside. He touched the funny wooden cart in the middle of the room, then noticed the upright piano. He played a middle C and it creaked through the room. It was out of tune. The room was eerie. The hole in the wall made sounds echo off all the cluttered surfaces.

Harpo thought of something. He jumped up, checked inside the piano bench. Nothing. He checked the sofas and chairs, the bookshelves, the card tables. Then he flipped through some of the books. Nothing. No presents. Not even a card. Something wasn't right. There were so many great hiding places in this room, so why hadn't Blima hidden anything in here at all? There had been presents in every other room in the whole lodgehouse. He'd even found a broken pencil hidden in a drawer in his room. Harpo sat down again and just then he saw little Blima herself, standing in the doorway, balancing on the wooden partition. "I hope that you're enjoying your stay, Mr. Harpo," she said.

He turned and played a bass note. It twanged as if from a honky-tonk piano. "Come here, monkey," he said. Blima touched the tip of her toe inside the room. Testing the waters.

Harpo made a face, his favourite one, the Gookie like Mr. Gookie the cigar man from the tenements, that crazy look he got when he was concentrating on rolling a cigar, puffed up cheeks, crossed eyes. When he had a daughter, that's what he'd do to cheer her up. Blima laughed the cutest laugh he'd ever heard, like a little xylophone. She crept into the room and swayed a little, right at his feet.

"You know what would make my stay better?" he said. "If you played Finding Stuff with me."

"Okay." Blima took Harpo's hand, and tried to tug him up off the bench. "I found some love letters in a guest room this morning. I take those and hide them. It's a mitzvah, and I can probably keep them anyway because nobody wires for those. I have a whole collection. We can look at those if you want. I can show you my collection." She pulled on Harpo's arm.

"I hid some things for you, you know."

"For Second Present?"

"You got it," said Harpo. "What about this room? I thought we could start right here."

"Did you hide them in here?"

"Well," said Harpo, "no. I guess I didn't."

"Good," said Blima. "Because we don't play in here." She leaned all her weight forward, tilted over completely, kept standing by Harpo's hand alone.

"Can't we play Second Present?"

"Never in this room," she grunted. "I told you. It's off limits. There's a hole. It's dangerous in here."

At that, Harpo stood, and Blima marched forward one laborious step.

"Don't you worry about the hole," he said. "I'll fix it tonight. But let's not leave so fast. There's a song I want to teach you on the upright."

"You're not allowed to play music before dinner," said Blima, grunting, tugging harder. "Everybody knows that. It's like you're not allowed to wear white after Labour Day or let the maid touch anything cold."

"The song is called 'Love Me and the World is Mine,'" said Harpo.

"We have to get out of here." Blima let go of Harpo's hand, panting. She motioned for him to kneel, and he did. "There was a ghost in here this morning," she whispered, hand cupped around his ear.

"A ghost?"

"That's because this room is haunted. There's a man whose soul is in here. If you see a lot of blue smoke, then that's what it is, it's the soul of a man who was mean and gave people needles. Also, he pinched. When he was alive, he liked to look inside people's faces and ears, so that's how his ghost tries to get in now. If you don't cover your mouth when you sneeze, then that's it, you're done for."

"Ghosts are like smoke?"

"Of course," she said. "They're not like people. You can't feel them. That's how you know the difference."

YOU SHOULD ONLY HAVE ONE LOVE IN YOUR LIFE

EMILY, 2003

As Emily crept out of her bedroom, she heard a sound, an angry kind of humming, but it was early, and what could account for *that* kind of noise? So she galloped up the stairs, taking two at a time, her heart beating to the rhythm of her footsteps. When she got to the landing, she saw Blima standing in the hallway with the vacuum cleaner. The noise was the vacuum.

Emily shrank into the doorway. She'd wanted to find Blima. She'd woken up with questions, wanted to know about Doran's story, the package she kept hearing about. But Blima was busy. This was a private moment. She shouldn't intrude.

Emily found herself looking around the wall. Blima was swinging that vacuum cleaner right in front of the students' room, Ryan and Amy's, closer and closer to their door each time. When Blima saw Emily, she waved. Her face was open and shining, and she was smiling wider than Emily had ever seen. Her expression was joyous.

Emily ran down the stairs, to where Jonah was fiddling with something behind the desk.

"Blima's vacuuming," she said.

"Yeah," said Jonah. "She does that."

"Upstairs."

"She likes to pretend that she's saving them from sin."

Emily craned her neck, to see the stairway again. "Because I didn't vacuum well enough?"

"Premarital sex." Jonah held up a lamp. "Do you like it?"

"Pardon me?" she said, feeling herself blush hotly.

"I tied a bow." Jonah fidgeted with the pink ribbon, and Emily saw that it was the same lamp from the day before.

"Oh," said Emily. "That lamp. Ryan's lamp."

"Yeah."

"But it isn't working, is it?"

Jonah thrust it into her arms. "She's been asking about you. She likes you."

"Jazzy." Emily stroked the glass cover. It was a cute little thing, if you forgot its practical uses. It looked kind of like an alien, like it had a lopsided little eye. "She misses me," she said, "clearly."

"Yes," said Jonah. "Clearly."

Emily hugged little Jazzy close to her. She tried to imagine that it was Jonah, but it was hard, because Jazzy was incredible bumpy. He'd tied a bow around her though. He'd remembered stuff from when they were young. That had to mean something.

Emily propped up her graphs and got to work like an adult. Well, she squinted at what she'd already written. It was a start anyway. And it was remarkable how little information family trees really captured. They didn't tell the reader who'd been involved in whose lives, for a start, who'd influenced whom. For example, she was connected only to her mother and father on the diagram, but really, she was pairwise connected to her grandmother as well, and that relationship was a significant one. It was Blima who'd explained her mother's moodiness, told her about sex and reproduction, and given Emily her first cup of coffee. She'd spent more time here than with her parents, growing up. And she was pairwise connected to Great-grandma Ayala as well, and they used to hide together, like under tables and in sofa forts—Ayala's idea, not hers. They'd watched Marx Brothers movies and giggled.

That was weird in retrospect. Ayala had told her everything about Harpo—everything but the most important thing: that she'd known him. Something was missing.

Emily made a new graph, and this one had Harpo at the centre. Then she drew more vertices, everyone who had known him at the lodge—Blima, Ayala, Sam, Moshe. Now Doran. That connection was a maybe. These people weren't biologically related, but related by influence, so she connected them all with dotted lines, from Harpo to all of them. Then Emily filled in all the other graphs with dotted lines too, from Blima, Sonja, Ayala, and Moshe too, all to her. They were edges of influence, though, so they should really be directional. So she drew in arrows. They terminated at her, the one who'd been changed. Because people changed.

In fact, everything should change, including, say, search patterns. This was stupid. The Mormons couldn't be the only ones interested in genealogy. Emily turned on her computer, opened a search page and looked for everything having to do with births and deaths in Russia, searched for anything having to do with genealogy there at all.

Jonah looked over her shoulder. "Find anything?"

"I'm making progress now," said Emily. "I've moved on from the Mormons. There are loads of message boards around. Here's one where they call themselves the cemetery men. They've photographed a bunch of cemeteries in the town where my family came from, every tombstone."

"Are the pictures posted?"

"Just a couple. They say that they'll send the rest if you ask. I'm asking. We'll see if they respond."

"This is fun." Jonah sat down beside her. He smelled like oranges.

"We can look at other message boards too," said Emily as a

feeling swelled in her stomach, the feeling of a tree growing roots, a cup overflowing, what Blima called awash with happiness.

Jonah pulled her chair closer, and they were on the trail, together, just like when they'd been little.

MAYBE THE POSTMEN SHOULD WRITE THE LETTERS TOO

HARPO, 1933

Blima held Harpo's hand tight, and pulled him into the stairway first, then into the dining room. A young woman in an impeccably pressed uniform stumbled past them, and Blima stopped and watched. "That was Bessie the maid," she whispered. "She's the help. Every time she touches anything cold, she faints. She believes in the evil eye and if you see her cross her fingers behind her back, that's why, it's for protection."

"Wait," said Harpo. "What did you say about cold things?" He watched the maid, the weavy one from the morning before, weavy again now and smelling like a cross between a fruit cocktail and a medicine cabinet. Sam probably kept her on staff because nobody else would hire her. It was Depression time. People needed protecting. Sam was a big old softie. Nothing should change that man. Men with the capacity for that much love should be protected fiercely.

The sad woman in his movie wouldn't be protected, would be the opposite of protected. She had to be in danger. There had to be more than sadness that the brothers could save her from. She could have a dangerous boyfriend, a man in her life up to no good. That would play.

Blima led Harpo back into the registration hallway. "I hid some things for my sister in here," she said.

Harpo touched his forehead, pretended to think very hard. "Did you hide a glove and a bear?"

"How did you know that?" whispered Blima.

"I hid something for you too."

Blima ran right to the chairs. It was just like he thought.

Harpo settled himself on one of the overstuffed chairs right by the doorway. "Okay, kid," he said. "We're writing a movie. We start with a beautiful girl. She's attached to a bad guy, a mobster maybe."

"Yeah," said Blima, "a real tough guy."

"Right." Harpo smiled. He'd never really talked to kids before. He'd clowned around in front of them, but they were cute when you let them talk too. "So she's attached to a real tough guy. But this beautiful girl, she still believes that she can find love." But that's quite the thing to think if you're stuck in a Mob-type of life. She must see a way out somehow. There must be a reason for so much hope.

"She knows a man," said Harpo. She sees him sometimes and he smiles to her, and he represents all her hopes for a better life. "This man is nice to her. She knows him…"

"She knows him from the post office," said Blima.

"Hey," said Harpo, Harpo the Postman, "that's perfect, kid. How did you know —"

"He works there, behind the desk." Blima attacked the sofa, pulling up the cushions and crawling under them. "And sometimes when she goes in all by herself, he gives her a sweet."

"That's why he knows all about her," said Harpo, "because he sees her when she posts the mail, he sees the letters she sends. He knows what she's like. More important, he knows her address. And that's why she expects him to write her a letter and slip it in with her mail. That's why she's waiting for a love letter."

"I know all about love letters," said Blima from underneath the sofa cushions. "I've read a million of them."

"Has your mommy ever written a letter? Say to someone other than your daddy?"

"That man, he writes her letters, except he doesn't mail them."

"Oh," said Harpo. "Wait. That's perfect."

"He hides them in a drawer or under his pillow. He probably has a hundred of them under there and it makes it hard for him to sleep at night."

"That's a great detail." Harpo looked around for paper, a pen, anything. He should be writing this down. Oh! He had papers in his pockets. "Why did you say that?" he asked, writing.

"My daddy doesn't like it when guests keep them beside their pillows." Blima scrambled to her feet and went about straightening up the sofa. "Because when they cry at night, the ink runs."

"Oh," said Harpo. He'd write Susan a letter tonight. He'd write her a million and send one every day.

Then he drifted over to the wall again, to the photographs. He posed like an old Russian man again, his hand behind his back. Then he noticed the funny picture of Blima again, Blima the tiny little sailor.

"Hey, monkey," he said. "Was this picture taken when you were in Russia?"

Blima ran over to Harpo and fit herself perfectly under his arm, like an armrest. He could get used to having a sidekick like this. He could see now why the tramp wanted one.

"That was when I wasn't allowed to wear any dresses."

"What?" he said. "Wait. Why were you not allowed to wear dresses?"

"When we took the train to Kingston, that's when I was allowed to wear a dress again. Also, I can wear a skirt if I want one, and a blouse too, but only if I promise not to get it filthy."

She had to look like a boy while in transit.

Blima looked up. "Don't be worried," she said. "My mom says I'm the tailored type anyhow."

Harpo closed his eyes, stroked Blima's soft hair, pretended he was her father to see what it felt like. Then he thought about that picture and the world shifted yet again. Had Simon given them a boy's papers for Blima? But why would he give them a little boy's passport when he must have known Ayala had a daughter? Well, what did Harpo know about these things? Maybe you couldn't be that picky on the black market. Maybe you had to just take anything you could get.

Harpo heard footsteps coming from overhead, and Blima ran to the stairway. She'd be running up to the attic to check on her mother. All Harpo knew for certain was that he wanted one of those. He wanted a family, his own one. He wanted to be a dad.

Harpo wandered until he heard one of his brothers clear his throat, and then he tiptoed into the room of windows like he was a tough 85th streeter, like he was about to start trouble. Really, he was just watching Groucho. Groucho, who could probably figure this out. There was a missing letter, a little boy's passport, an atticky girl and a sad little kid. Groucho was absorbed in a crossword. Harpo tiptoed closer, and flicked the paper right out from under him.

Groucho grabbed the newspaper before it could hit the floor.

"Where's Chico?" asked Harpo. He could use his big brother's input too.

"Where have you been every night? I haven't seen you at the parties."

"I don't know," said Harpo. "I've been around."

"You met a girl too?"

"I'm not like that," Harpo said quickly.

Groucho eyed him.

"I've changed."

"Sure, Harpo," said Groucho. "Fine." He turned back to the newspaper. "Then tell me all the words you know."

"Is that the crossword you saved for me?"

"I've almost got the bastard," said Groucho. "Go on. Give me a word."

"I'll get a dictionary," said Harpo, "no, a thesaurus. Thesaurus?"

"Don't you dare. I'm sick of putting in the right words. I'm gunning for all the wrong ones now."

"Fed up?" Harpo sat down across from his brother, leaned in.

"I'm destroying it," said Groucho. "With pen. Good luck to anyone who wants to have a go at the sucker after me. And that's the lesson to be learned, Harpo, my lad. If you can't do it properly, turn it into a big joke. Nobody will know that you didn't mean to do that in the first place. Now give me a word." Groucho squinted at him with that fake-o serious expression.

"Evil eye," said Harpo.

"That's two words."

"Give me a second then."

"Never mind, I'll use it." Groucho bent to the crossword and searched. "Seventeen across, seven letters, *evil eye*."

"What was the clue?"

"Tapioca source. See what I mean? We're learning things."

"Chico always told me tapioca was made out of fish eyes."

"Give me another word."

"*Kismet*."

Groucho searched the page, then wrote. "Perfect. The clue was 'utters impulsively.'"

"He did utter that word impulsively."

"What?" Groucho was searching through the crossword again. "Wait," he said, disappointed. "I know this next one. Seven across. The answer is *composition*. I don't know whether I should put it in though. It feels like that would be cheating."

"I have some ideas for our new movie," said Harpo. Composition. Like you compose a letter. Like you retire to your chambers to compose. The Gods of *The New York Times*. "It's really coming along."

"What new movie?" asked Groucho. "Our contract with Metro is up. *Duck Soup* was a flop. I was under the impression that we were out of a job."

"This one happens in a post office. I'm Harpo the Postman, and I pull things out of my mailbag, anything I want. You're the boss. Chico is the sorter. The romantic lead, he's the one who works behind the counter. There's a girl who comes in, and he watches her with moony eyes, and clutches his heart when she talks to him. A real romantic guy, the kid behind the counter, I mean."

"And who would pay for such a movie?" Groucho's expression was thoughtful.

"The girl is sad because she's attached to a hustler, the kind of guy that Chico would hang around. She doesn't like him, but he won't leave her be, and she's scared and all alone. Maybe he's her boss. Maybe her job depends on him, her livelihood depends on keeping him from getting mad. And maybe she's an orphan." Just like Harpo. Just like Groucho and Chico too. "Our job is to take her away from the bad guy and get her to marry the good guy. We do it with letters."

"Bringing down the entire US Postal Service while we're at it, I bet," said Groucho.

"There's also a little kid," said Harpo. "I forgot to tell you about her. She's the lady's daughter, no, kid sister, I mean. The lonely lady is stuck looking after her after their parents die. The kid works with us."

"Why do we need a kid?"

"That's the thing I figured out. If the hustler pushes a pretty little kid around, then we can do anything we want to him, we can go crazy, and the audience will still be on our side."

"I see." Groucho looked pensive. "Why does the postal service need to be brought down?"

"Why does that matter?" asked Harpo. "Anyhow. I have a reason."

"What is it then? Out with it. What did the US Postal Service do to you? Why do you want to destroy it?"

"Because..." and then Harpo stood. Because the postal service hadn't delivered the letter that would make Ayala happy again, that would make Blima less worried all the time, that would help Sam. Because the postal service didn't mail happiness. Because the postal service should be able to mail everything. "I just had an idea for the climax."

"The climax, you say."

"We need to make a quick getaway, so we mail ourselves. We get into one of those huge steamer trunks — you, me, Chico, the romantic leads, our costumes, pets, food of course, plates and plates of food. We mail ourselves to a person. Maggie. Then Maggie opens up the trunk and everything comes pouring out. The scene would take minutes and minutes. We could really draw it out."

"You might have something there," said Groucho. He looked hopeful, and it was the first time Harpo had seen the expression in a long time.

SO MANY SECRET COMPARTMENTS

EMILY, 2003

Emily walked laps of the first floor. She hesitated outside the room of doors. Her grandmother and great-aunt were talking. Someone leaned back on a chair. Emily could hear it groan. When she was little, snooping had been her go-to solution for most problems. It felt good to be back again.

"I keep telling you," said Blima. "It's a package. That's all I remember. I hid it because it was dangerous. Since our mother is gone, so I thought maybe the danger is past. But now I'm not so sure."

Emily hid in the doorway. Dangerous. What could be dangerous that fit into a package?

"Oh," said Sonja. "You hid it because of our mother."

"It's more complicated than that," said Blima.

"It's not complicated. Our mother was a broken barrel. She couldn't be filled up. We couldn't love her enough. If we made the slightest mistake, she'd retreat to the attic. And we did make mistakes, Blimushka. We were children. We were allowed."

"I don't like when you talk this way," said Blima. "Not when guests are here. Not with Emily close. Every mother makes mistakes, and you were happy sometimes too. Every heart has two ventricles."

"I only ever had one love, and she ruined it." Sonja's voice was hard.

"You mean Doran."

"Of course I mean Doran."

"You were young. He was an infatuation."

Emily flushed cold. Grandma Ayala said that Doran was miraculous, so why wouldn't she be thrilled that Sonja was in love with him? And Sonja had loved Emily's great-uncle. They told love stories about them.

"Tell me what you remember," said Sonja.

"If I tell you some things that made me unhappy," said Blima, "will you stop?"

"No," said Sonja. "Yes. Okay. I don't promise."

"There were things in my childhood that I didn't like. I had to summon Elijah."

"Never worked. Didn't happen. Move on. Tell me something serious."

"She ordered me around: turn on the stove, make more coffee, always make more coffee. I hated when we had to greet the guests and tell them goodnight. I didn't like that we had to eat dinner with them in the dining room and always know which cutlery to use. You used to hold up a fork and I'd shake my head. I'd pick up the right utensil and hold it under the table to show you. Well, I never really knew. I was making it up as we went along so you wouldn't be scared."

"That's not enough," said Sonja.

"Being yelled at," said Blima. "Learning to cry without sound."

Emily leaned her head against the wall. Grandma Ayala's face had been lined and soft and beautiful. She'd never been angry. She'd never yelled or raised her voice. She'd loved everybody, even the mailman.

"What else?" said Sonja.

"Learning to be loved less," said Blima. "I felt angry sometimes because of my pictures. I used to draw Elijah the prophet. She'd thought that Elijah had stopped coming, so I drew her pictures. But then I found them in her underwear drawer when she died."

"Pictures." Sonja was holding a drink. Emily could hear it clinking incongruously prettily. "She would hide for days, and we just wanted her to come out. And then she came out and she was furious. We used to hide in the coat closets. I cried under all the winter coats. I could hear you crying in the next closet over. And you talk about pictures."

"Every mother has bad days."

"Some nights we slept in the bathroom, because that was the only door that she didn't carry a key for. We saw the pin coming in through the door. You had to stay awake and force it out again."

"She had good days too," said Blima.

"You only tell those stories."

"Well, I can't tell my entire life, that would take almost eighty years. So if I'm picking and choosing, then I'm going to pick and choose the parts that I like best. Especially for Emily."

Then there was silence. Could they be whispering? Emily shifted to listen closer, but stepped on a creaky floorboard instead. The sound echoed. They must have heard it. There it was, the answering creak and shuffle, Blima and Sonja standing up. Emily walked into the room, sprightly like she had momentum, as if she'd been running in from another room. "I've been looking for you," she said, and awkwardly held up Jazzy. "One of the guests broke a lamp."

"Oh that's fine, lovie," said Sonja.

"I'll just ask Jonah to take one out of another room," said Blima.

"That's okay," said Emily. "I'll do it." She slipped out again.

Emily walked by the room of doors and peeked inside. She used to think this room was haunted too, but Grandma Ayala used to sit with her in here, had taken her by the hand and led her inside just to prove it was safe, she was sweet like that. She wasn't how Blima and Sonja were describing her. That had to be someone else. There had to be an explanation. Anyway the old folks never sat in here, and this room was a good choice to explore, it seemed. There were little lamps on all the card tables.

She went right to the big wooden table, the one made from the vegetable cart used in the family's so-called exodus from Russia. She knelt, and tried the lamp on top of it. It clicked on, cast a shuddering light. Good enough. She couldn't imagine anyone actually sat at those desks anyway.

She heard a creak, and turned to see Jonah in the doorway. "I'm just checking on Jazzy," he said, handing her a mug. "I brought her some milk."

"She was getting fussy. I had to take her for a walk."

"Yeah," said Jonah. "Sometimes she gets scared of old people. I hope it doesn't turn into a thing."

"It could be a phobia."

"Let's hope not."

"What's dangerous that can fit in a letter?" asked Emily.

"I don't know," said Jonah. "Explosives?"

"Where would my great-grandparents get explosives?"

"They're around."

That still didn't seem like an adequate answer to the question. Blima was a different kind of scared. Emily trailed her fingertips along the table. Sometimes she could almost see the vegetable cart this had once been. It was like that young beauty, old crone optical illusion that everyone looked at, sometimes an old table, sometimes the component parts of something else.

"It's dusty, I know," said Jonah. "We should hire Elijah to clean."

"He never shows."

"The problem is I always forget about this room. Blima never comes in here. I've never seen it happen. They always play cards in the dining room, or the room of windows. So sometimes I just don't bother."

Emily reached for the lamp. It didn't budge. It was stuck fast. But this was probably the best one to take in the entire lodgehouse. Nobody ever turned it on, and who would dare? Everyone must be afraid that the table would catch fire, that all the untreated wood would just combust, just get consumed. Before she came here, her mother had pulled her aside, grabbed her roughly by the arm and hissed, "No candles in that place. No incense. No open flame. Especially in the first floor, especially in the room of doors." Although all that was understood. All those books and things. Newspapers, old crosswords that they refused to part with for no reason that Emily could see, and now an old missing letter. What made better kindling than decades-old envelopes?

Jonah stood, then stretched, then crossed the room to the old piano. He used to call that thing an upright when they were kids, as if he was a miniature seventy-year-old. Emily had forgotten all about that. "Do you still play?"

"Sure," said Jonah, "when I get the chance."

"Do you know more songs now?"

"No song is as good as 'Love me and the World is Mine.' I can play it in three different keys."

"Right," said Emily. "I remember that."

Emily had rarely come into this room either. Once, when she was very little, she brought her toys in so she could play, and she was convinced the piano in the corner had played all by itself. Just one note, and it had echoed emptily. It had been the ghost. Except that might have been a dream.

"Do you know the one about Elijah and the old people?" asked Jonah.

"Elijah on the train?" Emily said vaguely. "The story with the man with the tight pants who whispered to Grandma Ayala and disappeared before Belleville?" She'd loved that one before she heard Blima tell it at the Seder.

"I meant one of the real Elijah stories," said Jonah. "From the Bible or wherever."

"Oh," said Emily, "no."

"Elijah likes to go for walks. Once, when he's wandering around, this guy sees him, and they decide to travel together for some reason. So they're going along and they come to an old shack. Inside it, there's a really old couple. And I mean gruesome old. I'd be shocked if they had any teeth."

"Did Elijah pray for teeth?"

"Outside, there was an old cow. The old man and woman loved the weird old thing like it was their kid. As Elijah was walking past it, all of a sudden, he dropped to his knees and prayed for the cow to die."

"That's not funny."

"That's what Elijah's friend said. 'Why would you do that?' Because then, seconds later, the cow falls right over. He died. He's just dead. But then later, Elijah tells the friend, 'I had to do it. The angel of death was coming to take the old woman, and as much as they loved the cow, they loved each other more. So I prayed for the angel of death to take the cow instead.'"

"I don't like that story," said Emily.

"Old stories are almost never nice," said Jonah. "Did you ever notice that? The ones we grew up with also. I've always thought it was because they didn't like telling them. My grandmother always talked about hobos. She'd always say, 'there are hobos on all the trains that come through Kingston.' They'd kidnap me if I didn't wash my hands properly because they'd think I was one of them. Eventually, I just learned not to ask for stories anymore."

Emily sat up on her heels and tugged. Then the lamp came away and she noticed the seam in the wood. She followed it, then crouched down and found herself looking at the underside of the wooden table. There was a latch there. And it looked like there was another seam. Could that be the legendary secret compartment? Wait. That would make a perfect hiding place. And this table had been here from the start of the lodge, by definition. It had come all the way from Russia.

"You okay?" asked Jonah.

"Sure," said Emily, straightening.

"Did you ever work things out with your thesis advisor?"

"Today I told him I had food poisoning."

"That's funny," said Jonah. "Except how long can you keep that up?"

"If he thinks he can catch me, he's crazy," Emily said absently. Blima never came into this room. Even Jonah had noticed. And why was that?

"Did you find something?" asked Jonah.

"In the family's exodus story, there was a secret compartment in this thing."

"Oh right. That was the cart."

Emily touched the rough wood with gentle fingers.

She ran her hands underneath and found a hinge. Why had she not checked this before? It seemed like a natural place to hide stuff. But she'd always been too scared to be in here by herself. There was the ghost of a man in this room, she remembered knowing, he appeared out of blue smoke. She couldn't account for either the certainty of so absurd a thing, or for the specificity of the image.

Emily lay down on the floor and slid herself under the table, her heart beating hard. She found the seam again, then the trap door in the table.

She forced the old door open. Inside, she found a package, a big brown envelope tied with lengths and lengths of twine, taped inside somehow. But the tape had long since lost its glue, and gave up easily. She eased the package out.

"Did you find something?" asked Jonah.

Emily slammed the door shut again, and the sound scared her, so she scrambled out like a wild thing, catching her hair, her clothes, scraping her arms. Then she sat back on her heels to catch her breath. Could this be Blima's letter?

"Are you okay?"

She held up the package, smoothing her hair back with her other hand. They looked at it carefully, at the accumulation of dust. The writing was in Grandma Ayala's pretty script, addressed to Russia. There were no stamps on it though, so clearly it had never been sent. Emily unwound all the string and dumped the contents. Two letters and a book. *Grimm's Fairy Tales*. A funny thing to send to Russia. She would have thought Ayala would send *Anne of Green Gables* or *Emily of New Moon* or something a bit more Canadian, if she was writing home. But maybe they hadn't been written yet. Emily was fuzzy on dates.

"What is all that?" said Jonah.

"I have no idea." Emily slipped open the first letter. It was in Cyrillic, so locked to her. Ayala never hid anything, but then of course Emily wouldn't have been born yet when these things were written, would she have been? She showed the contents to Jonah. "How are we going to figure out what it says?"

"Does your grandmother even speak Russian anymore?"

"I don't think so." She slipped the things back inside the envelope. "And I guess your grandmother never did."

"Well, we need some way to figure out what's written there."

"I'll ask my colleagues," said Emily. "Someone must have a contact in the Russian department."

"That sounds so academic." Jonah stood. "I'll search the Internet. See if I can come up with something too."

FEELING SORRY FOR THE ONE-HANDED CARPENTER

HARPO, 1933

If Harpo wandered for long enough, he always ended up right back in this exact spot, the clearing outside the lodge. He loved it, looking at the lodgehouse from the outside at night, watching how the joint glowed warmly against the dark of the forest. He stopped and watched it and held tight to his notebook. So far, he hadn't written any notes. But he did have script ideas. He had the beginning of the movie and the end—the crying girl to start, and the Marx Brothers and friends all falling out of a steamer trunk as the credits rolled. Now he just needed some scenes for in between. Maybe he should start with a story. Stories were doable. Stories were things he knew how to think about. Maybe he didn't have time to think about them right now though. He had other things to worry about too. He had an appointment tonight, didn't he? He was supposed to see a ghost.

He heard a sound and finally saw the dark figure he was looking for, William, peeking in the lodgehouse windows. He was moving, doing something. Harpo couldn't see what, could just make out a glint and shine, another bucket maybe?

"Mr. MacMarx!" said William.

"That's Exapno Mapcase to you."

William clapped him on the shoulder, pulled him into a hug, then let him go. Then Harpo was standing on his own again, only colder now. Abruptly, he remembered Blima's description of the ghost in the room of doors. You couldn't feel them. She'd explained it. They were like smoke.

"Why do you only come out at night?" he asked.

"It's so I can see in and they can't see out."

"Oh." Harpo took a deep breath of sodden, smoke-laden air. He remembered the first time they'd met, when William was asking how he was. He'd patted him on the back then too. "Why don't you want them to see you?" he whispered. But he didn't want the truth. He wanted to believe there were ghosts here. He wanted to believe he might see his parents again.

"There's no law saying you need to be friends with your neighbours," said William. "And most of their neighbours are terrible. They paint, throw stones, break windows. I try to fix it all before the family sees, but it happens often now, so, you know, I miss some."

"They don't like Jews around here," breathed Harpo.

"I wish I was their family. They would be forced to love me and my wife, and maybe my daughter and her husband too. I have a granddaughter the older girl's age, a tiny bit older. Her name is Mackie. They should be friends. If we were Jews, I'd have a reason to knock on the door. I'd know how to do it."

"I think Blima could use a friend." Harpo touched William's shoulder. It was solid. His coat felt soft.

"Well." William turned and clapped him on the back again, and Harpo pitched forward a step, then two. "It looks like everyone's gone to bed. I brought my tools. What say we get to work?"

"Well, this isn't the end of the world." They were sitting in the room of doors, and William was emptying his tool box piece by piece, quietly laying instruments on a threadbare towel whose fuzzy ends caught the lamplight and twinkled. "When you said a hole in the wall, I pictured something much worse than this."

Harpo touched each of the tools. They were all hard and cold and very physically present. He arranged them in order of length. He couldn't think of how else to help.

"Well, let's get to work then," said William.

"Okay," said Harpo. William had said this wasn't the end of the world, and he was right. That he wasn't a ghost didn't mean that ghosts didn't exist, or that other dead people wouldn't come back again.

William picked up a saw, his hand streaked with green again.

"What's that?" asked Harpo.

But William just pointed to one of the tools. "I think I need a bigger saw."

"Sawing didn't work the last time," Harpo whispered. "That's how we got into this mess."

"After we're done here, we have to see if there's anything else I can help with. You can tell me if anything else is broken. I've done this an awful lot. When Sam was building the extensions, I used to check on them, fix things up, come by in the night. I poured a proper foundation for him. Not proper. Just a bit better, I mean. I added braces, straightened a few things, added insulation to the walls. At first, I felt sorry. The stones. The taunts. But then I watched them. He's a good man, Sam. He loves his family. You can tell."

Then William chose a funny flattened out instrument, and waved to Harpo, beckoned for him to follow. Harpo scooted on his bottom, all the way over to where William was sawing at the wall.

"Do you need something?" asked Harpo.

"Yes." And William reached down and put his free hand on Harpo's bowed head. Harpo looked up. It had been so long since he'd felt such comfort. Not since Frenchie. Then William started sanding the bottom of the hole with his other hand. All night, William worked like that. Minnie might have said that Harpo was feeling sorry for himself, but Minnie would have been wrong. Harpo was feeling sorry for William. It must be hard to work with only one hand. And this, too, was what Harpo wanted. He wanted a family, and he wanted to be a father just like this, just like William.

CALLING IN THE SECRET AGENTS

EMILY, 2003

"My stay continues to be wonderful," Doran said without turning around.

"You beat me to it," said Emily, looking out at the dark lake, the deck, the forest.

"You're a good girl."

A breeze swept through the grass, and Emily shivered. She settled on the cold stair. "Do you remember meeting Harpo Marx?"

"I haven't seen his films in quite some time. I do remember seeing my first one. It was *A Night at the Opera*. I laughed so hard I had to hold my stomach, to keep everything in. I was unspooling, I thought."

"But you met him here," said Emily. "That's what everyone said."

"I don't remember that," said Doran. "Was he a guest?"

"Apparently." Maybe they hadn't met. Maybe their stays hadn't coincided after all. Emily let out a long breath.

"What are you working on all the time?"

"My research is in graph theory," said Emily. "I study social networks. But I've been doing a lot of work on family trees as well, family connectedness. I'm using that as an illustration. I've made a graph for my family and one for Jonah's. I might use Harpo Marx." Emily saw her opening. "I even thought I could include your family too."

"I would like that very much," Doran said slowly. "I was hoping that you were going to be the one to help me. That's what Blima seemed to think. She certainly has that hope as well."

"What do you mean?"

"I've only traced my adoptive family."

"Oh," said Emily. "All I can really do is the math. I don't know how good I am at finding people."

"I don't have much to go on."

"Did you remember anything?"

"Images. Sounds. A cupboard I crawled inside. I'm caught one time. I know this because I'm pulled out, and I see the whole office whirling past me. And then a pain. I've been spanked. Blima saw that cupboard too. That's the other reason I came. Verification. I wanted to know that they weren't all dreams."

Emily watched him carefully. Why would he think he remembered Blima's Russian room? "Do you remember where you're from?"

"That's a complicated question." Doran turned, and a spot of wet white tooth shone in the moonlight. He might have been grinning or grimacing, Emily had no way to tell. She tried to picture him as a kid inside a cupboard, saw him as long-limbed and strange, curled up like a bug and freakishly tall even then. That probably wasn't accurate though.

"You probably can't imagine me as a child," said Doran.

"No," Emily said, shaking her head fervently, hoping he couldn't see the flush of her cheeks in the dark under the veranda. "I mean yes. Of course—"

"But I was," said Doran. "I was a child then."

A breeze rifled thought the long grasses. Emily watched them shush each other and bow. For a moment, they just watched the grasses dance.

"Ayala came to our apartment," Doran said finally.

"What?"

"I remember. I'm sure of it now."

Emily shifted, looked at the doorway, at the light that was warm-looking and orange that shone out of the room of windows. She could hear a tinny sort of music too. Had they known each other in Russia after all?

"I have a father and a mother," he said. "For as long as I remember, when I'm upset or alone, I say their names to myself. Simon and Ekaterina. In the worst times, I've whispered their names out loud. But never when anyone else was present."

"Do you remember a last name?"

"They're saying those names to each other, giants standing in a hallway. They're angry. I'm afraid."

"You have first names," said Emily. "That might help." But how could it?

"I didn't take my adoptive parents' last name."

"Oh!" said Emily. "Right. Simon Baruch. Ekaterina Baruch. Okay. I'll look. I'll see what I can do. But I should warn you that I haven't found anything at all yet." And she'd already looked for Doran Baruch and hadn't found him, so what were the odds of finding Simon or Ekaterina? "What do you remember from the lodge?"

"Sonja," Doran said simply.

"That's so lovely." And it was. It was romantic. But he was having trouble connecting with her now. He slipped out of rooms right as soon as she walked in them. "Why did she mean so much to you?"

"Whenever I was with her, I felt like family."

"Do you still feel that way?"

"Maybe I should just talk to her?"

Emily nodded. He made it sound so simple. Maybe it was that easy to reconnect.

"You and I," said Doran. "We overthink."

"Yes," whispered Emily. "And you can't turn that stuff off."

"That's right."

They sat in silence, Emily shivering, Doran thinking, about what Emily couldn't fathom. She pictured monsters made of food, terrifying shadows, ghosts. Then Doran stood. He walked into the house, and she heard the low sounds of voices, Doran's and Sonja's. He was doing it. So she stood too.

Emily wandered around the side of the house. If Doran could do it, then she could do it. Friendship was easy. And she loved Jonah. That's all that mattered. Plus, they'd been getting so much closer in the last couple of days. She saw Jonah crouched in the shadows by the side of the lodgehouse, moving around, working on something, she couldn't see what. "Hey," she called out. "What are you always up to out here?"

"Nothing," said Jonah. He stood. "Don't go for a walk tonight."

"Why?"

"Tell me about the mystery," he said, grunting, from what possible exertions, Emily didn't know.

"Okay," she said, holding onto the banister, and trying to see him, to catch even just a glimpse in the dark. "We have three family trees: mine, yours and Doran's. They're not connected biologically, but apparently they met all at roughly the same time. And it was one person who introduced them, our families at least."

"Was it the same person who introduced all three?"

"That I don't know," said Emily.

Then there were just snapping branches in the dark of the forest. And then, "You've been researching Harpo Marx too," Jonah said softly.

"He was here in 1933," said Emily. "I wanted to see whether the lodge is mentioned in any of the books."

"Is it?"

"I haven't found it so far."

"The lodge would have had to have been influenced by him."

"I hadn't thought of that," said Emily, but it was true. There would be echoes of his presence here.

"What was Harpo up to, in that time?"

"Oh, that's smart," said Emily. "Let's make him a timeline."

"Maybe you should work on that by yourself."

And then Emily heard something, a splash by Jonah. "What are you doing over there?"

"Nothing," Jonah said quickly.

Emily waited for him to elaborate. He didn't. Maybe he didn't want to spend time with her after all. She turned and went inside.

Then Emily was in the room of windows, searching, pulling books off of bookshelves and flipping through the pages, and then, just as suddenly, she was caught. Blima took her arm. "I helped Harpo write letters," she said, steering her into the kitchen. "You wanted to hear things about the family. This is something I remember. I helped Harpo with his romance. He was sitting by the waterfall. No. He was sitting by the dock."

"Who was he writing to?"

"Susan Fleming."

"His wife!"

"Not yet she wasn't. But do you know what else I just remembered? His name. In Cyrillic, Harpo's name looks like it spells Exapno Mapcase." She wrote the word on a napkin.

"Could you tell me a lodge love story now?"

"You should go to bed."

"Sonja used to date a different boy every night," said Emily. "But then she fell in love with Daniel. Sonja started standing up all her other dates to see him. Then he stopped showing up, and Sonja stopped going out altogether, because she was waiting for him. She cried all the time, had red eyes and a runny nose and pretended to be sick with the flu. Finally, my great-uncle knocked on the door, except, instead of roses, he brought a box of tissues. Then he gave her another box. He'd only left so that he could buy her a ring."

"It is a good story, isn't it?" and Blima said nothing else. And Emily realized that she wasn't going to.

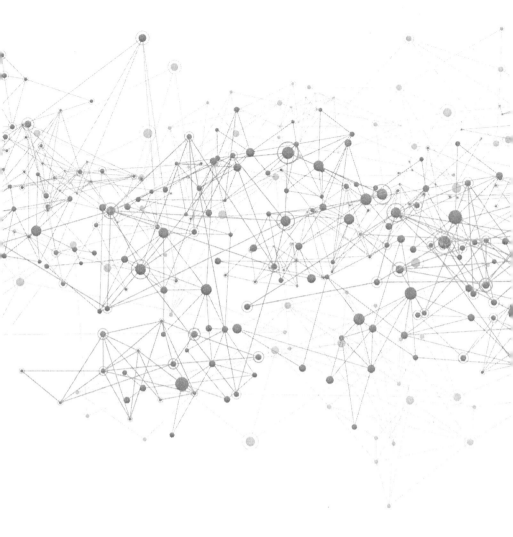

THE FIFTH DAY (OR THE FOURTH DAY OF PASSOVER)

SOMETIMES YOU JUST HAVE TO FIND A WAY

HARPO, 1933

"Harpo!" said Sam.

Harpo heard his name, then stumbled into Sam's embrace, then stumbled out of it again. He held onto the registration desk. Mornings were getting more and more difficult.

"Thank you, Harpo," said Sam.

Harpo felt the smooth surface of the counter, didn't look up at his friend. He shouldn't be thanked. He hadn't found them yet, the letters, whatever else Simon may have given, whatever else Simon may have done. He hadn't fixed anything. He would though. He wanted to, so badly. He'd stayed away from Sam's wife at least. At least there was that.

"The window is a masterpiece," said Sam.

"Oh." That, Harpo hadn't done either. Last night, William had sanded and straightened and pounded, then stained it all, while all Harpo had done was watched and breathed in the fumes. The room did look great, and the window looked dizzyingly good inside it. But it had nothing to do with him.

"I knew to believe in miracles," said Sam. "And I knew that you'd be miraculous."

"I think you're wrong," whispered Harpo.

Sam patted him on the back. "Come tonight," he said. "We'll smoke cigars. We have to celebrate the window. You're a good man, Harpo, and we'll celebrate that too."

Harpo escaped into the morning air. It was getting bigger, this problem he'd stumbled onto.

Harpo stumbled down the stairs, and beside the back window, he saw the faint mark of paint on the brick. He stopped, then edged nearer. There was the outline of words: *dirty jews*. Was that what William was always doing all alone in the dark? Cleaning graffiti? And what about the message itself, the fact that angry men were lurking close? Should he be concerned about that? Harpo looked around, at all the chattery guests, wearing bathing suits, holding towels, chattering and laughing. Nobody else seemed worried. He kept walking.

Harpo had a ritual too, he realized as he eased himself down beside Ayala. He loved this place, this time, these warm mornings full of pink sky and whispering lake. He didn't ever want to leave.

"You're easy to talk to," Ayala said suddenly. "I talk too much sometimes. But it's fine if I'm with you. There needs to be a certain amount of conversation, and you're certainly not doing it."

Harpo freed his arm so that he could touch her shoulder. She eased into his hand, her back concave. She was wearing a soft white sweater that reminded him of the nightgown from the night they'd met.

"Silences from you are comfortable," she said. "They're never uneasy. There's never that tension that happens right after I've said the wrong thing."

Harpo ran his hand up and down, and he could feel her spine under the wool. He drew a heart with his fingertips.

"Those bad kinds of silence follow me after they start. I drag them from room to room. All of this is easier for Sam, of course. He just loves people, and that's all there is to it. It doesn't matter who they are, Sam will love them. Getting along is easy for him."

"Was Simon like that too?" asked Harpo.

Ayala paused, but not for long. "I can't help what I see," she said. "These people, the ones who come to stay at the lodge, they've never had to run from anything."

"What does Simon do for a living?"

"These guests, they have their parents still. I had my mother until I was twenty-three years old. If you're forty and you still have a mother, and you see your mother two times every week, that means that you'll see her an average of three hundred times more than I saw my mother. That's not fair."

Harpo spelled out the word *mother*. Then *Minnie*. "I miss my mother too," he whispered.

"I have too many worries," said Ayala.

Harpo shifted so that he was sitting behind her now and she was between his knees. Now he could trace on her back properly. He needed a long word. Or a funny sounding one maybe. He wrote *filament*. He'd done this with Minnie once, on a balmy evening. He'd been walking back to the tenements when he saw her sitting out on the sidewalk, head in her hands and looking tired, so he sat behind her and patted her back. She hadn't pulled away.

"I talk about these worries," Ayala was saying, "and that's where the silences come from. Nobody wants to know. They don't want to hear about it because they know I'm right. I'm scared my girls will have to leave this country too. I'm scared the Jews won't be welcome."

Harpo blinked away the afterimage of paint on brickwork.

"Wars, *kinim*, *dever*, pestilence too, maybe, but that's not a major worry because I've never been squeamish about insects. Sam asks me to kill the spiders."

Harpo wrote *spider* in a loopy cursive. Ayala didn't say anything. Minnie had. Minnie had guessed: pencil, glass, tabletop, and Harpo had said, "that's right" every single time, even though he'd just been doing scribbles then. He hadn't trusted his spelling.

"I'm scared the girls will never find husbands," said Ayala. "I'm scared they'll choose the wrong ones. It's not like at home, where we just put the girls on the market and bargain between parents."

Harpo wrote the word *love*. He wasn't so good a speller, but that was one word he knew for sure.

"Here it's all so loose. What do you know when you're just eighteen? Can you really pick a husband on your own? You're still a child then. No. I know my daughters better than they know themselves and I'd do anything for them. Even if it's something that I shouldn't have done, I won't regret it. What I did, it was for my family. What I asked, I asked for them, because I love them."

Harpo rested his forehead on her back, breathing in her smell, the powder, the soft vanilla, then he wrapped his arms around her waist. That day in New York, Minnie had scooped around and pulled him into a hug, and for once, Harpo had liked being small. Harpo planted one chaste kiss on Ayala's cheek.

"When did you leave Russia?" he said into Ayala's fluffy, white sweater.

"Three years ago. No. Four. Almost four."

Harpo let her go. He lay down on the dock, suddenly too tired to stay upright. Ayala's smaller daughter couldn't be much older than four. She'd been conceived in Russia then, he'd bet on it. And she had blond hair and pale eyes and didn't look anything like Sam. Sonja was Simon's daughter.

He closed his eyes. When he opened them again, Ayala was gone, and he sat up to find little pebbles stuck to the side of his face.

Harpo picked his way off the dock.

Ayala had had an affair, a kid, an escape from Russia, but not in that order. And he was about to destroy the letter that she'd written to little Sonja's father. If he were a father, if he had a child somewhere in the world, he wouldn't want anyone to do that. He knew what Chico would tell him. If he wanted to be a grown-up, then he'd have to learn to make tough decisions. Sometimes, he'd have to do bad things. But he knew that already. He knew that better than his brothers did.

He knew that Minnie stole food for them. He'd never told anybody. He'd been skidding down 83rd past the grocery vendor one afternoon, pretending he was a marble in a box maze and the world was tilting him around, and that's when he'd seen her. She'd stolen things, taken them and slid them in her handbag, and then Harpo saw that the shopkeeper was watching her too, and the whole world stopped, and Harpo thought that his heart would just stop beating. Minnie might go to jail. This might be it. He couldn't catch his breath. But then the shopkeeper turned away, pretended not to see. Minnie had had to be formidable just like Ayala. She'd raised five boys with no money. Sometimes you just have to find a way.

So here's the deal. If Harpo could save this family, then he'd be responsible enough to have his own.

He had to find the father. He had to get Simon. No, he had to get word *to* Simon, and bring a letter back. He had to do it himself. He was going to Russia anyway, so he'd go playing Harpo the Postman. Then he'd tell Ayala that Simon was safe. He wouldn't tell her where he was though. He wouldn't give any kind of return address, just in case.

SOMETIMES ALL YOU FIND ARE CREEPERS

EMILY, 2003

Today was the day: Emily would write up her thesis, confront her advisor and finally decide whether to start the Ph.D. and be locked in Toronto for the next four to eight years, working on the same things. If she hadn't been fired yet, that is. She got to work. She had four days left, she could do this.

First she organized her books and notes on the table. Then she put Jazzy in the chair next to her. Then she breathed in coffee. She closed her eyes, and graphs and diagrams formed and disintegrated like images in a kaleidoscope, social networks sticky like spiderwebs, forming and pinching off again. Many of the people she'd interviewed didn't know most of the people on their own social networks, not even enough to remember why they'd added most of them in the first place. So Emily had established that people tended to connect themselves to acquaintances and friends of friends. That information travelled through these circuits seemed beside the point. People learned things from bus stop posters too, from graffiti on bathroom walls. She'd counted who clicked on the same links, read the same online articles, attended the same seminars. Nobody seemed to remember enough about any of those things to prove they'd been influenced at all. The numbers looked good though. Everyone agreed on that. Everyone had been impressed by her statistics. None of this belonged in her introduction though.

She sighed, watched coffee eddy around her breath. The beginning of university had been better than this, that could be the end of it. She remembered when she first lived in residence, the shock, the strangeness. One night after a class, she'd walked down to the laundry room, bought a stale sandwich from a vending machine and sat eating it, watching the dryers spin. Those were just the slack hours before time would pull taught again, but things felt different now. She might not be able to finish her thesis now that she was adding more stuff every day, and why couldn't she stop adding things? What if she did finish her thesis, and nobody cared about what she'd found? What if they figured out that those numbers didn't mean anything and called her a fraud? She couldn't fool everyone forever, that she knew for sure.

She opened her eyes. Technically, she couldn't be allowed a morning off her thesis since she hadn't started working yet. She opened her email. There was a message from Russell, so she upgraded yesterday's report. What had seemed like food poisoning was now the flu.

Then there was another email, a message from the cemetery men. It had a link to a page of pictures, to hundreds of image files.

She opened the first picture, labelled Cemetery 001. It showed the graveyard in a dreary bloom. That wasn't how she'd pictured Russia. There were dark things everywhere, mosses and creeper vines. The tombstone itself was damp, dry only in places, like the stone itself was weeping. The Cyrillic name on the grave wasn't visible, but the cemetery men had inserted a text box at the bottom of the image, with the name written twice, once in Cyrillic and once in English. It wasn't a name that Emily recognized.

There were over three hundred pictures to go.

Emily hid behind the door to the kitchen and peeked inside. Jonah was there, alone. "Hey," she whispered.

He looked up, his face filling with colour. "I was looking for you earlier," he said.

"I got an email back from the cemetery men. They sent hundreds of photographs."

Emily scrolled from picture to picture, watching Jonah's reaction more than the pictures themselves, and so found herself scrolling back again, apologetic. She'd forgotten to read the names.

"Don't worry," said Jonah. "I've been having trouble too. There's a lot of graves."

"Yeah," and Emily suddenly remembered her grandma Ayala's grave. She'd seen it last when she was eight, when her parents and relatives had taken turns shovelling in dirt. Emily had to scroll back once more. That's when she fell on a Robert. She stopped. It said Robert Baruch. The next one was Dimitri Baruch, and the next was Johannes. All her great-great-uncles, Papa Sam's brothers, but with Doran's last name. She looked up, and saw what must be a mirror of her own appalled expression.

"It's a coincidence," said Jonah, but the next grave said Israel Baruch, all the brothers now, side by side. The dates read 1929, around the time her family had left.

Emily slammed her laptop shut.

"I'm sure this doesn't mean anything," said Jonah, leaning forward. "Except what does that mean?"

"Could he be related?" breathed Emily. "Could his family have all changed their names?"

"People did that. To sound less Jewish."

"Except that Doran is pretty adamantly not Jewish. And the new name sounds more Jewish. I've never heard of anyone doing that. And Sonja is always looking through his keyhole when he's dressing for dinner."

"And creeping into his room late at night."

"She doesn't know they're related."

"Maybe they're not," said Jonah. "Could Sonja have been adopted? She has a completely different complexion from Blima."

"But they have the exact same face," said Emily. "They both look exactly like Ayala."

"We need to translate the letter," said Jonah.

REACHING FINGERS OF DUST

HARPO, 1933

Harpo peeked into Sam's office. Sam was gone but there was a globe on the desk so Harpo crept inside and spun it to look at Russia, no, the Soviet Union now. It was massive. He slipped out of the office, and into the big hallway.

Harpo walked past a pretty girl and leered. At first she glared, but then her eyes lit up with that look, the movie star recognition. She smiled, teeth dazzlingly bared, and Harpo saw a way forward, that familiar chess game series of moves that led right into her bedroom. He moved closer to her, now put his hand on her lower back, that lovely topography, that taper and swell, but then he was walking to the registration hallway again. He didn't even remember turning away. There had been no in-between between there and here, he was just moving, and he'd promised himself not to chase chickens anymore, so maybe it was working. Maybe he was turning himself into a better man.

Harpo took up his post, half crushed by the heavy door, when he heard footsteps. Then Blima was by his side. "The worst times are always in the mornings," she whispered.

"You know about the ritual too?" Harpo crouched down next to her. Then he sat. Then he wedged his foot in the doorway to keep it open a crack. Blima put her hands on his knee, and leaned forward, peering out the door. Harpo liked the tiny little pressure on him. He liked having kids around.

"Why do you like love notes so much?" he asked.

"Sometimes I hate love," said Blima.

"What?"

"I mean I hate letters. I mean, it's safer if I just hide them."

"I don't understand," said Harpo.

"They're dangerous. They only cause hurt. Sometimes love just causes hurt."

"Love letters are all about love."

"You shouldn't write about love," said Blima. "You should just do it. You should just love the people you have already. If you have to write about it instead, and send a love letter to somebody new, then that means there's something wrong."

Harpo let the ensuing silence stretch. Blima was a very loving little girl. You could see right away that she didn't hate love. Maybe she was right about just choosing to love. Again, he thought about Susan. He'd fix this. He'd prove he was a loving person and he'd run right back to her.

"We went to this place in the old country," Blima said suddenly. "They left me outside in the hallway. I was lying down on the bench so I could still see through the crack in the door. They were holding hands, I saw them."

"Who was holding hands?" whispered Harpo.

"My mom and the tall man."

"Was that Simon?" Harpo sat up straight. "Did you know Simon?"

"Mom gave me a book to read just before she went inside. So I dropped it off the couch. To make them stop. Then the boy did the same thing, with his book that his daddy gave him."

"The boy?" Wait. There was a little boy too? "What boy, Blima?"

"He always copied me. Every single time I did anything, he did the same thing too."

"Who was he?" Harpo shivered, like someone poured cold water down him. There was a little boy.

But just as abruptly as she'd started, Blima stopped talking. She slipped away, and Harpo watched her run out into the hallway.

Did Simon have a son?

Harpo peeked out the door. He saw Ayala shuffling behind the registration desk, and their eyes met.

Harpo ran out into the hallway. His heart was pounding. The whole place was throbbing, the colours too vivid, the sun too bright, and it wasn't what Ayala thought. Could she think that he was spying? Well, he'd fix this, whatever the problem was, and then she'd understand his intentions. He'd have to find that letter.

Suddenly, Harpo could hear his brothers, somewhere close, he didn't know where. He drifted toward the sound. Then he tripped on a throw rug. Rugs. Mats. Sure, everyone meant to clean under those, but nobody actually did. Harpo knelt and rolled up an oriental carpet. He searched under it. Nothing. He unrolled it again and crawled to the next one. This time, he found a tiny little sock. Second Present. It had to be. That's exactly the kind of gift adults thought to give little kids. He crawled farther, until he came upon a pair of legs. Guest. Guests. Two of them, and the female legs weren't bad. He looked up and saluted, and the people to whom the legs belonged shuffled away. Harpo sat down on his heels. He was getting close. He could feel it.

Then Harpo heard a whoop of laughter, Chico's, so he let his search take him in that direction.

If Simon had a son, then it could be that he had a wife too. Probably he did. It was more likely than not. Kids had to come from somewhere. Harpo shivered. It was warm out, but still, he had goosebumps. Had Simon put his own family in danger when he'd helped Ayala? Where were the wife and kid?

Harpo crawled under one of the long couches that lined the hallway. It smelled like dust. It was overpowering. And there was nothing under there but balls of lint. He pictured little Blima lying on top of one of these couches, dropping heavy books to remind Ayala that she was still there.

After a moment, Harpo crawled out again, then kept right on going, all the way to the room of windows. He looked up. His brothers were here — Chico on the sofa pressed far too close to a girl too young to have ever heard of vaudeville, Groucho lounging on an overstuffed chair, reading a book. Harpo scrambled to his feet and tiptoed to the doorway. He had to look in here. He had no choice. This was Blima's favourite room, so the letter must be hidden here.

Chico whispered something to the blond girl, and she twittered like a woodpecker. Then Chico put his hand on her thigh, his thumb just inside her skirt. Then he eased his hand higher up her leg. That was a patented move. They'd worked on that one for years. The girl didn't object. She just moved closer. Harpo leaned in the doorway, lured by equal parts fascination and revulsion. He and Chico looked so much alike that nobody could tell them apart. So this is what it looked like when Harpo did this. He must look like an old man too. He felt sick.

Chico kissed the girl's cheek, and Harpo looked away. Chico had a wife who loved him, had a child at home. His family was alive and safe. They could be happy too, should be happy. Their biggest worry must be where Chico went to at night. He had no idea how lucky he was. He had no right to hurt other people this way.

Then Harpo just couldn't take it anymore. He burst into the room. Chico looked up at him, smiled and winked. He must have glared back, because the girl blushed cherry red, stood, excused herself, then pushed past him and fled into the hallway.

Chico looked unfazed. "Howdy, stranger," he drawled.

Harpo sat down on the opposite couch.

"Where have you been all this time?" asked Chico. "I haven't seen you at cards. I'm on a winning streak. You should join."

Harpo looked away.

"Why do you always look so busy?" asked Groucho.

"I've been looking for something," said Harpo. And he had been, it was true, he'd just temporarily forgotten about the letter. He stood again, looked around.

"I'm hot," said Groucho. He'd put down his newspaper and was taking off his jacket. "Harpo, you look hot, and it's making me even hotter. Do you mind unbuttoning your shirt?"

"Did you have hidden things when we were growing up?" asked Harpo.

"I think you should take off your socks."

Harpo crept around the room. He'd already checked the sofas and the cushions, the underneaths of the chairs and inside all the drawers. There must be more hiding places. "Did you have special things?"

"I had this bun once," said Groucho. "Except my brother stabbed me with a fork and stole it."

"That was me," said Harpo.

"Yes it was."

"Except, did you have anything that you hid from the family?" Harpo had hidden pets, a cat once, three dogs and a moth, all in empty tenement basements. He'd creep downstairs to feed and play with them. But the neighbourhood kids always stole them. He'd hidden money too, all the things and buttons he'd found in the alleyways. He'd pulled a doll's head out of the Hudson once, and put it in Chico's pillowcase. He knelt down and rolled up the rug. Nothing.

"I had forty-seven cents I never told anyone about," said Groucho.

"Where did you keep it?"

"The sock drawer."

"I would have found that," said Harpo. "I always looked in there. I would've taken it."

"I know you would have." Groucho fanned himself with his

newspaper. "So I tied it to the top. I had a very advanced system with twine and a pulley. It should have been foolproof."

"Did it work?"

"Chico found it."

Chico opened his eyes. "Hardly worth looking for. The way you snuck in and out, I was expecting a hundred bucks."

"So to answer your question," said Groucho, "no. The sock drawer was not a good place to hide things. He even stole the twine."

"Finder's fee," muttered Chico.

Harpo tried the cabinet in the corner, opened the top drawer, then felt along the inside. Nothing.

"I hid things in my socks," said Chico. "I didn't take them off. That's how I kept them safe."

"You should take off your socks now," said Groucho. "That might make up for it."

"Socks wouldn't work for a letter though," said Harpo. You could always tape it to your leg. But not forever. That wouldn't work for more than a day or two, a week tops if you were a little kid, or just didn't take enough baths.

Groucho ripped a page out of a magazine and folded it into a fan. "Do you need to hide a letter?"

"How would you hide one if you wanted to?"

"The vent?" said Groucho. "Listen. Could you hide all those *Duck Soup* reviews while you're at it? No. Don't hide them. Burn them."

"Burn them…" Harpo found a vent mounted in the wall, dragged a chair to it and jumped up. He peeked in and saw nothing, an empty hole, gnarled fingers of dust stretching out toward him. He quickly closed the cover.

"Are you stripping?" asked Chico. "Harp, is he stripping?"

Harpo wheeled around and saw Groucho's rolled up pants and bare ankles.

"What's the point of being in Canada if it's going to be so hot all the time?" said Groucho.

"It's not so hot," said Chico.

"I like the warmth," said Harpo.

Groucho eyed him. "I'd feel better if you'd take off your socks too. I'd be cooler if you didn't look so hot."

"I remember taping something under the table leg once," said Harpo, still balanced on the chair. "I don't think that worked. It was a dime that Uncle Al gave me, but it was gone the next day. Frenchie was gone at the time, selling door to door I guess." He remembered because as he was looking for the lost loot, their tiny little apartment had felt cavernous.

"Hey." Harpo hopped from the chair to Groucho's loveseat. "I just thought the word *cavernous*."

"Good," said Groucho as Harpo slid in beside him. "Now spell it."

"Not on your life."

"Take off your socks," said Groucho, and Harpo kicked him. It felt so good that he did it again. Then he nudged Grouch's bare ankle with his foot.

"Are you scratching my leg?" asked Groucho. "You're probably getting my skin all over your socks. You'd better take them off in that case. It's more hygienic that way. Now spell *hygienic*."

"If I get cooler, then you won't get cooler," said Harpo. "I don't think that's how it works." Then Harpo put his head on the arm of the loveseat. He wanted to talk so badly. And now Groucho had even asked what he'd been doing all this time. But he had no idea how to start to tell him.

CEMETERY MEN

EMILY, 2003

Emily edged toward the door. Names weren't matching up, family things weren't adding up and nothing made sense.

Blima and Sonja were just outside in the hallway. They were arguing, it sounded like, but it didn't matter. Emily was on a mission. She burst right through the door. "Is Doran related to us?" she asked. "I need the truth."

"Do you mean, are we friends?" said Blima. "Sure we're friends. He's a friend of the family."

"Are we biologically related?" asked Emily. "Do we share chromosomes?"

"No," Sonja said quickly. "Of course not. He's not even Jewish."

That's what Emily had thought. And yet. "Are you sure?" she asked.

"I'm positive," said Blima. "We're not even close to being related. Two different families. Two different communities. I remember, from back in Russia. Different parts of town even."

"You knew him in Russia?"

"We weren't supposed to have anything to do with each other. It was a secret. It was hidden."

"I didn't even know the families were friends," said Emily. "Can we please just talk about how all these families are connected? There are so many things I don't understand."

"Darling," said Blima, grabbing Emily's arm tight. "There are things we need to ask you."

"Can you answer my questions first?"

"We've been having an argument," said Sonja. "Or rather Blima was arguing. I was just trying to have a civilized conversation."

"We were trying to decide about our mother," said Blima. "Was she bad at loving us? Or is it our fault? Are we just bad at being loved?"

"Maybe you just didn't understand each other," said Emily, suddenly remembering the soft smell of Grandma Ayala's perfume. "Anyway, it's hard to figure out what happened when there are so many stories, and you don't even know which ones are true anymore. I don't understand this family at all."

"Still," said Sonja. "Emily, you studied science. You should know how love works. How do people love each other?"

"I have no idea."

"But your mother says you work very hard."

"We don't study the transmission of feelings."

"What do you learn in university if you don't learn about that?"

"I took science," said Emily. "We learned science."

"Didn't you do anything practical?" asked Blima.

"That's what I mean," said Sonja. "What did you learn that's practical?"

"People are going to be married for most of their lives," said Blima. "Doesn't it make sense that they should learn how to live together? How to sleep with another person, for instance. That doesn't come naturally. It takes practice. How to share the blanket. How to never flatten another person's pillow. How to make a schedule. How to keep a house. These are the subjects they should teach."

"There would be less therapy in the world," said Sonja.

"Oy gevalt," said Blima, "if they just taught how to love."

Emily ducked her head, smiling despite herself, despite her frustration. What would they call a course like that? Love delivery systems. Or the transmission of love, maybe. Who would teach it? Maybe that magnetics guy in the physics department because he had a face like a waning moon, and he liked to clutch his heart when he lectured. He seemed like a romantic kind of guy, in a physics prof kind of way. But wasn't that a strange thought, that love might be explained by field theory.

"I know that I'm capable of doing it," Sonja was saying. "Emily used to cuddle while we watched movies, and I knew what it was to love."

"I loved her more," said Blima. "She's *my* granddaughter. Moshe would make an elevator and lift her into the bed and we would snuggle." Emily remembered that. Papa Moshe would lower his cupped hand and she'd step into it, and then hang onto his hairy arm as he lifted her into the blankets.

It would definitely be an offshoot of field theory. The field theory of love.

"This is kind of strange," said Emily. "But I just thought of it. What if love works like magnets? Magnets all have two poles, a north pole and a south pole, and opposite poles attract each other. But that ability to attract—the magnetism, I mean—that's not in the magnet itself. It's in the space around it. There's a field around any magnetic object."

"There's a field of love around all people," said Sonja.

"I guess not," said Emily. Put into those words, it sounded ridiculous. "It's a bad analogy."

"Of course that makes sense," said Blima, clapping her hands together. "It's like a soul."

"Okay," said Emily, "no. I'm certainly not talking about souls here."

"So how does the soul work?" asked Sonja. "How does it go through the air? And how far does it go? It doesn't make sense that it would go on forever. We'd be too wrapped up in each other, there would be no way to feel when one person ended and the next started. And why are some magnets stronger than others, since we're having the discussion?"

"Magnets?" asked Emily.

"Yes," said Blima. "Tell us more about magnets."

"Well," said Emily. "Magnet strength depends on a bunch of things. Material. Radius. That's one of the factors. The field gets weaker the farther away you get. See? None of this works out."

"You're better at loving close up," said Blima. "No. That can't be right. My great-aunt Olga. She was your Papa Sam's auntie. I remember her from Russia. She was a loving woman, but you couldn't get near her because of garlic and halitosis."

"I love by post sometimes," said Sonja. "That has to be taken into account."

"And I just learned about the Internet," said Blima. "There are strange sorts of love there, from what I've observed so far, but intense all the same. So great love, greater distance."

"But what about the radius of a waist," said Sonja. "Bigger magnets work better. So fatter people love better."

"This doesn't work out," said Emily.

"Of course it does," said Sonja. "Our mother was very thin."

"So was dad," said Blima.

"Oh, that's true," said Sonja.

"This isn't what I meant," said Emily.

"We'll figure this out," said Blima. "Dorothée. Fat and good at loving. I only knew her when I was very small."

"Who was she?" asked Emily, hoisting her laptop under her arm, reaching into her pocket for a pen. "Who was Dorothée?"

"That was your Papa Sam's mother," said Blima. "Then there was his father. Isaac. Thin with a very big head. He looked like a stop sign. Affectionate, but with suction-cup kisses, so not effective for a child. I used to cry when he came too close, but he just loved children. Then there was Johannes. I don't know him except for pictures. Fat. Reputation as a loving squeezer."

"Who were these people?" asked Emily, breathless. "What was their last name?"

"This is your Papa Sam's side of the family," said Blima. "These were the Kogans. Some of them married and changed their names. Not all. Not many, from what I remembered. They were an odd lot."

Sonja sighed. "No," she said. "I can't picture it. It doesn't look like there's a relationship between size and love."

"I never meant there was," said Emily.

"We'll keep looking though," said Sonja. "There has to be some way to explain it. This is the scientific method, right, Emily?"

"Then there was Angelica," said Blima. "Thin. She pinched. To her, that meant love. To me, that meant torture. I always worried that she'd pull too hard and a piece of my face would come right off. I pictured a gaping wound, and, for the rest of my life, facial disfigurement, and she never understood why I burst into tears as soon as I saw her walk into a room."

"You're just showing off that you remember people from Russia," said Sonja.

"We'll keep thinking about this, lovie," said Blima. "We'll let you know."

They heard footsteps on the stairs, loud and oddly lurching, unmistakably Doran. And then Sonja ambled out the door, around the corner, after him.

Emily stopped her grandmother.

"I'm trying to figure things out," she said.

"I don't think I can help you."

"Do you know any more names? Can you tell me that, at least?"

"That's all I can think of for now," said Blima. "If I remember more, then I'll tell you right away."

"Can you tell me a love story now?" she asked. "Can you tell me the one about Auntie Sonja and my great-uncle?"

"Are you ready to hear the real story?"

Emily didn't know what to say to that. So Blima shuffled out into the hallway and left Emily standing quietly by herself.

ALL THE USUAL ARGUMENTS

HARPO, 1933

Harpo crept through the forest that was creaky and dripping with a recent rain, carpeted with a mist that rose up from the mud. He heard a strange sound, and froze. Seconds later, a deer loped out of the trees, shining sparkling white in the moonlight, like something out of a dream. It turned so Harpo could see it in profile. He stumbled toward it, held out a hand, but the deer turned again and disappeared. He stumbled onward. Suddenly a branch like a crooked finger poked him in the top of the head. He gasped. Blima was a dutiful girl, if she'd run out in a dark forest in the night. There were things out here. There were noises.

He heard a crunch, unmistakably a footstep. Footsteps. More of them, and a guttural muttering in the dark. Harpo froze. Those were angry sounds. Then he saw a beam of light swing toward him. He turned and ran.

And then he saw it, the lodgehouse lit up from the inside, the very air around it seeming to glow. There was the silhouette dark against it, William peeking into the window, crouching where the greenish-blue forest light met the bright orange mist that surrounded all the windows. He wasn't just listening inside. Harpo had been right, before. He had a bucket beside him, and a sponge. And beside that, something else. A hammer. Harpo ran to him.

"There you are," said William, pulling him into an awkward embrace. "I didn't see you in the party room. I was so worried."

Harpo turned back to the woods, in the direction of those voices. Maybe he'd prefer not to know, to feel safer than he really was. "Why do you just look in the window?" he asked. "Why can't you just knock on the door?"

"I'm not Jewish," said William.

"They don't care about that."

"They dress for dinner."

"I'll lend you a jacket."

"Sam wears suits with things in the pockets. Ayala wears gowns and pearls, even in the attic sometimes. She tells the little girls about their family in Russia. They come from royalty, you know."

"And I'm related to Karl Marx," said Harpo. "Hey, do they ever argue about the littlest girl?"

William turned. His eyes shone a twinkling white. "They love both their daughters."

Harpo nodded. Sam was too good a man to wonder about Sonja. Your kid was your kid, and that was the end of it. Anyway, Sam probably just assumed Simon was a good guy, helping them get away. He probably thought Simon was being a good neighbour. He believed in miracles, after all.

"What *do* Sam and Ayala fight about?" whispered Harpo.

"Oh, the usual things." William edged closer to the window. "Russia. The move. The family they left behind, who might have died just after they left, they think, fighting the order to move, to stop worshipping, whatever it was that happened."

"Their family is all dead." Harpo exhaled, and watched the white mist of his breath rise and disperse. He couldn't imagine anything so terrible. "Do they argue about letters?"

"Sam says it's useless to send things to Russia," said William. "He says the mail is searched."

Harpo stood on his toes, and saw a glowing hearth, in the middle of all the fancy people. He crept closer still and saw little Blima sitting in front of it.

"The older girl tends to the fire." William had noticed Harpo's interest, and was pointing. "Isn't she a helper? She's a good girl that one. She has a good heart."

Blima *was* a good girl. And she was practical. And self-sufficient. She probably didn't even ask her parents for kindling. She probably made do with what she had around, like old newspapers and love letters written to other families.

Finally, the guests started standing one by one. They filed out, toward a party in another room. Blima left last, a stumbling little sleepwalker. Minutes later, Ayala drifted into the room. She was wearing the nightgown, the one he loved. His heart ballooned. He could have floated away, circled the world like a second moon. Ayala folded herself neatly on the side of the couch. Harpo bit his lip, hard. He was not that kind of man.

"They're talking about you now," William whispered.

"Can you hear what they're saying?" All Harpo could hear now were the forest drips, the pops of frightening things in the dark behind him.

"Ayala is saying that you're going to Russia. She said that you're going to set everything right."

Now Harpo felt worn out, like old twine, like he was a bale of hay. He sat down in the mud.

"Now she's talking about prophets. I don't understand. It usually makes more sense than this."

ALL THE LATE-NIGHT DRINKS

EMILY, 2003

Emily crept toward the dining room, Jazzy in one arm and her computer in the other. The floorboards in the hallway groaned, and started off a series of creaks and bangs in the walls and ceilings, an arthritic house settling in for the night. Then she heard another noise, one that was new. Jonah was in the dining room. Emily crept inside. "Jazzy was getting scared," she said. "I think she had a bad dream."

Jonah took the little lamp and cradled it. He was silent. Maybe he was just interested in the mystery. Emily started up her computer. She found the Robert Baruch pictures. Then she looked at the next grave, Dimitri Baruch, and then the next, Dorotheé Baruch, then Angelica, then Isaac. Dimitri, short and nice. Dorothée, fat and affectionate. Angelica, chubby and weird. And Isaac, who had a body like a spoon. "All the names match," she said. "Two can be a coincidence, but five is a pattern." She scrolled through more pictures. "At least five," she whispered. "No, eight. Nine. There may be more."

"I have no idea what this would even mean," said Jonah.

"We're connected somehow."

"He could have converted, I guess. *Are* you related, do you think?"

"No. I don't know. Maybe." There was a new sound now, a hiss of rain on the roof, a wind that whistled in through the window cracks, and Emily shivered. Jonah patted her back. She leaned her head into his shoulder, hadn't planned to do it, just suddenly felt the soft material of an overworn shirt and saw the skin of his neck way too close, and smelled the dryer sheets and the spicy scent of his soft skin. He smelled like a coconut again. He had a birthmark in the gentle curve between his neck and shoulder.

"There has to be an explanation," said Jonah. "Maybe he's a long-lost cousin."

"Sometimes cousins is just a thing that people say." Emily sighed. "Except nobody's saying that. I asked. Blima said they're from different communities, weren't allowed to talk. He can't be a relative."

"So what's your theory?" he asked. "I know you must have one."

"I don't know," said Emily. "I honestly have no idea what to think. He's not a Jew."

Then there was silence, and Emily sat up, absently tapped her fingers on the table.

"So your mother said you were a mistake?" said Jonah. "That's cool. I think I was one."

"I wasn't a mistake," said Emily. "It's worse than that. She said she never wanted me. Only my dad did, and she agreed because he said he'd walk otherwise. And it wasn't even love that kept her there. She said it would have taken too much work to find someone else."

"That must have been rough to hear," said Jonah.

"She invited me over for dinner," said Emily, "then drank too much, maybe. Or maybe she just wanted to get unburdened. She said she'd wanted to focus on her career. She told me I should do the same."

Jonah sighed. "It's getting pretty late," he said.

When Emily found Doran, he was sitting under the veranda. Emily suddenly remembered that he'd grown up in Russia. Blima didn't remember any Russian, but he might. He might be able to read the letters to her.

She crept out the door. The rain had stopped, but the whole night was dripping anyway. It was so misty that she couldn't see the lake, but she could smell it, the water plants and weeds. She sat down on the step and clutched the first of the two letters to her side, unsure how she should start.

"My stay continues to be wonderful," said Doran.

"If you keep beating me to it," said Emily, "then I might be out of a job."

"Then I'll make sure to forget to update you. On my status. Until you ask."

Emily's eyes were adjusting slowly. She could see the path now. She could see a giant puddle on the stones, getting whipped by the wind so hard that it had its own little waves, looked like the roof of a wide open mouth. "Do you speak Russian?" she asked. "Can you read Cyrillic?"

"I used to."

"Can I show you something?" She handed him the letter.

Doran took it, and scanned it, then turned it over.

"What does it say?" But suddenly, Emily realized that she shouldn't have shown him this. It was private. There was a secret. She should have waited, taken this to the Russian department at school; anything could be written there.

"Do you understand it?" she asked, hating herself for doing it. She should stop this. She couldn't.

"It says, 'I love you,'" said Doran. "It says, 'I love you, Simon.'"

"Simon?"

"I think Simon might have been my father's name."

"I remember." And she craned her neck. The letter was in Grandma Ayala's writing, covered in her artistic swirls, and Grandma Ayala had loved everyone, even the mailman, so this wasn't surprising. "What else does it say?"

"'Those are names that I've kept in secret for years,'" said Doran. "'Decades. Simon. Ekaterina. Their names are here.'"

Grandma Ayala had loved Simon.

"What else does the letter say?" asked Emily. Watching Doran read was exasperating. He was giving nothing away. "Please."

"It says, 'You told me that every heart has two ventricles so that we can all have two different kinds of love in our lives.' It says, 'I'm trying to love this country.' Who wrote this? This is Ayala's handwriting. I recognize Ayala in this." Doran turned to the other side of the page. "Is there more? Where did you get this?"

"I don't know." Emily felt for the second letter in her jacket pocket. Now she didn't know whether she should show it. "There might be. Maybe. I just stumbled over this." She felt like she herself had something to hide. She didn't, she reminded herself. She'd done nothing wrong. "Is there more?" asked Emily. "What else does it say?"

Doran bent to look at the letter again. "She talks about Sonja here."

Emily took a deep breath. The outside smelled smoky now, and it sounded like there were a billion things buzzing around in the darkness.

"She describes Sonja in great detail. When Sonja was very young."

"Blima too?"

Doran turned the page back over again. "No. I don't see Blima. She promises that her love has continued. That's all. Are there any more letters? Is there anything more, like this?"

Emily clutched her pocket. She needed time. She needed to think. "I'll see if I can find anything."

"Do Sonja and Blima know about this? Have they read it?"

"I don't think so. No. They were looking for something, but they had no idea—they couldn't remember the contents. And maybe we shouldn't tell them quite yet."

Doran nodded slowly.

"If I can find more," said Emily. "I'll bring them to you." But she might not. This was private, strange somehow, and she couldn't tell Blima and Sonja about it. She didn't know why, but she knew that they'd be furious. That she'd found it. That she'd shown it to someone else. Except there was nothing in the letter, just a description of baby Sonja, so why was she so afraid?

"I'd better go to bed." But Emily didn't move. A drip fell onto the letter, with a sound like a footstep in the grass. The paper was a translucent silver where the rain had touched it, and a streaky blue was bleeding radially outward. Emily willed the stain onward. She didn't know why.

As Emily walked back up to the porch, she saw Jonah again, in that same spot near the side of the house. He was crouched over a bucket, then stood. Emily stopped walking. She wanted to tell him, but she had a sick feeling in her stomach, a foreboding.

"Emily?" Jonah called out.

She closed her eyes. "I thought you were sleeping." She couldn't say it, couldn't tell him.

He stood, put his hand lazily to his head, mussed his hair.

"What are you up to?" she asked, finding her voice at last.

"I was going to bed, but then…" Jonah shrugged. "It's nothing really. Graffiti."

"What?" asked Emily. "Still now?" And then she saw it, bright green paint already streaked and dripping because of Jonah's ministrations. But the message was still clearly visible: *Jews Go Home. If you stay here, we only have to use one bom.*

"Don't worry," said Jonah. "It comes in waves, that's all. It'll die down, and there'll be nothing for months."

"That's terrifying."

"I wouldn't worry too much. Not until they learn to spell the word *bomb* anyway."

"Sure," said Emily, but she knew the family rule. There are always threats just outside the door.

"It's really not a big deal," said Jonah.

Emily watched him. She tried again to tell him about the letter, that terrible feeling in her stomach, the certainty that she'd done something very wrong. But she couldn't do it.

After a moment, she turned, hurried back inside. And she heard the low murmur of voices, Doran and Sonja, Blima and Moshe. Doran had beaten her inside. She stopped to listen, hugging herself to suppress violent shivers. But they were talking about the weather, about people long dead, about all the same things they usually talked about. Doran was giving nothing away. At least there was that.

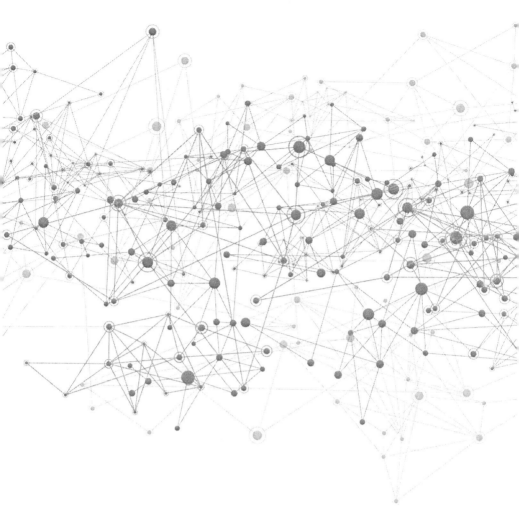

THE SIXTH DAY (OR THE FIFTH DAY OF PASSOVER)

LOVE, LIKE LIGHT, FILLS EVERYTHING

HARPO, 1933

Harpo patted Ayala's head hard enough to mess up her hair, to take strand after strand out of that tight elastic. She laughed. So did Harpo. Because she looked like a scarecrow, and, of course, she wouldn't know that until later. Sometimes it was the little things. He could be happy. He wouldn't fail this family.

"How do you think love works?" said Ayala.

"Oh no," said Harpo. Not this again. He rubbed her back. Loving wasn't complicated, it really wasn't. Love was like light. You flicked a switch and the room was lit. You loved someone and they were loved. But that did seem too simple. How did love get sent? How did light get sent, for that matter, now that she'd asked the question, and how come when you flicked the light switch the whole room lit and not just a small part and the rest incrementally? *Incremental.* Amazing. Two down, the Saturday that Frenchie was in the hospital. He and Groucho had been sitting in the waiting room and he'd figured he'd never use that word in his life. Harpo rubbed his eyes. Frenchie would never have worried about things like these. He never felt sorry for himself one minute of his life. Harpo would be like that. He'd figure this thing out and then move on to his own family, would be a family man just like his father. "Can you tell me things about Simon?"

"You know," said Ayala, "sometimes I dream that my love is inside a balloon that's attached to me by a cord. And when I complete some task, I get a pair of scissors and I cut it. Then the girls catch it after that and I can give them my love. And Sam. Simon too."

"I've run out of places to look," said Harpo. The letter had been burned, he'd bet on it. Little Blima had probably fed it into the fire, months before, or years. "I need help. Is Simon tall?" And his voice cracked. He made a lousy detective. "Does he have dark hair? Is he Jewish?" Oh God, please answer no. The Jews are having a rough go of it in some places, that's what people were saying. "What's his last name?"

"But it never works in the end," said Ayala. "No matter how successful I am in the dream, I wake up and it's all just the same. And I'm worried that it's going to be too late. Soon I'll lose my chance."

Harpo lay down on his back. "Too late can happen," he said.

"What?"

He rubbed his face. You never knew when too late would come. At least with Frenchie, they'd been expecting it, he was a while in the hospital, and the doctors had told them to say their goodbyes. When Minnie went it was sudden. There was no knowing that the dinner party at Zeppo's would be the last time they'd talk to her, that when they hugged at the door, it would be the last hug ever, and after that, never again. Nothing more.

"Nightmares, at least, bring a measure of relief when they end," Ayala was saying, "because they can be over. But this doesn't end. I mean to say I love you, and I can't. Even when I wake up."

Harpo remembered that night with breathtaking clarity. He bent forward, put his head in his lap. That night, the last night of Minnie's life, Frenchie had led her to the car and the boys had stayed for cards. An hour later, Frenchie was back again, pounding on the door. Minnie was in the car. Something was wrong. Something had happened. She couldn't move or speak. Could he bring her back into the apartment to die with her family? Harpo didn't remember getting her up into the bedroom, but he must have helped. He didn't remember taking turns sitting with her in the dark bedroom, stroking her hand and waiting, but that's what everyone said happened. He didn't remember much of that night, just the end.

"I mean to say, 'I love you,'" said Ayala, "and I say, 'Do up your shoes, you look like a homeless person.' I want to say, 'You look beautiful,' and instead I hear myself telling Blima that the hobos will see her untied shoes, think she's one of them, and steal her away to live in trains and eat tin cans."

"So stop," said Harpo. "Just stop it. Life can be simple." He closed his eyes and could feel the weight of Minnie in his arms as her laboured breathing had slowed and slowed then stopped. And he was back again, in the dark room in Zeppo's apartment, holding on to his mother's body, begging her not to go. He didn't care about the hard times. He just loved her. That's all there was to it. That's all that was left.

Ayala stood up, turned and walked off the dock. And Harpo sat up and watched the water, and a long time later, he followed to the lodge.

Harpo felt numb as he installed himself in the office doorway, sitting against the wall, foot thrust out to hold the door open a crack. A long time later, Blima appeared. She lifted Harpo's arm, and curled into his lap, hugging his arm around her. Harpo let the door shut. He closed his eyes. He didn't need to look, to know what was happening now.

There was the crack that meant that Ayala had passed behind the registration desk.

And there was the soft hush, the drawer opening.

Abruptly, Blima squirmed out of his lap. By the time Harpo

looked over, she was already gone, clear out of the room. The office door opened all the way. There was a whoosh of cold air, a breeze that lifted Harpo's hair, and Harpo didn't move, not even to take a breath. Ayala was standing in the doorway, towering over him. Her eyes were shining brightly, and there were tears on her flushed cheeks. Harpo's head was blank. He saw falling snow. Every time he blinked, he saw mounds and mounds of it.

"Harpo." Ayala's voice was hard. "There's a wire for you," and she handed him a card.

Harpo didn't know what else to do, so he turned it over in his hands. It was from the government, not the Canadians, the Americans. They requested his help in his upcoming tour of the Soviet Union. They wanted him to be a spy probably. Aleck had warned him this might happen.

And suddenly, Harpo had an idea of how he'd get Simon's family out. He laboured to his feet, and left the room, measuring his steps so he wouldn't show that he was afraid.

THE UNNATURAL CONNECTIONS WILL BE MADE

EMILY, 2003

It was an ominous morning. Emily had woken up to the sound of a door that slammed, and her entire body had jerked with the sound, the pressure change, like someone had shaken her roughly awake. Why hadn't Ayala sent that letter? All night Emily had asked herself that question. Why was it hidden away? Was that a family game too? Withholding Love wasn't cute like Wall Mouse or Finding Stuff. It didn't seem like a particularly nice game if it was one.

Emily stumbled into the room of windows to find Jonah sitting on an easy chair, flipping through recipes. She watched over his shoulder. She didn't want to think about the letter anymore. She didn't want to worry about Doran or family secrets. "Is Passover really that bad?" she said.

"It is if you're cooking."

Emily put her hand on Jonah's back. He felt so solid. She could feel his soft shirt, and under it his shoulder bones and muscle, and he smelled like dough and musk, and woodsmoke, somehow, and, bitingly, of oranges. If the Harpo and Groucho axes of personality were north-south, and east-west, respectively, then the Chico axis would be up and down, measuring impulse control. She dropped her hand.

She sat across from him instead. He had Jazzy, Emily saw. He'd propped her up in his lap.

"So how are things with your boss?" asked Jonah. "Are you still missing in action?"

"I raised the stakes. Yesterday, I told him I have the flu."

"Will that work?"

"Russell has WebMD bookmarked. He checks it the way some people check their horoscopes."

"I don't think I understand why you're doing it."

"Yeah..." They were sitting together, talking. They'd connected as kids with silly games, but they needed to connect as adults. She needed to start a conversation, a real one, a human-to-human one between grown-ups, and she had to do it now. If Sonja and Doran could reconnect, then so could she. "What do you want to do with your life?" she asked.

"That's a light topic of conversation."

"I'm serious. Do you have life plans?"

Jonah put his feet up on the coffee table. "Pipe-dream plans, or real plans?" he said. "I guess it's all the same. I want to open a café, a student hangout. A safe place for lost people like this was a safe place for the Jews."

"That's funny," said Emily. They were talking. Maybe it was that easy. "It's a good idea."

"Sometimes I feel like I'm stuck, though. Like my life is blocked like a trapped sink. I feel like I need something to happen before I can actually do anything."

"I know what you mean." And she put her feet up too.

"What about you?" asked Jonah. "How is all this genealogy helping with your thesis? What's really going on?"

"What do you mean?" asked Emily, putting her feet down again. "I told you. It's an illustration."

"Yeah, but it doesn't really sound that mathy."

"The problem is that all the other grad students have projects that show more insight than mine does. They can do more stuff."

"So if you're worried you're not good enough—"

"I'm not worried I'm not good enough." But she was. That was precisely her concern. And she'd wanted to talk about it, couldn't figure out why she was getting so upset. But her throat was constricted, her face flushed, she could feel it, and she just wanted him to stop. "I showed the letters to Doran last night."

"I hadn't thought of that," said Jonah. "Could he read them?"

"He translated the first one."

"Why didn't you tell me?"

"I don't know," said Emily. "I mean I just did."

"You're really into this letter stuff," said Jonah. "Why you don't study history instead?"

"You can't just move from department to department," she said. "And I'm not a historian. I'm a mathematician." But she wasn't that either. She wasn't anything.

"If you're not happy, then you should consider doing something else."

"I am happy. I love math."

"I'm sorry—"

"You're the one who doesn't understand the first thing about it. Did you even finish high school?"

And that was wrong of her, unforgiveable, and Jonah's eyes widened.

And just then Blima walked into the room. Emily could feel Jonah stiffen. He squirmed to get out of the chair, and it took seconds and seconds. He was struggling with Jazzy, wasn't used to getting caught, and this was all her fault.

"I didn't know all the work was done," said Blima as he scrambled to his feet, finally upright. "So the help could put his feet up."

Jonah was already leaving. He hurried out of the room.

"I thought of some more names for you." Blima took Jonah's chair, and Emily was still buzzing with all the things she should have said, thrumming like a guitar string.

"You wanted some more relatives," said Blima, unrolling a piece of paper. "So I made a list."

Abruptly, Emily stood.

"You don't want the names anymore?" asked Blima. "Oh. I see. You're going to work on your thesis?"

"I'm going to read about Harpo," said Emily. "I got, like, fifty books out of the library."

"I thought you were behind on your thesis."

"It's research," Emily muttered, gathering up Jazzy. "Harpo is connected to us. Anyway, he's connected to everyone famous back then. I'm going to look at timelines. See if he affected their art or research or something."

"I don't see what that has to do with math," said Blima. "You *are* studying math?"

"I'm studying connections, social interactions, and it makes sense that Harpo would have affected science too. You don't discover new things by always thinking about the same old stuff. You need to put one thought next to a completely different thought, and see if you can connect them somehow. So Harpo would be important. He'd make people think in a whole new way." That's the argument she should have made with Jonah. She was trying to think in a whole new way. So it was math. It could be thought of as being slightly related, at least.

"It's not natural," said Blima.

"Well, it's a new thing that I'm doing in my work. It's part of charting connections and connectivity, figuring out how new ideas are formed. That's the whole idea behind what I'm doing."

"What I'm saying, darling," Blima said slowly, "is that it's not natural to love someone who's dead."

"What?" Emily had never thought about her love for Harpo in those terms before, but it was true, he was a man who was dead.

She loved a man who was dead and buried, no, whose ashes had been scattered.

"It's a thing against life," said Blima, "against nature. You should never have more interest in the dead than you do in the living. You should think about real people more."

"Whatever." Emily turned to leave. Then she turned back. "Jonah isn't the help."

"Sure he is. He's on the payroll, lovie. Don't think that he would pay so much attention to you if we weren't giving him money."

A TRAMP LOSES HIS COMPANION

HARPO, 1933

Harpo found Blima in the room of windows. He stood in the doorway, caught her eye and cocked his head, and out she came, running. He felt a surge of something like affection, only more so. He needed a sidekick. Maybe he'd take the tramp's. Maybe Blima would be great in the pictures. He took Blima's hand and led her out the door. "There's a place I want to show you," he said as they walked down the stairs. "Also, I need to know everything you remember from Russia. I'm trying to solve a mystery. I need your help."

"My bed was metal," she said. "We had a maid who snored like a train engine. And I had a toy house that had furniture made of *metal*, but it was too big, so I wasn't allowed to bring it."

"What about leaving Russia?"

"I had a brown coat. It smelled like mothballs. That's because the woman who gave it to me wasn't a good housekeeper, that's what my mother said."

Harpo nodded. Brown coat. Bad housekeepers. The agents would probably need something more in the way of coordinates. If he was going to enlist their help, he would need concrete information to give them.

"Sometimes the old man with the tooth taught me poems. Then I recited them door to door. It was one poem for a kopeck, or three for a denezka, it was a bargain. Our neighbours paid me to recite because I was the cute one then. And when we first moved to Canada, people used to call me adorable. Then I always said ding-dong. Then I had to stop because adorable and a doorbell are two different words."

"Do you remember what it looked like? Where you lived in Russia?"

"There was my favourite tree."

A place with trees. "Did the trees look like these ones?"

"Oh no." Blima looked at him soulfully. "They were much higher."

Trees that were high as seen by a girl who was little. The path swerved, and he could hear the waterfall now. The roar of it was starting to drown out his thoughts, and wasn't that some luck, because he didn't know what to think. Blima clutched his arm. He needed details. Concrete information. Anything. Except Blima must have been nine minus three, so very young, when they moved away.

"What else do you remember?"

"One time, we went into the big city for the day. I was playing on the docks. There were boys jumping into the water. Then one of the boys jumped in, except he didn't float up again. There was just red water. He'd hit an anchor. Everyone was shouting."

"That must have been scary," said Harpo. And yet. He'd figured something out. If there were anchors, then it must have been a port town. Odessa, maybe? Could they have come from a small place just outside?

"My daddy picked me up and carried me away again."

As they got closer, Blima held his onto his fingers tighter and tighter, scared by that roar, by the sound that had scared him too. But then the falls became visible and she ran off like she was one of those race car toys, and Harpo had to run after her. She climbed up the tiny mountain, then turned and ran back to him. "I also remember a lamp."

"What?" said Harpo, panting. "From Russia?"

"It was really tall, and I wasn't allowed to walk behind it. And there was an office. It had a drawer with needles inside. Inside the office, there was a hidden door for the goyim to go in."

"Did you say golems?"

Blima spun on her feet and ran back up again. Harpo stumbled after.

At the top of the hill, Harpo sat down on the rocks. He took the movie notes and Susan letter drafts out of his pocket, and put them on the mossy ground beside him. Then he took a sheet of paper and folded it into a boat, then set it in the water. Blima ran after it as it crashed down the falls. Harpo folded another one as Blima ran back up holding the sopping mess of paper.

It had been hours of repetitive folding and chasing when the boats finally disintegrated and couldn't be put back together again, and Harpo took Blima's hand to walk home. When they got to the lodgehouse's back door, Ayala was waiting. Her cheeks were red and she was smiling thinly. The guests on the waterfront path laughed and waved, but they seemed to exist in a whole other world. Harpo and Blima squeezed each other's hands. Ayala was furious. They could tell. Both of them. They knew the signs.

Harpo opened his mouth to say something, but Ayala took Blima's other hand roughly. "It's not your fault, Harpo," she said, pulling the little girl away from him. "Blima knows better than to go outside without asking for permission." She dragged Blima into the lodgehouse, and Harpo stood still and mute. He'd made a mistake, hadn't been a good guardian, a good father figure. Harpo stumbled inside, to make it up to them, to Blima.

The dining room was full and cheerful, and Harpo was frozen like a ventriloquist's dummy. He was watching Ayala, who had her hands around her daughter's shoulders. She shook her. Then she shook her again. People would notice and why wouldn't Ayala just stop? It was his fault, not Blima's. He was the adult.

"You don't care if I take Sonja for walks." Blima's voice was shaky.

"You can't go that far," said Ayala, "never. You know better than that."

"You love Sonja more. You wouldn't be this angry if Harpo had taken her instead."

The blood running through Harpo's veins chilled. If he tried to move to Blima, he'd crack right open, shatter, fall to the floor in a million pieces. Minnie had let Chico get away with anything too. A new feeling thrummed through Harpo, like his stomach was a giant guitar string. It was anger, maybe. No, not anger. Desperation. Despair. Where were the Gods of *The New York Times* now? He didn't know what to say, what to do. Blima would be so embarrassed. Everyone in the room was dressed for dinner. Why hadn't he thought first? Why had he let this happen? All he wanted was to prove that he could be a good father.

"They've been spray-painting on the wall again," hissed Ayala. "Last night, your father saw tire marks, bats made of wood. Outside the window, there was a hammer."

Harpo flushed cold again. Ayala was right. It wasn't safe, and he should have known that, should have known it better than anyone. It was his fault.

"You're a big girl now, Blima," Ayala was saying, "but it's still my job to keep you safe."

Harpo looked around the room full of people talking, bustling, pretending that they didn't see. Across the room, someone sneezed. Harpo heard it, but through a filter like there was cotton in his ears, like his ears should pop.

"You have to listen to me, Blima. You have to remember what I tell you to do."

Harpo looked at the floor. He was vibrating at a frequency that should make all the glass in this place explode. He willed Blima to look at him. After a moment, she did. She fixed him with a hurt expression and Harpo felt like his heart and his insides were suddenly liquid. He sat down, collapsed right into the chair beside him, suddenly without the power to stand, without any bones at all. When he looked up again, Blima and Ayala were gone. He heard a door slam shut down the hall. Poor little kid.

STANDING ON YOUR HEAD CAN BE AN IMPERFECT SOLUTION

EMILY, 2003

Emily opened her door to find Moshe standing right outside. He looked anxious.

"Can I help you?" she asked.

Moshe leaned into the bedroom a little. "It's not a catastrophe," he whispered. Then he turned and walked, and Emily quickly followed.

"I've already done most of it," said Moshe.

As soon as she walked into the room of windows, Emily was met with the smell of coconuts.

"People have brought up just about everywhere over the years," he said. "This used to be a wild place, you know, so don't worry too much."

Then Emily saw Jonah lying under the table by the window. And she understood. He was drunk. He'd been drinking, all those days. Coconut rum. Orange liquor.

"I don't want to ask your grandmother," said Moshe. "But you see, there's still the stain there, that's what I don't know what to do about. We just need to make sure nobody can see a mark."

Emily watched Jonah carefully. His chest was rising and falling, so he was alive at least. Although, even if his chest wasn't rising. He was a person who knew how to hold his breath.

"I feel responsible," Moshe was saying. "We've been drinking together in my office. He's been so celebratory the past few days. I don't know. I kept refilling his glass. I shouldn't have, I know how you young people can't keep up, but I did it anyway."

Emily knelt beside Jonah. "Are you okay?" she whispered. She felt very close to him, suddenly. Maybe they had reconnected. Maybe that wasn't something that you worked at. Maybe it just happened.

Jonah looked at her, eyes like two harvest moons. "I've had better days," he said, and Emily laughed.

"This is like old times," she whispered. "We used to play games under the table."

"We should get this cleaned up quickly though," said Moshe. "Before Bubbie and your Auntie see."

"I'll get it right out," said Emily. There was already a cloth on the floor, and bottles and bottles of solvents and a huge metal bowl full of water. She mixed proportions, took a cloth and started to scrub.

"I'm so sorry," said Jonah.

What would Harpo say in a situation like this? He'd probably find something positive and say that. "It smells really nice in here," she said, and it was true, it did.

"Oh God," said Jonah.

"No really," she said. "It actually does." She'd expected to be disgusted, but she wasn't. The whole room smelled like a cocktail, or a rum cake. "It's really more coconut than anything."

"You should let me clean up," said Jonah. "Just an hour to sleep and then I could do it."

"I don't mind."

"You don't?" He sat up painfully. "Usually these things make you snap."

Emily sat back on her heels. "I snap?"

"You don't like these kinds of surprises," Jonah said quickly. "Not that anybody should. Especially from the help."

"I'm not like that," whispered Emily, but maybe she was. She listened to all the family's stories about being Russian royalty. She didn't even seem to want to hear the real ones. She'd been given the opportunity to hear a story that was true, and she hadn't pursued it. Great-aunt Sonja's love story was clearly untrue, and she hadn't asked any questions at all.

She put all her weight into her shoulders and scrubbed as hard as she could. She felt like a cord had caught around her neck and pulled tight. All she'd wanted was to be nice and forgiving and happy like Harpo. But she was a Groucho. Still.

Jonah reached for her hand, but Emily sat up, pulled away. "The stain will set," she said. "I have to get it out. It's just lucky you're not dead."

"All those times..." But Jonah didn't continue.

All those times. Emily blinked away the memory of dark nights, dark rooms, laughter filtered underneath the dining-room door, and so many tears that she felt like she was drowning. "Next time, it might not be a joke," she said.

"What?" said Moshe. "Alcohol poisoning? I don't understand the two of you."

Emily scrambled to her feet, then reached for the bowl. "I'm going to get more water." Moshe followed her out the door.

Emily stopped outside the dining room and watched the crack beneath the door. There was always a little draft, a breath of cold air that came through no matter how hot it was. When she was little, she used to lie there and listen in on the grown-ups' parties. She heard Moshe walking to her side. She didn't turn around.

"The first time Jonah died was when he was nine years old and I was six," said Emily.

"I don't think Jonah really died though," said Moshe.

The first time might have been a Seder, but it probably wasn't.

The adults were all in the dining room, having a fancy dinner. Beneath the door, there was a tiny strip of bright yellow light. She was playing by herself because Jonah was in one of his moods.

"I don't think he was really dead," said Moshe, "not for any appreciable amount of time, anyway."

"I was only six," said Emily. "Five maybe."

"Did he tease you? Is that what happened?"

"He used to do it a lot," she said, and her voice was brittle. "He used to pretend that I killed him."

Emily could always tell that it was coming. She could sense an edge to his jokes, an energy building, a strange upsetting tension that she could neither account for, nor explain. Then he'd tease her. He'd tease and he'd tease until she'd turn around and shove him. Then he'd always fall down dead.

"He'd goad me into hitting back, then would fall down and pretend to die."

"That's too bad," said Moshe.

Emily didn't respond. It was more than too bad. It was scarring. It had scared her. After a moment, she heard Moshe leave the room. She continued into the kitchen and wrung out her cloth.

Emily hurried back to the room of windows, but Jonah wasn't on the easy chair, or underneath it. She ran to the table. He wasn't under there either. She sat down heavily right in front of the stain.

She remembered seeing him dead on the ground, where she'd shoved him. All those times. She'd picked up his hand, dropped it, and, when it fell back to the ground, she thought that meant he was dead because that's what she saw on TV. She'd never understood the pulse part of things. Then she'd always rushed to get her mother's compact, click open to the mirror, hold it under Jonah's nose. Jonah had explained earlier that when a mirror didn't fog up, it meant the person wasn't breathing, he was dead.

"He probably went to sleep it off," said Moshe, from the opposite doorway.

"It wasn't just playing dead, you know. He'd lock me in the cellar, hold the doorknob so I couldn't get out. Sometimes he paddled me to the dock and left me there."

"That I remember." Moshe was trying not to laugh. Emily could hear him trying to silence it, and that effort to stop was infuriating.

"I was little." Emily scrubbed vigorously. "He told me that we were all the way in Kingston. And that the lights from the lodge were really prison lights. I believed him."

"He was just trying to get your attention," said Moshe.

"He had my undivided attention. He always did."

"He felt self-conscious because you were always so smart."

Soon, she heard Moshe leave the room. Emily dipped the cloth in the water and swirled it around. It had been so long ago. Jonah had been nice to her for decades, and she should just let it go. That's what Moshe must be thinking. He was right too.

When the carpet was clean, Emily tiptoed to Jonah's room, then to the kitchen, then to the room of windows again. Finally, she found him in the room of doors, curled like a larva beside the big wooden table. She found a blanket and covered him up and sat beside him. Here's what she remembered most. She was sitting on a stair just outside the dining room, crying without sound, when Jonah appeared at the bottom of the stairs. She threw herself into his arms, and he nearly overbalanced, but grabbed onto the railing in time to save them both. But then, "Next time, it might not be a joke," he whispered right into Emily's ear.

"So I hear it's been a long day for you, Emily," said Blima as Emily wandered back into the room of windows.

"It's not that bad," said Emily. "Where's Auntie Sonja?"

"She's upstairs, looking for Doran. So. Jonah drank too much. That's like our chef who used to drink too much. These men. Your Great-uncle Daniel nearly drowned the chef in the lake, he got so mad."

"I'm not that mad," said Emily, interrupting. For once, she didn't want to hear another story. "I'll just watch *A Night at the Opera*, then I'll feel better."

"All of this business with Harpo Marx," said Blima.

"He's somebody I can depend on."

"How can you depend on a man who died in nineteen sixty-three? He's dead, lovie. It's unnatural when there are living men around."

"It's not like that. He's just comforting. I put his DVD on, and I laugh, every time."

"It's easier for a man who's dead," said Blima. "He doesn't have to do as much."

"He never makes me sad. He never lets me down."

Blima stood. "Let me tell you about Harpo Marx letting you down. A pretty girl walks by, who's older than you and has long legs, then he's off."

"That was just in the movies."

"That's what he was like. That was Harpo. Except the real man knew what to do with the girls once he caught them."

"What about Elijah? He wasn't perfect. He went to those old people who loved that cow like it was their kid. And what did he do? He prayed for the angel of death to take their pet away. And it died. And those two old folks were devastated."

"That's easy," said Blima. "Everyone knows that one. He did it because he saw the angel of death coming. He asked the angel to take the cow and to leave the old woman."

"And he couldn't have asked the angel of death to leave them both alone and just not come? He could have saved everybody. He had a pretty direct line to God, that's what everyone says. Those people were old and poor and he just made them more miserable."

"Sometimes, that's the way things have to work."

"Sometimes, people just want to look clever."

"You don't know Elijah. Anyhow. I'm the one who knew Harpo. You want to know about him? This is who Harpo Marx really was. One day, I had a fight with our mother. Harpo and I had just been out for a walk, and for a few minutes, she didn't know where I was. She pulled me right into the great room in front of everybody — this was in the old days when the lodge was packed — and then she yelled at me in front of all those people. And Harpo didn't help. He didn't defend me. There was probably a girl there, he was always chasing after pretty girls. At first, I thought he just didn't notice. But then he gave me a long look in my eye and I knew that he saw. He just did nothing. He just stood there while I cried in front of everyone."

"That's not true," said Emily. "That can't be true. Harpo was a good man."

"He didn't stand up for me. That's your hero. A man who will leave a little girl alone."

"Whatever." Emily stalked away. "Everyone else says he was great."

Emily slammed her door, and for minutes after, she could still hear the echo, the pop of air, the vibration in the walls. She hadn't slammed a door like that since she was fourteen years old, and why had she ever stopped? It felt great.

She walked around the room, lap after lap, then stopped at the cabinet. On it was the postcard of the three most famous Marx brothers, the one she'd stolen from Ayala's file. The Marxes were pressed into the frame, smiling boyishly, clearly caught in the midst of some great movement. And beside that, there was the picture of Harpo Marx without his fright wig and costume. Harpo just looked like a normal guy. She picked up the Harpo picture, the au naturel one, and took it with her on her next lap of the room.

Harpo hadn't been mean.

Emily felt a breeze, and suddenly she knew what Harpo would do right now.

She ran to the window, then hopped onto the ledge. As she swung herself outside, she hit her leg and it made a horrible sound, thunderous, and she froze, half inside and half out.

Then Doran's face appeared out of the window of the adjacent room. He leaned out, farther and farther, not saying anything, just fixing her with his weird dish-plate eyes. Emily's leg started to throb. A bruise was forming, she could feel it. Should she go back in? What would she say to him if she did? He'd come around for sure and want to talk, or he'd just stand there in the doorway, silent and maddeningly weird. She manoeuvred the rest of the way out the window, and let herself drop.

She fell to the ground, stunned. That had hurt.

Emily picked herself up again and looked up. She had just jumped out of a window. She'd been caught at it too. Doran was still leaning out the window, looking at her with an unreadable expression. Well at least there was that. A normal person would have been appalled.

"Hey!"

Emily wheeled around. Ryan was walking toward her, Amy standing sullenly beneath the oak tree.

"Hey, Emily!" said Ryan.

Emily turned and limped down to the woods as quickly as she could. She'd just jumped out a window. And she'd been caught at it twice.

Emily limped farther and farther into the forest.

Harpo used to get tossed out of his school when he was in the second grade. His class was on the second floor, and two bullies used to grab him, hoist him up to the window and let him fall. Emily had always read that particular anecdote as mostly funny, and admired the scrawny little kid who picked himself up and marched himself back to the classroom until the day he just didn't anymore. But now she knew that it hurt.

THE CAPACITY FOR INFINITE HAPPINESS

HARPO, 1933

Harpo sat against Sam's closed office door. He shouldn't have taken Blima so far. They could have played indoors. He should have known this would happen. He'd seen the paint on the wall, had heard the voices in the woods. Of course it wasn't safe.

He'd had a dream last night or the night before maybe, and it came back in a rush. He was supposed to be performing on Broadway, that he knew, only he forgot what play he was in, what he was doing, and all he knew was that he was standing all alone on centre stage, caught by the spotlights. He called for Minnie and after a moment heard her climbing onstage. He explained, as the footsteps creaked nearer, that he'd forgotten his lines, and wanted his brothers, and was embarrassed and afraid. Minnie made her slow way into the well of light. When she got to the spotlight, Harpo's breath caught. Her cheeks were red, her lips pinched. She was furious. Then she yelled at him for minute after minute, about *Duck Soup*, Ayala, Simon, Blima, everything. At some point during the tirade, Harpo realized that the audience was still watching. He'd forgotten about them. But now he could hear them, shuffling around in the dark. Someone opened a hard candy, and he could hear the crackle of the wrapper and the sharp clack of teeth.

Harpo had no idea what to do next. All he wanted was to talk to Sam, to be comforted, but that wasn't right. If he wanted to become a good father, then he should be the one to give comfort, not to receive it. He should talk to Ayala, explain the situation, make things right. But she was mad. She probably wouldn't listen much right now. He should comfort Blima. But she'd be furious with him.

He had to do *something*.

"Hey, Sam," said Harpo, peeking around the door into Sam's office.

"Are you ready for that cigar, Harpo?"

"I need to send another telegram. It should go to Aleck Woollcott. Alexander, I mean."

Sam took out a form. "I can do that," he said. "What's the message?"

"If they want my help, I want theirs. Stop." Then Harpo was silent, and he knew that Sam was watching him, and he didn't even know how to start.

"I have an idea," said Sam. "I just thought of another project for us to work on together. I've been inspired by your windows in the room of doors. You know that vegetable cart I want everyone to gather around? What if we turned it into a table? That would help people gather there. They'd have no choice. That's where their cards would go."

Harpo sat on a tool box. He stared at his hands. Sam always knew what to do. He was just a born family man. What if Harpo hadn't been born that way? He let people comfort him. He went to others for help. Here he was again, acting more like a son than a father.

Sam turned a bucket upside down and sat in front of an upturned chair. "What's the different between a vegetable cart and a table? Give up? The answer is nothing. I just realized that. They're the same thing, except that a table has legs."

"You're going to take the legs off the chair?"

"Why not?" said Sam. "The tree won't mind. It's long dead."

"I'm worried that I won't be a good father," Harpo said quickly, before he could lose his nerve.

"Of course you will."

"I never know what to do. And I always end up doing the wrong thing. And I never know how to act. How can I raise a child if I'm not finished being raised myself?"

"We're none of us finished," said Sam. "And nobody knows how they'll act in a situation until they find themselves acting. You're a good man, Harpo, and that's all that's needed. You have to trust that the rest will work itself out. That's the real secret."

"I want to be like you."

"I never know what to do. Not really. I'm always groping around in the dark. I think the secret is not to lose your sense of humour, and I can't believe that you ever would."

Harpo blinked back tears. He focused on the old vegetable cart, prodded one splintered edge with his foot. "Do you like remembering the trip from Russia?"

"The trick is to tell it better than it really happened." Sam turned the chair over, grabbed it by the seat and sawed. After a moment, one of the legs came off with a resounding crack. "The trick is to remember only the good things. If I tell the story that way long enough, then that'll be what really happened."

Sam looked up, and caught Harpo's eyes, and Harpo felt like his blood was suddenly electric. He knew. Sam knew everything, about the other man, about the baby, everything.

"God gave us a selective memory," said Sam, "and an imagination, and with those gifts comes the ability to remember things any way we want."

"I think you're right," whispered Harpo.

"And with that comes the capacity for infinite happiness," Sam said sadly. Then he turned the chair around and sawed the other legs right off.

LOVE LETTERS IN CULINARY NOTATION

EMILY, 2003

Emily walked back up to the lodgehouse. She saw Doran and stopped. She couldn't deal with him right now. She couldn't have another Morse code conversation.

"Emily!" he called, as she walked to the stairs.

She wanted to walk right past him, pretend she hadn't heard. He'd probably want to talk, and he went about everything like Michelangelo staring up at the Sistine Chapel, waiting to start to paint.

"You found him," he said. And that did it. Emily stopped walking.

"What?" she said. "Found who?"

"The man on your door. He's the man who brought me home from Russia."

"That's Harpo Marx."

"Imagine that," said Doran.

"Wait," said Emily.

"I guess I did know him."

"Are you serious?"

But Doran was already walking into the woods. He was probably making fun.

Emily slunk into the lodgehouse, and this, also, she remembered from childhood. Walking back inside with her head down, feeling sad and chastened, just wanting to apologize. No. Just wanting to be forgiven. She poked her head into the dining room. There was a lump of a blanket under the table, where Jonah had been sleeping. And abruptly she remembered something else, lying under that table with Great-grandma Ayala.

Emily crawled under. She curled into a ball, then looked up. There were pictures under there, stuck to the bottom of the tabletop, a million crudely drawn little sketches in hundreds of colours and curl after curl of peeling yellow tape. Emily reached to stroke them, and got the strangest feeling, like she was too big for her body, two sizes at once. It was dizzying. She remembered things: putting her head on Grandma Ayala's leg, colouring, Grandma Ayala bending to look at her as the sunlight swung by to hit them right in the eyes.

Emily reached up to touch the table, and that's when she saw all the words. There was a border around all the pictures, *I love you*s pasted up there, in hundreds of different kinds of paper, in hundreds of different hands.

She lay on her back as minutes passed, then hours, and she read the *I love you*s, mesmerized.

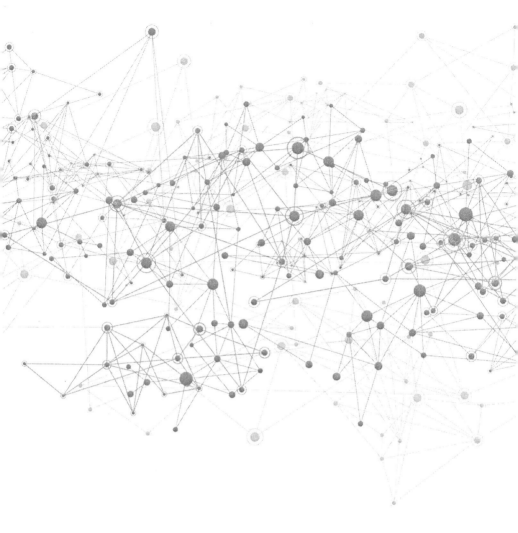

THE SEVENTH DAY (OR THE SIXTH DAY OF PASSOVER)

LOVE ME, ETCETERA

HARPO, 1933

The sun was just thinking about rising when Harpo crept into the room of doors and sat at the piano. This morning, he'd trick Ayala. She'd walk out to the lake and get all ready to ditch him, but he'd beat her to it. He'd ditch her first. He just wouldn't go.

He opened the piano's dust cover. This was how Chico used to start when they were kids: Chico played a single chord, and the music vibrated exactly where Harpo's heart was. Even Mr. Levi — the piano teacher with the wrist-smacking ruler and drooling Bronx lisp — clutched his heart like the hammiest of romantics. Harpo needed that. His heart hurt. He needed something to mend it, and music seemed just the thing. He didn't look at the keys. Maybe the trick was to not overthink. He looked out the window, at the pastel clouds and lit up water, and played. The piano cried, a sound felt in the stomach, not the heart.

Then he heard a creak outside, answering footsteps, then Ayala tiptoed into the room. She hadn't gone to the lake either. She'd tricked him first.

Harpo played a D minor chord, the sound guaranteed to break any heart, coincidently the first chord in the first song Harpo had ever learned—"Love Me and the World is Mine," sad version.

"I used to play for the pictures, you know," he whispered as Ayala sat on the bench beside him. "I played this song over and over, in different keys, different tempos, depending on what was happening on the screen." He played the song in a minor key. The world could have been mine. If you'd only loved me.

"I'll never love them properly," Ayala said after a minute. "My poor motherless girls."

As Harpo played, he pictured a beautiful woman looking out a dirty window, waiting for a letter that hadn't come. Across the city, a man looked at the unfinished love letter that he knew he'd never send.

"Maybe I should leave," Ayala whispered. "Maybe their lives would be better without me."

Then Harpo took his foot off the sustain pedal, switched from minor key to major and played the song again. Now in the movie, Harpo would be appearing with the mailbag. He'd start insinuating himself into the sad man's life, convince him to let the brothers see his secret love letter.

"Or maybe I should stay," said Ayala. "Maybe a bad mother is better than no mother at all."

Harpo stepped up the rhythm of his playing, quick and plucky now. Love me and the world could be mine. Now he'd grab the letter and run, tearing across bright green lawns, ripping up bright-coloured flower beds, vaulting over shrubs, right to the lonely woman's house, where he'd pause and peek in the window.

"Or maybe I don't have to be a bad mother anymore. How hard can it really be, turning your life around, turning yourself into a better person?"

Harpo played faster. This would be where he delivered the letter. He'd ring the bell, and put it right in the lonely lady's hand. She'd wipe her eyes.

"Maybe I just need help."

This would be the part where the man knocked at the girl's

door. He'd be holding flowers in shaking hands, a happy ending, a high note and a major key. Harpo sat back. There were some in-between bits that still needed figuring out, sure, but that seemed like a story that could work.

"I'm willing to work on other things," Ayala was saying, "so maybe I can just work at this."

"Maybe you could write a love letter for Blima."

"Yes." Ayala stood. "That's exactly what I should do." She ambled out of the room.

Harpo moved to the couch, lay down and draped his arm over his head. He'd go to Russia. He'd find Simon and the wife and kid, give them his passport. It would be easy. He'd pretend that he'd lost his somewhere and someone would bail him out, they always did now that he was a celebrity. But there were three of them now, weren't there? Would one passport be enough? And wait. He'd forgotten something about the movie. There was a bad guy in it. How would they get the hustler out of the sad lady's life?

Harpo opened his eyes. It wasn't Ayala sitting on the piano bench across from him now. It was Groucho, working on a crossword puzzle from a magazine. He wanted to go back to sleep. Napping seemed like the only solution to his problems now.

Harpo sat up and something fell to his chest. He picked it up. It was a piece of paper folded into tight accordion sections and squeezed in at the bottom. A fan. As he unfolded it, another landed on his lap.

"I just wanted to tell you," said Groucho, throwing another, "I'm your biggest fan."

"Minnie used to call you the whiner."

"You were no Chico yourself."

"We still did everything she said. What could we have done—"

"There's nothing we could have done."

"Okay," said Harpo. Then he looked at the floor. "Do you forgive her?"

Groucho ripped out some more glossy pages and folded them. "Sure."

Harpo pictured Ayala in the doorway. Another fan hit his nose, and he threw it back, hard.

"You can't just throw those things around," said Groucho. "Imagine if everybody did that. It would be *fan*demonium," and he threw another.

The fan landed on top of Harpo's head, and Harpo kept still to balance it. "Are you bored?" he asked.

"I'm making art," said Groucho. "*I'm* just fine. *I'm* gainfully employed. *I'm* doing something with my life. You're the one who looks miserable. What's been wrong with you the past few days?"

Harpo readjusted himself. "I'm thinking," he said, and it was true. "Do you think it would be hard to get out of Russia? For people who live there, I mean. Some people were living there and had to escape."

"You're referring, I assume, to the beautiful Ayala and her family."

"I'm just talking in general. No. Hypothetically. Hypothetically, how would a family get out of the Soviet Union?"

"Are they Jews, these hypothetical people? This isn't a particularly good time to be a Jew."

"If they traded papers," said Harpo. "What would happen to the people they traded with?"

Groucho threw another fan. "That would be a lunatic thing to do, Harpo. Don't give away your passport when you're there. I don't care why."

"But if someone did."

"You won't."

"If someone already has."

"The only reason I could think to do it is if you were a wanted person anyway. Maybe you're a criminal, and you think you're better off as a Jew."

Harpo nodded slowly. You would also do it if you were in

love. You might do it to save an unborn child. Another fan landed on Harpo's arm, and he unfolded this one, pulled it out and smoothed it. It showed a beautiful woman in an evening gown. "If I were to forget my papers when I get to Russia. If I lose them—"

"You won't do that," said Groucho.

"There are these government guys who want me to do something for them."

"Just settle what they owe you before you go."

"That's an idea." Talk to them before he went.

"Good." Grouch held up a paper fan. "Do you like these? I thought you should wake up to *fan*fare."

Harpo thought, but he didn't have as many words as his brother.

"Hey, Harpo," said Groucho, looking back down at his crossword again. "What's a seven-letter word for infinite sadness?"

"Oh God," said Harpo. "Don't ask me that. That's not a word that I want to learn." He curled up in a ball. He shouldn't fall asleep this time though. When he woke up this time, he knew, he would be buried under a mountain of little white fans.

SOME PEOPLE LOVE SO FREELY

EMILY, 2003

Emily woke up early, her mind whirring like a broken fan. She checked her email. Still more messages from Russell. Just days to go before the final draft of her thesis was due. He must be mad. He'd liked the old draft and the new one was so different. He hadn't approved the changes, she hadn't even shared them yet. She considered opening the messages, but shut down her computer instead, then crept down to the dining room and crawled under the table like she used to do when she was little. Now that she'd remembered that secret space, it was all she could think about.

She looked up and scanned through the pictures and *I love you*s.

Ayala had written *I love you* to Simon. Why was that bothering her? Why couldn't Emily herself ever say it that plainly? That was another dimension of the personality graph, but Emily didn't know how she'd quantify that one, or what it would be labelled even, not self-awareness, but emotional maturity maybe, or emotional generosity, the Frenchie Marx axis from what she'd read last night in Harpo's autobiography. Frenchie had been a man just full up of love. Ayala had been like that too. Ayala had loved everyone.

But as Emily kept staring at the dining-room table, the *I love
yous* seemed to melt and distort, the tape that covered them flashing
like lightning, beautiful and terrifying. They seemed ominous now.
Threatening. Sometimes an *I love you* was something that could
freeze your blood.

Emily slowly pulled herself up the stairs. Forget the letter. The
contents didn't really make a difference. They didn't pertain to her
research at all. She should concentrate on the math. Or maybe she
should graph love connectedness instead of biological relation-
ships. This community was complete. Everyone here would be
connected to everyone else. Everyone loved everyone, sometimes
inappropriately, staring at them through keyholes as they dressed.
That was a topic that should be discussed, and maybe her thesis
was precisely the right forum for it.

Emily crept down the first floor hallway, felt herself being
pulled like she was attached to a string and someone at the other
end was pulling. She touched the doorknobs as she passed them
and tried to imagine this place when it was popular. Because it had
been popular. Jews weren't allowed anywhere else, so the lodge
used to get stuffed to capacity and beyond that, guests sharing
rooms with other guests, ones they didn't even know sometimes,
just for the privilege of being here for a day or two, of meeting
people and then not seeing them until the next season or maybe
never at all. Connections, in that time before email, that meant so
much for a weekend, then vanished after that. Like how you used
to have to really listen to music back when you couldn't just buy
the MP3. No grasping on to digital signatures.

She crept up the stairs. It was just the morning, she reminded
herself. Her research often felt useless and derivative before noon.
Anyway, forget the letter and follow the connections. She was
connected to Blima, and Blima was connected to Harpo Marx. At
least there was that.

And that was something. Emily sat down on the stair. She took out her notebook. Ayala had known Harpo. Harpo had helped Papa William dynamite the basement. She put the family stories she remembered on a timeline, and that was the first time that William had ever appeared. So far she had two family graphs connected by Harpo, like he was the angel on top of a Christmas tree, and he was the only connection she had. He was the maven, the connector dot. There was only one point he wasn't connected to, that gangly little orphan vertex, Doran Baruch, who just thought he recognized a famous face, who wasn't connected to anyone at all. But that wasn't right. Doran had known the Kogans in Russia, presumably. Then he'd gone to the States, then come here, then gone back, rolled around the world like a marble in a box maze. There had to be a reason for all that movement. People didn't travel much back then. They didn't even have planes, well, not commercial ones anyway. If he'd made his way here, then there must have been a reason.

Emily drew in the Doran dot. He remembered a father and a mother, Simon and Ekaterina, so she drew in those too. She hadn't really asked herself how Doran's family might fit into the rest of the graphs, and she wasn't asking herself now, because somehow it was in the realm of things that she knew. His family should be charted right alongside her own. There should be a dotted line connecting Ayala to his father. Ayala had had an affair with Simon. Those letters that Emily had found. They were love letters. Obviously. She'd said, "I love you" right out. Maybe Doran was really Ayala's son and they pretended, but no, that couldn't make sense, the mother was too easily verifiable. It was the father who was forever in question. The father was still in question. If Ayala had sent for the son, why hadn't she sent for the father too? She'd loved him. It was right there on the page.

Emily crept into the dining room. She wedged the door open with a salad bowl so that she'd hear the gurgle of the coffee maker, be closer to the smell. She took the package out of her bag, dumped the contents. She'd sort this out.

There was the letter that she'd shown Doran, and the second letter, and of course *Grimm's Fairy Tales*. Emily set the letters aside and picked up the book. She flipped through it, and, like most old things, it was weighted funny, felt strange in her hand. The front cover tended to fall forward. Emily flipped it open. Tucked inside were three identity cards, and folded papers attached to each. She flipped through them—one, then the next, then the next—and then laid them out on the table, and she saw three faces she didn't recognize: a man, a woman and a little boy. She didn't recognize the faces, but she did know that name. Blima had taught her to write that Cyrillic word on her first morning back here. Kogan. She'd practised, written it on a napkin. Strangers' faces, and her maternal family's last name, her grandmother's maiden name. She felt like she was made of ice, might break apart at any second. The man had light eyes, the little boy too. That little kid must be Doran.

She quickly stuffed the passports back inside the book's pages, into the groove that they'd pressed inside after so many years, decades now because Doran must be in his seventies at least.

Grimm's Fairy Tales.

Doran's father had given his family's passports to Grandma Ayala.

Ayala got Doran out of Russia, but his father had gotten Ayala's family out first. They'd assumed false identities, no, not false, someone else's, Doran's and his parents'. Oh God. That's why Doran had needed rescuing in the first place, he wasn't Jewish, his family wouldn't have been threatened in the pogrom, unless of course they couldn't prove that they weren't Jews. And what had happened to his family? What had happened to the two other faces from the identity cards? Why hadn't Ayala gotten them out of Russia too?

Emily checked the envelope. There was no postage on it, no stamps, no evidence that it had ever been sent at all, any of it, not even the identity cards. They'd taken the papers and made no attempt to send them back. And then the son was sent halfway across the world, alone. What had happened to his parents?

Emily tucked the letter in the book, then the book back inside the old paper package. She thrust the second letter into her pocket. She couldn't show any of this to Doran. What if something terrible had happened to his family? What if it was Great-grandma Ayala's fault?

He never even got his name back. He didn't even know who he was.

INTO THE GREAT, WIDE HALLWAY

HARPO, 1933

Harpo heard footsteps and stiffened. He wasn't ready for company, couldn't perform for strangers. Then Chico walked into the room, and Harpo settled down into the cushions again.

"I got you some coffee," said Chico. "To make up for that night on the dock."

"What night?"

"The night we left you on it."

"Oh," said Harpo. He craned his neck and saw that there were two mugs of coffee on the table in front of him, one brimming, the other mostly empty, both rimmed with a slick of coffee oil. "Thank you."

"We did go back for you, you know," said Chico. He was slouched on the chair like a real tough guy, like an 85th streeter at least. "You were already gone."

If Harpo was going to pull this off, if he was really going to work with government men and boost a whole family from Russia, he'd need to look the part. He had to look tough like Chico. Harpo slouched. It worked. He felt tougher already. He jumped up. He should get the Chico walk down too. Start with stance. When he met those agent guys, he'd be standing like this, like Chico from the tenements, hustling, playing cards, placing bets, you never knew what he'd just been doing, but you always knew that it was dangerous.

"Are you okay, Harp?"

Chico looked more worried than scared. He needed to make some adjustments then. The Chico walk had to start with the right posture. Harpo adjusted himself.

"Did you sprain something?" said Chico. "Did you pull a muscle in your groin?"

Harpo added forward momentum, steps bouncy but not measured. He loped around the room. Then he got his arms swinging. Then he knocked over a lamp. He caught it before it fell.

"That mug is yours." Chico pointed. "I carried both mugs of coffee together. It was harder than I thought. I had to put my thumbs in them, because otherwise they would have spilled."

"I need to talk to you," said Harpo. He needed this new movie idea to work. Because he'd decided. He'd go to Russia, save these families, then he'd come home and start his own, whether he felt ready or not. He'd need to have a job to come back to though. That was the only thing. "I have an idea for a movie."

"I heard that," said Chico.

"The idea is this. We take over a post office."

"Do you think we'll be able to find producers?" asked Chico. "MGM is out. That I know. I guess that MGM isn't the only game in town. You're right about that."

"Groucho's the supervisor. He sorts the mail, and we take it to the houses, you and me. At first, I rip up the letters as they come in. I get mad because I can't read. But then you and Groucho start reading the pieces, then pasting them back together. Then we start playing around, messing with the mail on purpose, rewriting letters because we can. We take lonely girls and set them up with the shy men who love them, that sort of thing. Unhook good girls from the bad guys."

Maybe the sad man couldn't finish his love letter. Maybe they should do it for him, they could take other love letters and paste one perfect one together for him. This was getting so complicated. Usually, the Marx Brothers had a whole writing team and he was only in charge of the Harpo bits.

Chico scratched his face. "Wouldn't work," he said finally. "Letters wouldn't keep a picture moving. Not enough action. You don't mind that I put my thumb in your coffee?"

"We could solve mysteries. How about that? That could have lots of action."

"I put my thumb inside your coffee. That one there."

"I know," said Harpo. "You said."

"Do you mind if I put the rest of my fingers in?"

"No," said Harpo. "Wait. Yes I mind. The letters would count for something now. I could still have that stupid look on my face while I rip them up, as we cut and paste. You and Grouch would be mad at first, but you'd get into it too, as soon as you saw how well it was working. We'd manipulate the whole world. We'd mess with everybody. We'd be able to. We'd have their mail."

"I'd just feel better if all my fingers went in. I would feel more complete."

"I'd be sending for things as well. I'd be learning to write, my little sidekick would help me, and that's how we'd practise. By writing to catalogues and ordering things. Pets. A dog. A lizard. A dark suit. Disguises. They'd all arrive slowly, a running gag. Audiences love running gags. They'd all be used in the climax, all the things that come for me in the post. It would be chaos." He'd put on all the disguises as they came. By the end of the picture, he'd be a mile thick.

"Harpo?" said Chico. "Can I put my fingers in your coffee?"

Harpo slumped back into the plush open palm of the easy chair. "Of course," he said, "please do," but when Chico leaned toward the mug, Harpo scrambled forward and blocked him. Then Harpo manoeuvred himself back into his seat. After a moment,

Chico tried again, and Harpo kicked at him, and they both struggled, but neither fell out of their chairs. They sat back, both at once. Harpo shifted so he was lying across his chair again, facing his brother, his legs hanging close to Chico's shoulder, just in case. This movie would work. It would reunite them. It would make them actors again. It had to work because Harpo didn't know how to do anything else.

"It's too much reading for a talkie," said Chico. "The audience would have to read the originals, then the new letters. Wouldn't work."

"Groucho could read them out loud."

"It would slow things down. My gut says no."

"Well my gut says yes."

"Harpo?"

"Yeah?"

Just then, Chico went for the coffee mug again. He moved fast, but Harpo beat him to it, arching his back and kicking him, and Chico slid out of his chair. He landed with a bump, but then shot to his knees and dipped his fingers into the coffee mug.

Harpo let himself slide off his chair and onto the floor.

Then Chico wiped his hand on his pants and slumped back against the couch, looking thoughtful. He pointed to the upright. "Maybe your idea could work for music."

"Nobody sings letters."

"People pay big money to listen to the opera though."

"Nobody would pay to hear me sing," said Harpo. "Not when they can get a record of 'Minnie the Moocher' for twenty-five cents."

"That's a good line," said Chico.

"That's a good line," he repeated in Chico's Italian accent. The dangerous accent. The accent that his brother had developed in New York. So that people would think he was Italian. So that they'd stop beating him up for being a Jew. God, what was Harpo thinking about? The world was a scary place. How could he hope to manoeuvre through it alone? How could he hope to usher another person, a whole family through the world when he was so scared himself.

Harpo heard quick little footsteps down the hall, like rain on a patio, and suddenly the little footsteps turned into little people. They rounded the corner right into him, Blima with a tumbledown carpet bag and Sonja trailing a pillowcase behind her. Blima wouldn't look at him.

"Where are you two off to?" asked Harpo.

"Blima is running away," said Sonja.

Harpo knelt. Blima turned to face the wall, and Sonja held up her unevenly stuffed pillowcase.

"What's in there?" he asked.

"My bear called Dodo," said Sonja, "and two books and a jacket."

"Are you leaving too?" asked Harpo.

"I have to be with my sister," said Sonja.

"I need to talk to her first though." And Harpo turned to Blima. She still wouldn't meet his eyes, turned again, to face the banister. She had a choice. She could turn around and let Harpo hug her, or she could run down the stairs and out the door. She could feel like Harpo loved her, or she could pretend he didn't and she was all alone in the world. He'd had that choice before. He remembered being a kid as little as Blima, and feeling his options out on a dark stage after the audience had left and the managers had swept up. He'd never wanted Minnie to feel bad.

Abruptly, Blima turned and threw herself into his arms, and he grabbed the railing to keep from overbalancing, from falling right down the stairs.

Then suddenly he didn't know what else to say. He wanted so badly to make everything better. What were the words he'd learned in the crosswords recently? *Corporeal, tacit, torrent, enumerate. Consistent. Topography. Limbless,* but that might have been in a dream. None of them helped, anyway. But he had to do something. This was his chance to redeem himself.

"I have a question for you, monkey," he said finally. But he didn't really need to ask what had happened. Ayala had meant to do something nice for her, but it had gone horribly wrong. She'd wanted to say, "I love you," but instead had called her an upstart or a gorilla. He'd never seen anything like it before, except maybe for Minnie, and Groucho sometimes too. They made no sense. Loving was so easy. And they were people who loved so deeply. Harpo could tell Blima that. That she was easy to love, that it was clear to everyone *else* how much her mother loved her. "Would you watch a movie about a postman?" he said instead, surprising even himself. "I mean. If the Marx Brothers made a picture about mailmen, would you watch it?"

"Yes," whispered Blima. "Can we watch it tonight?"

"Before we run away?" said Sonja.

Harpo smiled. He knew it was a good idea. "I haven't made the movie yet," he said. "Remember? You're writing the story with me, monkey. Now, Sonja can help too."

"Oh yeah," said Blima.

"I can't quite remember where we were," said Harpo. "So I'll set the scene. Chico and I play mailmen. We're partners and we go door to door together. Chico knocks on the doors, and when the women answer, he goes inside and takes chocolates and flowers out of his mailbag. I sit down outside on the porch steps, and all the neighbourhood dogs sit beside me, and I pull dog biscuits out of mine."

"Because you like animals," said Blima, clapping her hands.

"That's right."

"I know that from the pictures. One time, you whistled a love song to a horse."

"So I did," said Harpo. "So. One day, while I'm delivering mail, I see a woman through a dirty window. She's waiting for the mailman and crying."

"She's sad because she's in love with two people. Only, she can just marry one of them."

"Oh?"

"She's in love with the doctor, but that's only because he was her childhood sweetheart. That means that they played with the same toys sometimes. She's also in love with the other man. She might not know it, but she loves the second man more."

Harpo's fingers were tingling. Simon was a doctor. He'd figured something out. "Tell me more about the doctor," he whispered.

"The sad woman's mother makes her marry the other man," said Blima, "because they pray together in the same temple. And the doctor married someone else too. Sometimes the sad woman pretends she's sick so she can visit the doctor during the day. When they kiss in his office, her daughter hides in the cupboard even though there are boxes of needles in there. Sometimes they talk about dangerous things and the daughter gets scared. She wants them to stop so she acts up."

"Were there lots of doctors where the woman lived?" whispered Harpo. "Or was there just the one?"

"Just one," said Blima. "She doesn't really love the doctor at all, I changed my mind. She just thinks she does. And the doctor doesn't love her at all either. So when she tries to send love letters in the mail, since she doesn't mean them, they don't get there. That's the rule. You have to believe in the letter for the mail to work. So he doesn't get the letters and that's why he never writes back. That's why she doesn't get any letters. That's why she's crying. Except then how would people get the bills they have to pay?"

"Bills?"

Blima slumped. "My daddy gets bills, and he says he doesn't believe that he should have to pay them. They still get here though."

"How about this," said Harpo. "One day the beautiful woman gets into a fight with her husband. It's nothing serious. Just a little thing. An argument about socks or dishes or something silly.

She writes a letter to another man, not a man she loved, just a man she knew when she was a kid, a friend. She only wrote it because she was feeling sore at her husband. After she sends the letter, she feels just awful and she regrets what she did. That's why she's crying."

"Yes," said Blima. "That's why she was crying all along."

"She wants to get the letter back so that she can get rid of it. She doesn't want it to get there; she's scared she's going to ruin her family. So she tells Harpo everything, and Harpo the Postman finds the letter. He tracks it down, and rips it up, and everything is saved."

"Except can he do that?"

"Harpo the Postman?" said Harpo. "He can do anything."

"Can he write a new letter instead," whispered Blima.

"Okay…" Harpo scratched his chin.

"Let's write a letter from my mother to my father."

"Let's write a letter that's just for you. I can do that. Letters can't be that hard to write."

"I already have some," said Blima, and she shuffled to her carpet bag, and pulled out letter after letter. "Sometimes when pretty ladies check out, they leave letters under their pillows. I'm allowed to keep them because our parents never look at what's inside, and the maids don't know that I can read."

Harpo opened the envelopes. "These are great," he said. This was research too. It would have to be.

"I know they're love letters," said Blima, "because there are *I love you*s on every page."

"That's it!" said Harpo. "Let's cut out every time someone writes *I love you*, and tape all the *I love you*s to the underside of the table." Because wouldn't that be the perfect love letter? What mattered more than that?

Blima nodded seriously. "I'll get the scissors and the paste."

When they were done, they lay under the table, Blima's head on Harpo's stomach, Sonja curled nearby.

"Can you tell me more about your mischief stories?" asked Sonja.

"I've done loads of bad things," said Harpo. "I get into lots of mischief. I went to a black-tie dinner, and I wore a black tie, but no pants. I ran out of the bushes with no clothes on once so my friend would miss his shot in croquet. Oh and I caused mischief one time in a hotel in Montauk, Long Island, not far from here. I wanted to go on a fishing trip with my friends. I booked our stay and I got a wire from the hotel the next day that said, 'Trust you are Gentile.' So I checked into the hotel as Harpo MacMarx so they wouldn't think I was Jewish, and I brought a walking stick and tam-o'-shanter. I was afraid my friends wouldn't like me anymore if I caused them trouble. But then that night I told them, and they were angry on my behalf. We left. And I got the last laugh, anyway, by asking the concierge for directions to the nearest Jewish temple."

Harpo sat up on his elbows. Blima was fast asleep. Sonja too. He took off his sweater and tucked it around them. He felt kind of like a father, doing that. He crept away.

Harpo padded into the forest, listlessly touching the tree branches as he walked, shaking their bony hands.

There would need to be a climax in this movie. There would have to be great danger, and a great resolution. So the sad lady was stuck in the company of a bad man. A good guy loved her, so that was good, but the hustler would have to show up one last time. It would have to be scary. So the hustler, he'd come to the post office where they were hiding out, and he'd bring his crew. They'd have guns. Harpo would pack them all into a steamer trunk. No. Not scary enough. He would sneak the lady out through the back entrance, into the night. But they'd be caught. The hustler would fire. An explosion of glass. The only light bulb shattered. But then Harpo the Postman would run right into the hustler, protected by all that extra padding of disguise after disguise after disguise. The hustler would pull off Harpo's jacket, and he'd have another jacket on underneath. Then the hustler would pull that one off, and he'd have a dress. But then the hustler would pistol-whip Harpo, and that would hurt, so Harpo would cower…

Harpo stopped. He heard a creak, footsteps in the darkness. So he edged forward, and saw them, a group of men huddled by the lodgehouse, great buckets of paint in their hands, flashlights. One man held an axe. Another swung the beam of light to the wall. *Dirty Jews*, the graffiti read, *your not safe here either*.

At first Harpo cowered. But then he straightened and edged forward. He couldn't hide forever.

"That's not how you spell that," and he was surprised to hear his own voice. The men all turned toward him, their faces contorted with anger and surprise. The biggest one looked like a boot, another like the tip of a pencil. Mean-looking men, all of them. He should have stayed hidden. He edged away.

"You need an apostrophe." Harpo sounded calm, but he was having trouble breathing, couldn't catch his breath. "Because you really mean to say 'you are not safe.' You're is a contraction of you are." At least Groucho would be proud of him. He hadn't realized that he remembered that rule. Or the word *contraction*.

"Are you one of them?" growled the pencil top.

Harpo turned and ran into the woods.

After minutes and minutes of running, Harpo slowed, then stopped, then realized nobody was following. He was safe. So he looked up. He saw trees without a break, and strange plants—lichens? He'd never even seen them before, had just read about them in books.

He wasn't safe. He was lost.

THE MAN WHO LOOKED LIKE LOVE

EMILY, 2003

When Emily woke up again, she was still under the table. The sun was up, struggling over the lake, smudging colour all over the shimmering water. In front of her was the brown paper package, and, on top of that, an envelope. The Russian letter. The second one. She picked it up. She should tell Jonah about the letter, about the whole affair. She'd wanted so badly to have a mystery, something that they could figure out together, the two of them against the world. This was perfect. And she was excluding him.

Emily slid the thin sheets of paper out of the envelope. The note wasn't addressed, and there were none of the formal greetings that she'd grown used to in other old correspondence. There was a date, that was it, and a mess of jumbled script.

Doran had asked for more letters, and she'd promised that she'd bring them. But she couldn't show him anything now. He'd know what all this meant, of course. It meant that Grandma Ayala and Papa Sam had taken his name, stranded his family in Russia, and then, for some reason, only Doran had made it out.

She smoothed the letter out on the floor, and ran her fingertips over the indents. The cursive Cyrillic was tight but uncontrolled, the shapes oddly angular and pressed firmly in the page, not like Ayala's writing at all.

She'd make an excuse. She'd say there had never been another letter. She'd say she'd been mistaken, there had only ever been one.

She flipped to the next page and felt line after line, pretending that she could read it herself, that she didn't need Doran to unlock it for her. But her fingers stopped in the middle of the page. She'd found probably the only Cyrillic words she knew, save for the name Kogan. "Exapno Mapcase." Harpo Marx.

She flipped back to the first page. 1933. Oh God. Harpo went to Russia that year. He was the first Western artist to perform after Communism. He'd written about it. He wrote that he'd gone, that he'd played secret agent while he was there. The American government asked him to smuggle out a letter taped to his shin. It couldn't be this one though. It didn't make sense that the letter would have wound up here.

Anyway, Emily shouldn't get her hopes up. And she shouldn't get worried. This might not mean anything. Maybe the writer of the letter had simply seen his performance. Apparently, Harpo had gotten standing ovations every single night he was there. In all the Russian papers, they'd said that his performance was something to write home about.

Emily sat up on her arm. She reached up and let the curling little bits of tape tickle her fingertips. There were people who could go through their whole lives not knowing how things fit together, how they fit into the world, but she hadn't ever been one of those people. She needed to know. She had to find out what that letter said about Harpo.

Emily found Doran sitting by the lake. When she sat, water from the deck stairs soaked into her pants. She didn't move. She deserved to be uncomfortable. What she was doing was wrong. The first time had been a mistake, an accident, but this was inexcusable.

"I found another letter," she said quietly, and handed it over.

Then Emily watched the lake as Doran slowly flipped through the pages. "What does it say?"

"It's about Simon, Ekaterina and Doran. Doran must be me."

"Probably," said Emily. "Maybe." She didn't want to verify anything until she knew more.

"This doesn't seem to be how you spell my last name though," said Doran.

"What?" said Emily. "How is it spelled?" How stupid could she be? Of course the other last name would be there, the switch would be evident. She wanted to stand and run, had to force herself not to move.

"The writing is strange," said Doran. "I can't make it out. All the words are misspelled. The writer wasn't so literate, it seems."

Emily released her breath, relief rushing over her like a swell on the lake. "What does the letter say?"

"It says that my parents are dead."

Emily put her head on the banister, submerged again.

Doran bent to read, "'They were sent away with their little boy, all three of them.'"

Was that because they didn't have papers, identity cards? Could they have died because that book was never sent back? Emily couldn't imagine ever asking anyone those questions, not Doran, not her family, not anyone from the Russian department at the university. She had to take this back, keep Doran from knowing what he now knew. But how? Her head was blank, her thoughts, snow.

"They were sent to the north," said Doran.

Emily looked up, and the snowflakes in her head eddied.

"I think that's what this says," he said. "They were sent to a farm in the north where nothing would grow. The authorities were angry because my father had the wrong papers, it says, or he'd lost his papers, or couldn't produce them. He was the doctor in the town, and he assumed, therefore, that nobody would pay attention to what he did, what was hidden behind his office. I don't understand that, but that's what's written. That's what it says here. He thought he was more important than rules. He was wrong. He was arrogant, that's what it says, that even in the settlement, he was arrogant."

"Oh God."

"This letter, it looks like it was written by another survivor, someone who had known him before. Yes. Yes. It says right here. He'd known him in their town."

"I'm so sorry," Emily said. "Listen. You don't have to keep reading."

"He says he's not surprised that the doctor found an American to rescue his child. He's not surprised that an American sent for the whole family, and that the doctor assumed that he and his wife would make it, would survive. They didn't. This man writes that Simon and his wife are dead. The child has been cared for by the community." Doran looked at Emily. "I would say that he didn't like my father."

Emily didn't know what to say.

Blima would be heartbroken. There was no room in the family mythology for a story like that, and Blima seemed to believe those stories with a sincerity that was touching, that was heartbreaking, now that Emily thought about it, now that she saw the whole thing in context.

"I never thought they'd still be alive," said Doran.

Emily shouldn't have brought out the letter. She should never have shown it. All this for the love of Harpo Marx, a ghost, a man she'd never met, to satisfy the most useless of curiosities.

"That can't have been what I was expecting, coming here," said Doran. "That I would find them living still."

Emily could have spent this entire week keeping to herself, typing. That's what she'd imagined this trip would be like. She'd pictured herself sequestered in the room of windows, just listening to the clicking of keys. "Do you remember being there?" Still, she couldn't stop. "Do you remember being in Siberia?"

"I remember a ditch. It's less a memory than an image. It looks like the ground has a jagged scar. But it might have been a dream. When all this time has passed, it's hard to know. What's real. What I saw in books, movies. It all feels the same sometimes. That, also, is why I came. I wanted confirmation. Proof that what I'm remembering is possible."

Doran bent over the letter again. He read, "The little boy is being sent to Canada, and then to the United States where a quick adoption has been arranged, he understands. To the celebrity that has been pulling strings, it says, we cared for him well, the little boy, regardless of who his father was. We felt sorry for the woman and the boy." Doran looked up.

"The celebrity," said Emily.

"I remember him, the man the writer addresses. Although the writer is too angry to make much sense. To do much, in the way of logic."

"Who was it?" whispered Emily, but she knew. Exapno Mapcase. Harpo Marx. Doran already said that he recognized that picture of him. And Moshe had said there was a connection. Her whole body tingled. Despite the discovery, the series of awful discoveries, she was sickeningly excited.

"I remember men," said Doran. "They didn't speak to me, and I didn't speak to them. I pretended I was mute. They took me in a car, and then I'd been given to this other man. I was prepared to pretend the same with him and to go through life that way, never saying another word to another human being. But then this man, the man with the soft black hair, he knelt down and looked at me. He had a smile that was sad. It looked like love. That's what I remember."

"What's his name?"

"I remember now," said Doran. "The air was cold and wet and I was frightened. When he saw me, he closed the space between us quickly. Then he knelt and hugged me, pulled me right to him."

"Is it written there?" asked Emily. "His name?"

"As soon as the men in suits left, I talked to him. I had some English, some German and French too, and so did he."

"You spoke to Harpo."

"Yes," said Doran. "It was Harpo Marx."

Emily shrank away from the sunlight. She wished for rain. She wanted thunderclouds. The weather shouldn't be this cheerful.

"Imagine," Doran said after a silence. "Ayala sent Harpo Marx to rescue me. That makes sense though. He was there anyway, in a professional capacity. Your grandfather told me that yesterday."

Emily curled a little. Of course Moshe would have bothered Doran about that, about Harpo's visit to Russia the year of Doran's escape. Moshe had memorized Harpo's autobiography too.

"Harpo Marx performed in Russia in 1933. He was doing favours for people too, carrying letters for the government. So it makes sense. But nobody would have thought to ask him but Ayala. She was the only one who knew what to do."

"Are you mad?" whispered Emily. His father had given them all away, had given their identity cards to her family, and because of this, they'd died. She couldn't make herself say it. Maybe he didn't even know. What had he pieced together?

"I remember sitting with Harpo at the end of our journey. We were here, on these steps. He was crying. I was crying too. They wouldn't let him keep me because he wasn't married yet, and a child needs two parents. That's what they told him. He said he'd get married the second he got home. There was a girl he loved who he'd beg to be his wife. But it was too late to adopt me. There was a family who wanted me too much. And he would adopt a million children, Harpo said. There was no way he could wait nine months."

"Why did you stop coming here?" she asked.

"Sonja got married," said Doran, "and I'm a SINK."

"What?"

"Single income, no kids. SINK. So you see the problem."

Emily held the banister. She didn't see the problem. She didn't know how to tell him that. But Doran smiled, and his face was transformed. Suddenly he was almost handsome. "I don't think I missed having a wife, children," he said. "But some grandchildren, I think I might have liked that."

THE LAST HAND

HARPO, 1933

Harpo had no idea where he was. He couldn't see the lake, or the lodge, or the path. He knelt, to look at the moss on a tree, but the moss seemed to wrap around the entire trunk, so it couldn't point him south, or north, or wherever moss grew. The shadows were all stretching and pointing out some direction, but Harpo didn't know what that meant either, and didn't they turn throughout the day? What time was it, anyway?'

"Hey Harpo," came a voice from the trees.

Harpo stood. It was Chico again. His brother was magic. First Chico and then Groucho struggled through the straggly branches, and he was saved.

"We're going canoeing," said Chico.

"Let me guess," said Harpo, fighting the embarrassing need to throw his arms around his brothers. "You found another island."

"Except this time," said Groucho, "we'll all go together."

"I have cards," said Chico. "It's nice out and you're going to Russia. We thought it would be fun."

"There are only three of us," said Harpo. "We need a fourth."

"We'll think of something when we get there."

"You won't pretend that the dock is an island? It'll be different this time?"

"Of course this time will be different," said Chico.

There was a trick in this one too. There always was.

"Well?" said Chico.

"Of course I'll come," said Harpo.

Off they went onto the dark lake, Harpo slumped in the middle of
the canoe, curled up like a little kid, his brothers pulling the oars.
The dark and the rocking made Harpo close his eyes. He
remembered the fishing trip. He couldn't help it. He couldn't stop
thinking about Montauk, Long Island. He remembered the nice
part of the trip, in that other hotel, when they'd sat up and played
cards, and they'd laughed and talked until the waiter nodded off
in the corner of the room. At the time, Harpo had thought, who
could sleep? Now he understood. He knew how the waiter must
have been feeling, like he was sitting still and the whole world was
floating away from him. Maybe that was the lesson that he should
be learning. He'd survived all the hard times. He'd found a way.
So what if he'd asked for help sometimes?

"Harpo," said Chico. "Harp. Get up. You fell asleep."

"I did?" He didn't feel like he'd fallen asleep.

"You missed the card game," said Groucho. "Needless to say,
you lost."

"We've been gone for hours," said Chico. "Grouch and I
couldn't get you up, so we just paddled around. We're back now."

"Wait," said Harpo. "We're back at the lodge?" He *must* have
been sleeping. He didn't even remember turning around.

"Oh no!" said Groucho. "I see Sam on the dock."

Harpo opened his eyes, but he couldn't see anything it had
gotten so dark. Sam was waiting? Was something wrong? Oh God.
Maybe he knew what Harpo had been doing, with the lost letter,
Simon, his family. Maybe Harpo had been thinking too loud. But
wait. Those men. Harpo had forgotten all about the angry men in
the woods.

"He looks mad," said Groucho.

"We're not supposed to canoe after sunset," said Chico. "I promised we wouldn't do it again."

"Oh," said Harpo. At least it was only that. Although he still couldn't see Sam, or the lodge. He blinked and blinked but his eyes just wouldn't adjust.

"You get out," said Chico. "Talk to him. Smooth things over a bit. We'll put the canoe away."

Harpo scrambled forward and felt for the dock. If there was one person in the world he didn't want to be mad at him, that was Sam. He loved him. He still hadn't figured out how to fix his family, not really. He pulled himself up onto the dock, and looked up, but still couldn't see Sam. He couldn't see anything, not even his brothers' canoe, or the island, or the lodgehouse.

Harpo sat back on his heels. He wasn't back at Treasure Island. He wasn't on an island at all. He was alone on the dock again, afloat in the middle of the lake. But beside him, there was a deck of cards. His brothers must have thrown it after him before they'd paddled away.

Harpo shuffled the cards. It was a bit cold, but it was a nice night anyway. And this was a nice place to think. Really, his brothers had done him a favour. He could plan for the trip, finally compose that letter to Susan. But he couldn't focus on any of those things. All he could think about were the strange, still moments in his life. Looking at Frenchie, those minutes when he was pinned by the hospital bed. Frenchie was so close, but he was far away too, far away and gone, not really his father anymore. Harpo shut his eyes tight to black out the image, felt tears on his cheeks, dripping hotly. He flipped a card into the lake. It splashed quietly. The memory was gone. Then he remembered holding Minnie as her breathing caught and finally stopped, feeling alone like he'd never been alone before in his life, used up and empty like a discarded soda bottle bobbing up and down in the Hudson. He'd felt like he would never be happy again. He threw another card. It worked. That memory was gone too. The feelings also. Then he remembered looking at that wire he got from the Long Island hotel. "Trust you are a Gentile." He remembered that hot flush of shame, then being angry at himself. He should be proud to be a Jew. Trust you are Gentile… trust you are a bigot, my friend. He threw another card.

Then Harpo remembered Susan's face, that adorable nose, those red cheeks. When she laughed, she got crescent moon–shaped splotches of pink that covered her cheekbones. Suddenly, Harpo could remember exactly what Susan's face had looked like on that disastrous last date, when she'd curled up on the rug. "I guess you're not a marrying man." Harpo threw a card, then another, then another. He wanted to marry her. He was ready now. He just had one last thing to do, one last trip to Russia, this one family to save, then he'd ask her, no, beg her. He was ready.

Harpo stood. There was a hole in his heart, and it was exactly in the shape of a person. He wouldn't have thought that such a big thing could fit in such a small space, but it did.

He paced.

First, he called for Ayala, then he called for William. Then he sat down again.

Abruptly, he remembered Minnie again, Minnie from when he was little, when they lived in the tenements. Minnie lifted his face, wiped his cheeks. "Nobody can be sad all the time," she said. "Can you imagine if you cried when you woke up in the morning, and cried when you went to work, then cried when you went home and made your supper? Have you ever seen that happen? If lots of people did that, then the Hudson would overflow and all of New York City would sink. We'd all be under water. And I've never seen that happen. Have you?"

Harpo felt a bang, and, unaccountably, he looked up. He saw nothing. Stars. That was all. When he looked back down again, William was beside him. Seconds later, Ayala appeared with the canoe. She crawled up and sat on his other side.

For a moment, they just sat together, the three of them, and Harpo had a feeling of space inside his head, like there was a lot of empty air whistling around in there. He didn't know what to say.

"Harpo," Ayala whispered finally. "There is a man on the dock."

William seemed to shrink behind Harpo, like he was a little kid.

"I rather hope this man isn't a guest," said Ayala, "because I'm in my nightgown."

"This is William," said Harpo. "He's your neighbour on the island."

"I don't know him," said Ayala.

"He knows you," and all Harpo could see was the sparkle of William's watery eyes catching the moonlight. He was looking out over the lake. "William probably knows you better than anybody, minus Sam. He's like your guardian. Your foster father. He's the one who fixed the window in the room of doors. He does the plumbing when everyone's asleep. When Sam was putting up the extensions, William always used to sneak onto your property to fix the work, so it wouldn't all come crashing down."

William said nothing. Finally, Harpo broke the silence. "Okay," he said, "I'll admit it. I'm scared to go to Russia."

First William touched one of Harpo's shoulders, then Ayala touched the other.

"You're a brave man," whispered William.

"Yes," said Ayala. "Yes, precisely."

"I'm the opposite of brave," said Harpo. "I can't even travel in New York. When I went on a vacation to Long Island, they didn't let Jews in most of the hotels. I couldn't figure out what to do on my own so I lied. I put the reservations under Harpo MacMarx. My friends had to clean up the mess, find another place. What's going to happen to me in Russia? What if they don't like Jews? What if they don't like me?" What if he couldn't figure out this problem of Ayala and Simon and Sam?

"Then you'll just come home again," said Ayala. "You'll come right back here, and we'll take care of you. That's why we made the lodge." And she peeked around Harpo and spoke to William for the first time. "I would also like you to visit," she said.

"I'm not Jewish," whispered William.

"The lodge is also for Gentiles who help Jews," said Ayala. "You belong here as much as anyone."

"Thank you," said William.

"I'm in love," Harpo heard himself say. Well, he was just enumerating problems now. Enumerating! Thank you, *New York Times*, he thought bitterly. If he'd never learned that word, then maybe he wouldn't have known how to use it, wouldn't be doing this now.

"Tell us," said William.

"Her name is Susan," said Harpo, unable to stop talking for once in his life. "When I first asked her out on a date, she asked whether she could bring her mother. But then our last date didn't go well. She said she didn't think I was ready for a family."

"It's nice, being in a family," said Ayala.

"I can't think of a better thing," said William.

"Let's talk about this inside." Ayala stood up and herded them to the canoe.

"I'll meet you there," said William. "I'll take my motorized dock."

They all three bent toward William's invention, a tiny little dock with a motor, that he could use to sneak around the lake. Harpo knelt down and touched it. Suddenly, he was on his knees on the dock, his face in his hands, and he was crying, was he crying? His hands were wet, he knew that for sure. "I just want to go back," he heard himself saying. "I want go back to when I was small and my parents were big. We slept together on a mattress, and I was always in the crook of my mama's arm, and my dad and all my brothers were with me. I can never go back there again." There were hands pressed against his back. The night was cold, but those palms felt very warm.

ONE MORE ORPHAN VERTEX

EMILY, 2003

Doran paused in the doorway. "I marched in here so sure of myself," he whispered to Emily. "But now, I don't know what to say."

"Doran, our mother called you a miracle," Sonja said as she and Blima walked into the room of windows. Emily wished they hadn't shown up just now, that she hadn't invited Doran, hadn't set any of this into motion. She felt bad for what she'd done. She was sorry now. "Blima and I were just talking about the old days. Our mother always said that you should have been lost forever in Russia, but you got out."

"Yes." Doran sat straight-backed and leaning forward, like he might jump up again at any moment. Emily willed him to sit back, to calm down, to forget everything that had just happened. It didn't take an acute observer to see that he was sad. And how could he not be? How could she have shown him that?

"Our mother said that Elijah himself went back to Russia to rescue you," said Sonja, taking his hand as Doran sat down next to her. "She used to say that he was your special friend."

"I think that my parents were Ayala's friends," said Doran. "Do you remember that, Blima? Could that be true?"

"I don't know." Blima rearranged the cups and napkins on the table. She wouldn't look up. "That's something that I might remember."

"This I didn't know," said Sonja.

"I remember my father and your mother," said Doran.

Emily looked at Doran, and he was already staring at her, those milky eyes unreadable. She felt like she was buzzing again, like she'd downed a quart of coffee. She wanted to stand and run. This wasn't fair. You were only supposed to be on one side at a time.

"Maybe everything in my father's life happened because of love," Doran said after a moment. "And I don't think he cared about me less, for loving other people more."

Emily willed him to stop, stop this line of thinking, stop talking, stop everything.

"Do you remember him now?" asked Sonja. "Is that what's happening?"

"There are things I'm starting to remember," said Doran. "In one of my favourite memories, I'm sitting on a stair beside him. We didn't sit together like that often—he was a busy man. I sat very still even though the floor was cold. I was afraid that if I moved too much, he'd stand up and walk away—I thought, at first, that he didn't remember I was there. But then he turned and looked right at me. He said to me, 'The heart has two ventricles.' He was a doctor, you see. He said, 'Everyone should have two loves in their life, to fill both ventricles up.' He said he had my love in one ventricle, the right one. He didn't tell me whose was in the other."

"That's funny," said Sonja. "That's what our mother always said. She talked about ventricles too."

"Did she love him?" whispered Blima. "Did our mother love your father?"

"That's what ventricles are for, my father said. To be a reservoir for love. I didn't remember anything until I turned seventy-three, and then it all started coming back to me."

"I have the opposite problem," said Blima. "I couldn't ever

forget. I tried to. But then I turned seventy, and I'm losing everything, it's all leaking away. I don't even know what these memories are that used to upset me so much. I remember the feeling of them. The dread. But nothing more."

"I used to think I was losing my father again every time I remembered him," said Doran, "but it's the opposite. I have to keep reminding myself of that. There's a measure of love that comes with all these memories. I remember looking up at him, a tall man, towering, and I remember the breathtaking adoration and fear. And I was happy with my adopted family, happier than I'd ever been in Russia, even in the good times. My adopted father spent time with me on purpose."

"Well isn't this turning out to be a party?" said Sonja.

"There are some things that I still remember," whispered Blima. "I remember sitting in your apartment, Doran. When our family left, she loved him still. She wrote him letters. I was afraid they might be love letters. I felt sure they were. She didn't like going outside then, could never go all the way to town. So she asked me to mail them. Of course, I never did. I was afraid that my own family would come undone, that I'd be given away."

Emily looked at the floor, didn't want to make eye contact with anybody. Maybe Grandma Ayala hadn't hidden the package. Maybe Blima had done it. Blima must have been given the package to mail, and had hidden it instead, and she wouldn't have been older than five or six when they first got here. She wouldn't have known what was inside. She wouldn't have understood the significance if she had.

But what did Doran understand of this?

"This also," said Sonja. "I didn't know this either."

"I feel just terrible," said Blima. "I should have sent them."

"You shouldn't think about it," said Doran. "He must have died not long after you left. He wouldn't have been around to get a letter. Did you know? Many people did survive. There are hidden churches in Siberia, still, hidden synagogues too, through secret doors. Every building there is one third bigger than the authorities believed because all the interior spaces were hidden."

"Wait," said Sonja. "There were love letters? Our mother and Doran's father? You thought they were having a romance?"

Emily looked at Sonja and Doran. "Does anyone else in the family have blond hair?"

"I don't think so," said Blima.

"Sonja and Doran both have very light eyes," said Emily. She thought that this story couldn't be any worse. "What if you two are related?"

Sonja dropped Doran's hand. She pulled her arm away.

Emily didn't let herself breathe. She shifted slightly, winced at the squeak of leather. She didn't want to call any more attention to herself. She shouldn't have said anything. Maybe she shouldn't have come back here at all.

Finally, Blima sat up. "So what?"

"Blima," breathed Sonja, "this is terrible."

"Why? You were thinking of having sex?"

"Blima," whispered Sonja.

Emily held her breath. What had she done?

Doran stood.

Then Sonja stood too. She turned to Emily. Her cheeks were red, her lips pressed into a thin line. "Is that what you were looking to find?" she asked. "Was this the purpose of your trip?"

"Let's be honest here for a moment," said Blima. "Are you worried about having deformed children? Because I hate to tell you this, Sonja, but you're almost eighty years old. There is no risk of children. And nobody knows about this but us. You can do anything you want. And besides, we're all Russian royalty here."

Doran chuckled a little. "That's true." But then he bowed, first to Sonja, then to Emily and Blima. And then he shuffled up the stairs.

Then Sonja left too, Blima close behind her.

Emily curled up in her seat. This wasn't what she was

hoping to find. Now Jonah was mad at her, and her beloved grandmother and great-aunt wouldn't even make eye contact. She wasn't connected to anyone at all anymore. She was the orphan vertex now.

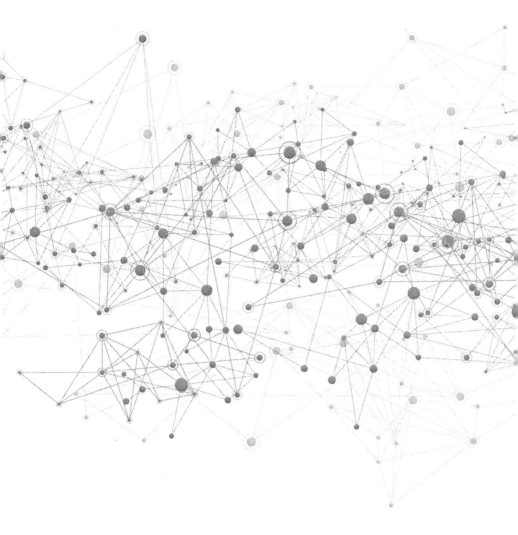

THE EIGHTH DAY (OR THE SEVENTH DAY OF PASSOVER)

DON'T LEAVE

EMILY, 2003

Emily kind of knew that she was dreaming, but that wasn't important. What was important was that she not wake up.

Harpo was standing in front of her, and Emily couldn't decide what to do. She knew that she wanted to close the space between them, but how? How could she do it without scaring him away? What if she spooked him and he remembered that he was dead? This was a fragile moment. He couldn't disappear again. She wouldn't let that happen.

Abruptly, Harpo fixed the problem. He closed the four steps between them all in a rush, grabbed Emily under the arms and hugged her tightly, lifting her bodily off the ground. He felt incredibly solid. She could feel his back under his coat, the muscles moving as he lifted her up higher. Then he put her down again. Emily didn't let go. She just hugged him tighter. The fabric of his coat was soft, so much softer than it looked in the movies.

"I've been looking for you," Emily said into the raincoat. She hugged him tighter still and felt an answering pressure, Harpo's hands on her back. She'd wanted him to hug her so badly. She realized now, that's all she'd really wanted. "Please don't go."

Now Emily was awake. She was lying in bed, watching lights play on her ceiling, and these were the things that she knew. She was alone. Harpo Marx wasn't here, and he wouldn't fix anything. So she tiptoed out of her room, and that's when she saw Doran walking down the stairs, dragging a suitcase. He saw her, stopped, and put a hand on her cheek.

"Do you have to leave?" asked Emily.

"I'll be back," said Doran. "I'll come soon, and for a much longer stay. I'll bring more things. See how long I can impose myself. If I can't make myself into family too."

Emily watched Doran walk out the door, and fought to get control of her breathing, of her feelings, of all these things that she knew now that she couldn't unknow. She'd inflicted some of the knowledge on other people too. That was the worst part. Some people preferred to go through life not knowing, and who was to say they weren't the smarter ones.

Sonja sidled up beside her. "You're sad to see Doran go?"

"Do you forgive me?" whispered Emily.

"Of course I love you," said Sonja.

Emily nodded, mute. Classic deflection. Loved and forgiven were two different things.

"Everyone seems to miss Doran terribly," said Sonja. "It's funny, because I'm the one who should miss him the most, and I feel oddly free."

"He said he's coming back," said Blima.

"Oh yes," said Sonja. "I should have mentioned. He said he'll be back in a few weeks."

"Will he really come?" asked Emily.

Sonja just shrugged.

"Of course he'll come," said Blima. "He's family. He was our mother's special friend."

"Emily," said Sonja, "do you know who else was our mother's special friend?"

"No," said Emily.

"Harpo," said Sonja. "Now I'm remembering things too. I don't like to be excluded. Harpo Marx was our mother's special friend. I remember that now."

"Oh yeah," said Emily. "Bubbie Blima told me."

"She cried when he died, you know," said Sonja.

"I didn't know that," said Blima.

"You were too busy crying to notice. You couldn't see anything through your own tears."

Emily heard footsteps on the staircase, Doran trundling back up for a last look, maybe. She rounded on Blima. "I thought you were mad at Harpo."

"Only for one day," said Blima. "You can get mad at a person and still be his friend after that. You can still love him terribly."

Emily heard the front door click shut. She looked at Blima, who was looking out toward the door, watching the empty space with an expression that Emily couldn't decipher. Suddenly, Emily felt electric. What did *Blima* know? Had she looked at that package since she'd hidden it so many years ago? She wouldn't have understood then, but she would now. But she'd hidden the thing decades ago, seventy years at least, maybe more. Maybe she didn't remember where she'd put it. Maybe she didn't remember doing it at all.

Blima sat heavily. "Our mother had two ventricles," she said. "One had love for a man, either Doran's father or ours. The other ventricle had love for you, Sonja."

"That's not true," said Sonja. "It was for both her girls."

"She loved you more. Me, she used to boss around. Microwave the soup. Turn on the element. Make coffee. Check the stove."

"I have a letter I want to show you," said Sonja. "Mackie and I were looking for whatever *meshugas* you needed and she found this letter instead. Mackie found it in her mother's old things." She pulled a letter out of her purse, carefully unfolded it and scanned the contents. "Let me get to the good part," she said.

"I don't want to hear it," said Blima.

"'Well, I've just learned that my farts can be heard over the phone,'" read Sonja.

"Grandma Ayala wrote letters about farts?" asked Emily.

"'I'm writing to apologize to you,'" Sonja went on. "'I'm not calling you because I don't want to embarrass myself further. Also, I'm not sure what else can be heard over the telephone lines. Technology is a dangerous thing.'"

Blima reached for the letter. "I didn't know she wrote about that. Let me see it."

Sonja stood. "'What about thoughts?'" she read. "'Sometimes you pick up the telephone and you hear someone else talking. My Blima tells me that it's the wires that are crossing somewhere, but what if it's someone thinking? It could happen that sometimes our thoughts happen at the frequency of a telephone.'"

Sonja walked away, holding the letter up, away from her sister.

"It's true, Emily," said Blima. "Our mother didn't know that other people could hear these things. Her hearing was going, and she didn't know that just because she couldn't hear it anymore didn't mean that everyone else couldn't hear it."

"Our mother was a hoot," said Sonja.

"The guests would laugh," said Blima. "She'd leave the dining room, then there would be a second, two, then everyone in the room would burst into laughter. Everyone loved our mother. You couldn't not. You could hear her giggling down the hallway and we'd all just laugh louder. Those were good times."

"'I'm going to use this to my advantage,'" said Sonja, reading again. "'What if sometimes our thoughts travel at the very same frequency as a microwave? Would our appliances talk too? So I'm encouraging Blima to use the kitchen appliances as much as possible. Make more coffee—in case the coffee machine can talk. Roast the beans yourself—in case it's the stove that can hear my thoughts. Heat the soup. Run the dishwasher. I imagine that while she's in the kitchen, she's hearing a chorus of *I love you* from all the machines, because I'm not good at saying it anymore. I used to get help, but now Harpo is gone.'"

"Harpo?" said Emily. "What did she say about Harpo?"

"Our mother really wrote this?" asked Blima.

"'Harpo cut up all the lodge love letters,'" read Sonja, "'and then he taped *I love you* all over the underside of the table.'"

"That was him?" asked Emily.

"'So I could take my daughter under the table. Harpo made me a script. Then I started writing it myself and taping it up there. But Blima is an adult now, and married, so she won't follow me anymore. So we'll just drink more coffee instead, just in case the coffee maker can help me say *I love you*."

"Harpo did that?" said Emily, her voice catching, barely a whisper.

"'When Blima was a little girl, she used to draw me beautiful pictures,'" Sonja read. "'I put them all in my underwear drawer so I could look at them every morning because it's been a long time since I forgot to put on panties. After all these years, I still look at those pictures every day.'"

"This is real?" whispered Blima. "That was Elijah the prophet that I drew for her. I knew how much she loved him."

"The farts," said Sonja, looking up. "I'm the one who told her. She used to do it in elevators too. One day, we were at the mall, going down to where you park all the cars, and I had to tell her, 'Mom, I can hear that. Everyone else can too.' And she said she had no idea. She just giggled. She was just naturally funny."

"I want to read more letters," said Blima.

"Yes," said Sonja. "Me too. No, let's look at the photo albums." Then they stood and walked out of the room arm in arm, and left Emily alone.

As Emily was tiptoeing back to her room, she realized there was a room that she hadn't explored yet: the attic. She grabbed her computer and crept up the stairs.

Emily sat down on the cot and started her computer. She'd been working so diligently on these symptoms for the past few days. So maybe she could be honest now, tell Russell her real worries.

"Dear Russell," she wrote, and stared down at her computer. She didn't believe that her research showed anything. The numbers were great, but they didn't prove what everyone said they proved, or anything at all. She'd shown that there were tenuous connections between people, but she couldn't show influence. She should be focusing on genealogy, or including it at least. Because family influenced you. Even after they were gone, they lodged inside you and forced you to change and change and change. But that wasn't math. Jonah was right. There was no way to show it empirically.

When Blima walked up to the attic, Emily heard her coming, heard her footsteps from miles away. And she knew it was her grandmother coming to sit with her. She was relieved.

"I think he'll be back," said Blima, as she sat down beside Emily. "He'll come next year at the very least. I think this might be our tradition now."

"How about we set a place for him no matter what?"

Blima cupped Emily's cheek. "Yes," she said. "We'll extend the table. We'll set places for Elijah and Harpo too, and we should have been doing this for years. Why didn't I ever think to do that before? We should always set the table for everyone, living and dead."

"For Great-grandma Ayala."

"And for my father," said Blima. "Your old Papa Sam. He died when you were still so young. You would have loved him. He was like Harpo. Everyone in Kingston cried the day he died. I thought that Treasure Island would sink, and all of Ontario would be under water. Someone told me once that this could never happen, but I thought at the time 'today's the day.'"

"I want to hear the real love story of Auntie Sonja and my great-uncle," said Emily. "I'm ready now."

Blima settled onto the bed, and rusty springs cried out discordantly. "Our mother made Sonja marry your great-uncle. The marriage was arranged."

"No," said Emily.

"Sonja was boy crazy. That part of the story was true. She did go on a date with a different man every night. So our mother gave her a choice. Marriage, or boarding school."

"I can't think of anything worse."

"Arranged marriage doesn't mean that they didn't love each other. And it doesn't mean that Sonja didn't get a choice. For all her faults, our mother was good with people. She knew how to match. She got right with me too."

"What?" And Emily felt like she'd run over a speed bump, hit the bottom of a roller coaster, that the world was shifting and rearranging all around her.

"Of course I love your Papa. We've loved each other since I was eight years old and he was nine. And Ayala didn't arrange the marriage exactly, I mean, it wasn't an actual *shidduch*. But she did hint at it an awful lot. She always said, 'You should marry that boy.' I regret that I never told her that she was right. It was my fault anyway. I saw Doran and Sonja on the dock and told. Two weeks later, my sister was married. I should have known it was for a reason. I should have trusted my mother more. I loved her. I hope she knew that."

"I can't believe all this."

"Wait," said Blima, reaching into her pocket. "I have something for you. A special treat since you're too old for the afikomen." She handed her a letter. "It was given to me by Harpo Marx."

Emily unfolded it. It said *L* and that was it. "What is this?"

"It's a love letter," said Blima, as if that explained everything.

IT HURTS WHEN EVERYONE YOU LOVE IS TRYING TO GIVE YOU AWAY

BLIMA, 1933

Blima ran out into the woods. For forty-three days, they'd been happy, all of them, her mother included, but now there was a little boy who could ruin everything. She didn't know what to do. She needed help. She needed something. Or somebody.

She skidded down into the clearing, and there he was, Harpo sitting on the dock with his pants rolled up and his feet in the water, sitting still with a letter in his hands, just like the last time Blima saw him. Except this time, he'd come to the lodge with an extra suitcase and a little boy, the blue-eyed one from before. Also, he was holding a pen and a paper. Who could write a letter at a time like this?

Harpo shifted and Blima froze, and suddenly, they were playing a game of red light green light, and that would be the answer. If she won the game, then that would be a sign, Harpo would be able to help her. Maybe he'd brought the boy by accident.

When Harpo looked down again, Blima crept forward. She was winning and he didn't even know. When she got right behind him, she knelt. Maybe she'd be able to read the whole letter before he even noticed her, that would mean that she'd won for sure. But the letter was just an empty page, with a "Dear Susan" written at the top, and that was it. Blima sighed, sat down loudly and ended the game.

Harpo wheeled around. "I've been wondering when you would show up," he said, pulling her into a hug. "I've missed you. I've been looking for you everywhere."

"You were looking for my mother," said Blima. "I heard you when you came in."

"I have presents for you. But I have something I need to give your mother also." Harpo looked out at the lake. He looked sad. So probably he'd brought them socks. They lapsed into silence. Then, "I don't want to be Harpo the Postman anymore."

Blima felt a chill. "What do you mean?"

"I thought mailmen could choose to only deliver good news."

Even though it was a warm day, Blima felt freezing cold. She scrambled to her feet. Harpo had a letter to deliver. She saw it now. He was holding it in his other hand, under the blank sheet of paper. The letter was a bad one, it had to be. She had to get to her mother first. She turned and tore back to the lodge.

Blima ran up to the attic, heaving to breathe, forcing her feet to go up and up and up. It wasn't locked. Maybe she was still safe.

Blima threw the door open. Her mother wasn't there. There was just a little boy sitting on the bed, staring at her with big blue eyes flickering like the shallows. The boy she remembered. She backed away.

By the time Blima got downstairs again, it was too late. They were standing together in registration, Harpo and her mother, looking solemn. Why was he doing this? He was supposed to be her friend.

Blima tucked herself into the space between the open dining-room door and the wall.

Harpo extended the letter to Ayala. Blima willed time to stop.

But it didn't. Her mother took the letter, read it, then turned and walked up the stairs.

Blima leaned her forehead against the wall. The next few days, she knew, would be punctuated by hammer bangs like exclamation marks after every panicky thought. Her father would try to pry open the attic room. Blima would be scared that her mother would die because of no food or water. Nobody would talk to anybody else, there would be no eye contact in the entire family. Nobody would see their mother at all. She knew how to stuff things between all the door hinges.

When the attic door closed with a pop, Blima fled. Harpo saw her come out of the hiding place, she knew, but she didn't care. He called after her, but she didn't even slow down.

Blima sat down on her bed. She needed a plan. She imagined that the whirlwind of God appeared in her bedroom. If Elijah came right now, she would kiss him right on the mouth, just like she saw Mr. and Mrs. Levi do that one time in the back of the kitchen, behind all the crates. She pictured kissing the boy called Moshe, and she felt that wave of dizziness she got on Passover sometimes when she took too many sips from her dad's wineglass. She slid off the bed. That wouldn't do. She couldn't be dizzy for the rest of her life. Also, she wouldn't let the family break apart like that little attic boy's had. Moshe was the one they were all trying to give her away to.

Blima hopped off her bed and ran around the room, around and around again to see if she could cause the whirlwind herself and summon Elijah to come to her. Maybe this time it would work. If he came, then he would lead her mother out of the attic. Also, he wouldn't let Blima be given away.

Then Blima heard a knock at the door. She froze.

"Blima?" came Harpo's whispered voice.

Blima turned away. What if Harpo the Postman was here to deliver all the bad letters?

"Blima?"

She couldn't let that happen. She'd been guarding the last one for years, forever, and her mother would be so angry if she found out she'd never posted it. She had to get to it first. She climbed up onto the windowsill. Then she scooted outside, banged her knee as she swung herself around the window frame. She froze again, perched and wobbling, but there wasn't any response from outside the door. She hopped off the window ledge, right down to the garden. She ran around the lodgehouse and to the registration entrance.

Blima tore inside the lodgehouse again, ran from the mud room to the stairway to the dining room so fast that Mr. Echelstone the mailman, who wasn't the normal kind of Christian, shouted that she was probably possessed. She skidded into the room of doors, and stopped. Nobody was around. She crawled under the table, retrieved the package, and slid it under her shirt, tucked it into her pants. She ran off again, but this time, she didn't know where to go. She wheeled from hallway to hallway. Nowhere was safe.

When Harpo visited last, the world had opened up. Her mother had turned into her plain old mother again, weird but okay on the whole, not the pale ghost who hid from people and said things that were mean. And they'd had friends again, all of a sudden — Papa William, Mackie's mother and Mackie. Mackie had freckles everywhere, even on the backs of her hands. She was perfect. She was Blima's best friend now, it would even count in school, she'd said, in a promise that involved *fingers*.

Blima slid into the dining room. The package crinkled as she moved. Blima closed her eyes and wished for it to hush, please hush, someone might hear, and what if there were even more letters? Who knew what might be written in those things? Well Blima wouldn't let this new life go. She'd get Elijah. She ran in a circle, all around the room, and she prayed *hard*.

She paused and looked back but nothing was happening yet. No wind was swirling, no funnel clouds descending. Maybe she wasn't running fast enough. She made herself go faster, right into the room of windows. She whipped behind one chair and then another and then another, then dropped to her knees and scrambled behind the couches, and then she was blocked. There were people here, Harpo's brothers. She shifted to listen. The letter crinkled menacingly.

"I need a nine-letter word for overflowing with happiness," said one of the brothers from on the couch. Blima heard a newspaper sound. Crossword puzzles! They played those now, ever since Harpo.

"That's easy," said the other brother. "Chico Marx."

"I don't want to hear about your assignation last night."

"You do want to hear about that ass."

Curse word!

"Wait, I got it," said the first brother. "*Ebullient.* Nine letters. Overflowing with happiness."

"Now you have to use it in a sentence," said the other.

"Now you have to get lost," said the first brother, and there was a commotion, a rustling of newspapers, and then Blima heard her sister's giggles, and the commotion sounds got louder and weirder and everyone was talking all at once so she took the opportunity to crawl out from behind the couch.

But she got caught.

"Well look what we have here," said one of the brothers, a grown-up man who looked exactly like Harpo. This one was either Groucho or Chico.

Blima stood up. She held her shirt over the envelope.

"Hiya, monkey," said the second brother. This one was kneeling down, already holding Sonja around the shoulders. "Did you happen to see the newspaper this morning?" He pointed to the paper that was splayed out on the floor, at the picture of two tanks like giant tin cans rolling over a cobblestone street. "Did you happen to see what's on the front page?"

"Yes," said Blima.

The man waggled his eyebrows. He was Groucho then. He was in disguise as a normal person, but the eyebrows always gave him away.

"What's the picture on the front page?" asked Groucho.

"Tanks," said Blima.

"You're welcome!" said Groucho.

Blima giggled nervously, and then Sonja pressed her face to her ear. "That's because tanks sounds like thanks."

Blima turned. "I got it," she hissed, and now she did.

"Harpo was looking for you," Groucho said to Blima. "Last I saw, he was outside talking to your father. I think he's pretending to be an architect. It's going to be a disaster. If you go out there, make sure to put on a hard hat."

When Blima got out to the hallway, Harpo was already there, hovering in a doorway. She hid. And so when Moshe walked by, Harpo knelt down in front of him instead.

"Wait," said Harpo. "I know about you. Ayala was telling me. You're Moshe, Blima's friend. I think you should marry her."

Blima pressed herself against the wall.

"Mister Harpo," said Moshe. "I'm only nine."

"I don't mean right now. I mean eventually. I'm just telling you. Don't wait too long. You shouldn't let things get too complicated. I let things get too complicated."

Blima tore out of the lodge, blinking tears out of her eyes. Nobody knew how much it hurt when everyone you loved was trying to give you away.

She grabbed onto a tree and used it to rocket herself forward. It was getting hard to make herself run now. But she had to go go go, so she stumbled onward. She was rounding a bend in the path, when she heard people talking. She crouched down behind the shrubs. Just to take a small break. Just to catch her breath. Plus she was curious. There were people in the woods, and they were holding things and talking in hushed voices. Blima edged nearer. And then she saw it. One of the men was holding an axe. The metal blade winked menacingly. These were bad men, bullies, Blima could tell by the tone of their voices, their rough laughter, why hadn't she heard that boiling anger before?

She tucked herself behind the ferns and saplings. This was it, the danger that her mother was always telling her about, and it was exactly where she'd said it would be too, just past the equipment shed.

She backed away slowly. But then one of the men saw her. He whooshed toward her, grabbed her arm, and dragged her out into the clearing, squeezing tight.

Another man bent toward her. "Is she one of them?" he asked, his breath sour and terrible.

"Let's see if they'll Jew us out of the ransom," said the first man. "She might not be worth that much to them." Then he tightened his grip on her arm, and then they were moving, and Blima was trying not to cry. What *was* she worth to her family? They had told her not to wander away. She'd been disobeying rules all day.

Then there was a commotion, Blima couldn't see what was happening. All of a sudden, she was sitting on the ground. Then the man who'd been holding her went wheeling into the trees, and he fell too.

Blima stood up. Harpo was there. That's what had happened. Harpo had saved her. He'd pushed the man away.

Now the bad man was standing up again, and the rest of them were gathering around him too, all advancing on Harpo with their axes and bats of wood.

There was a sound like a shot, like an explosion. Blima fell to her knees again. The bad men wobbled on their feet too.

"He's got a gun," said the bad man.

"Um," said Harpo. "Yeah. That's exactly what happened." He pointed his finger and raised it at them. "Get out of here, or I'll shoot all the rest of you too."

The men ran into the trees. Harpo ran over and hugged Blima tightly. "It's okay," he called out. "I've got her."

Blima struggled out of his arms. "What's happening?"

"Are you okay?"

"How did you get here? How did you know to come?"

"Thank God we did this," he said. "Thank God I was looking for you. I sent my brothers on a walk with your little sister, but I needed to make sure you were safe. Your dad asked me not to evacuate the rest of the guests. He says he doesn't want to disturb anyone's stay. But I needed to find you, at least."

"What would disturb their stay?"

"I can't believe those men touched you."

Just then, Blima noticed how pale Harpo was. His face was covered in sweat. That's how her dad looked you know when, when he was kneeling with his head against the attic door, holding his pliers like the hidden old Russian men used to hold their Torah books.

"I'm okay, Harpo," she said.

"If I'd really had a gun, they wouldn't have stood a chance."

"You saved me anyway."

Harpo put a hand on her head. Just then, Blima heard the sound again. There was a click, and then another sound, and then another.

There was a muffled noise and the ground seemed to drop away, like when you put your foot in a canoe and the canoe sinks into the water. Blima felt like she was falling, even though she was standing on the grass. She stumbled into Harpo. There was another deep shaking and Harpo dropped to his knees and pulled Blima close. And then Blima was curled up and Harpo was crouched on top of her, and the whole island seemed to rock.

Then there was another loud sound, a sound like a big explosion, and, for some reason, Blima looked up. She saw flights of birds like a blanket over the lodgehouse. They shifted and covered the entire sky, a squirming, writhing sheet, flapping and billowing out in sections just like a blanket caught in the wind. They stayed that way for a minute, two, and then they dispersed, and they were birds again, flapping and squawking around the island.

Then Blima looked back to the lodgehouse. There was a cloud of dust in the air, so thick she couldn't see the bottom floor or part of the second storey. That was one half of the lodge, swallowed up and gone. But it couldn't really be gone, otherwise the second storey would have tumbled down. Whole pieces of a house didn't just hover in mid-air. There were laws against that. Plus now there was a stream of guests coming onto the porch and crowding onto the lawn, and they had to be coming from somewhere. Blima could hardly hear them though. She felt like she had cotton in her ears, like there were pillows pressed against both sides of her head.

Halfway between Blima and the porch, Dad and Papa William were hugging each other and whooping. And then Blima realized that Harpo was still crouched, still hugging her, hiding his face in her jacket. "Did the house cave in?" he whispered. "You can tell me. I can take it."

"Everything is still there," said Blima.

"Did it fall over? Did the first floor crumble?"

"What just happened?"

The wall of white dust began to settle, but now all the things were white. Everything looked ghostly, the shrubs, the trees, the stones leading out to the dock. All the people on the lawn even, they were covered in white dust and whispering. There were no sounds above a hush, and Blima felt that was okay because her ears needed to pop anyway.

That's when she looked up at the attic. There was her mom's face, pale as the moon. Her mother turned and walked away, and Blima couldn't see her anymore.

Blima remembered the package, reached under her shirt to make sure that it was still there. It was.

"Is it a disaster?" asked Harpo.

"The lodgehouse looks exactly the same," said Blima. "Except there's dust everywhere."

"Your dad and William just made a basement," Harpo said,

peeking around her. "And I think it might have actually worked."

"A basement," said Blima. "Wait, that's the same as a cellar."

"If it hadn't worked, then I think the whole house would have fallen in."

"They made a cellar in our house?"

"Monkey, it's your job to make sure that your daddy never listens to anything I say ever again."

"Okay." But this was sort of a miracle too. A cellar. That would have to make her mother happy. "We can make root beer now."

"How could I have known that William had explosives just lying around?"

"Also, we can make sauerkraut."

They both watched Dad and Papa William and all the guests inspect the house. Dad looked around, and when he saw Harpo, he flashed him a thumbs-up. And even though her dad's face was white with plaster dust, Blima could see that it was ebullient. Ebullient! Overflowing with happiness. She'd used it in a sentence. She'd have to tell Chico and Groucho.

"I've been thinking about it," said Harpo. "It's probably safer if you never let me tell anybody anything at all."

But before Blima could answer, there was a clap, the sound of a door being thrown open. They both turned back to the lodgehouse. And just then her mom ran out the back door, holding the hand of the little boy. Ayala picked him up and walked down the steps, and she was covered in white, and Blima didn't know what to think. She was outside. That was good. But she might be mad. She didn't like being dusty.

Her mom turned back to the house, and her dad caught up to her, and whispered in her ear.

Then there was a silence.

Then Ayala laughed, high and loud and lilting. It was a musical sound. It was happy. Everyone turned to watch. Nobody pretended they didn't see. And for a minute, that laugh was the only sound on the island.

Groucho and Chico staggered out of the lodge, down the stairs and right toward them. They looked like monsters, all streaked with dirt. Blima hugged Harpo's leg.

"I thought you were going for a walk," said Harpo.

"What happened here?" asked Groucho.

"I think I got a backer," said Chico, interrupting. "Well, we're in talks anyway. We're thinking, the Marx Brothers take over an opera. You wanted to rip up letters, how about you rip off costumes instead? The dancers are running onto the stage, you catch them as they come in and you rip off all their skirts. You wanted to change around a story, we can mess up an opera plot, tear pages out of the score."

They all walked back toward the equipment shed, Harpo, Chico and Groucho talking excitedly, and Blima trying to tug at Harpo's shirt. It wasn't safe in the forest. They both knew it now. And these were the brothers who'd left him all alone in the middle of a lake.

When they got to the equipment shed, the brothers stopped.

"Hey Harpo," said Groucho. "We still haven't been on a proper canoe trip, the three of us."

"I had a premonition you would say that," said Harpo.

"Premonition!" said Groucho. "Good man."

Blima grabbed Harpo's leg, thinking 'danger!' These brothers always left him on the dock!

"So what do you say?" said Chico.

"Of course," said Harpo. Then he knelt in front of Blima. "I want you to watch this," he whispered in her ear. "You don't have to get your mother this time."

Blima held a tree and watched as the brothers paddled Harpo to the middle of the lake and left him on the dock again. This was mischief. She was a witness. She didn't know what to do about it though because both her mom and dad were busy now.

Then Harpo jumped off the dock and Blima heard the sound of a motor. It was Papa William's motor-dock. He must have stashed it away there this morning. Harpo skidded out into the lake on the motor-dock, faster than the brothers could paddle, and he turned circles around them, whooping like a loon.

EVERYONE NEEDS SOMEONE

EMILY, 2003

Emily walked toward the laundry room. She'd send the thesis tonight. She had no choice. But what would she include in it? Sonja might have been in love with someone else instead of her uncle, might have been in love with her own half-brother. Her life was modelled after Greek tragedy, or could have been. Emily had followed the connections. She'd found out more about the family, but now she felt worse. Plus, math had betrayed her. Family traditions and the scientific method too. Maybe secrets were secrets precisely because nobody *should* know them. Maybe the very idea of connection was a false one. What did anyone know about anyone else, really? Maybe she wasn't lonelier than other people. It could be that she was just a little more honest.

Emily slowed when she saw the open laundry-room door, crept into the room, to where Jonah was folding clothes.

"So what did the letter say?" he asked after a moment.

"I wish I hadn't found it," said Emily, hanging onto the doorway.

"I have rugelach."

"Oh God," said Emily. "I can't break Passover now. I did something horrible, so now I have to do something that isn't wrong."

"I didn't mean that you should eat it." Jonah opened the bag quickly. "I thought we could throw pieces of it into the water bucket. Like on Yom Kippur."

"When we throw pieces of bread into the river? And think about our sins?"

"Oh," said Jonah. "I'm sorry. I didn't realize that's why we did it. It was Jazzy's idea."

"Jazzy wanted to throw bread in a bucket?"

"She has bad days sometimes. I think she wants to get rid of worries too."

Emily pulled out a pastry. "I think it's perfect, Jazzy. This is exactly what I need to do."

"You can tell Jazzy anything," said Jonah. "You know that."

Emily ripped off a piece of rugelach and threw it into the water. She turned to Jazzy because maybe Jonah was right, maybe that newspaper had been telling her to confide in inanimate objects all along. "I found papers in the book," she told the lamp. "They were personal identity papers, folded inside. So I took the letter to Doran. I suspected that it talked about a terrible thing that our family did to his. I knew that I shouldn't show it to him, but I asked him to read it to me anyway."

"What happened?" asked Jonah, and then he picked up Jazzy and held her in front of his face. "I mean... What happened to Doran's family?"

Emily threw another piece. It clanged off the side of the bucket. "When the people in their town went after the Jews, Doran's father gave Grandma Ayala his papers. They traded names. And then Doran's family died, and they never traded back." Emily ripped another rugelach apart. But some sins were too big to assign to bread.

"That sounds like Doran's family did something good, "said Jonah, "not that your family did something bad."

"You don't understand," said Emily. "They didn't make it out."

"Your family didn't kill them," Jonah said mildly.

They threw pieces of pastry in silence.

"So how's the flu?" asked Jonah.

"It's progressed. It's basically Ebola now. Speaking of my potential firing, how is the lodge doing?"

Jonah shrugged. "Better than you'd think, I guess," he said after a minute. "They get a lot of sentimental traffic, after obits especially."

"Everyone remembers the lodge in their obit."

"It's not what it was. People don't have to stay here. Jews can go other places now."

"So how does it keep going?"

"The money comes from their investments," said Jonah. "You won't get fired though."

"The thing is, I used to be on a track. You do well in high school, get into a good university, then grad school. But that's done now. I'll never just know what to do again."

"Maybe you just need to think bigger with your math. When the Marx Brothers were kicked out of vaudeville theatres, that's what they did. They shot for Broadway, and they broke through. Maybe you should do the math equivalent of that."

"How did you know about the Marx Brothers?"

"Moshe lent me Harpo's autobiography."

Emily laughed. Of course he did. "Maybe I don't need to think bigger. Maybe I should just think different."

"What do you mean?"

"Do you think there could be a future here? What if we tried to bring in younger guests? We can make this place a safe haven for lost people."

"Finance is a kind of math," said Jonah. "Isn't it?"

Abruptly, Emily remembered her dream, felt Harpo's hands pressed against her back. "I dreamt about Harpo Marx last night."

"Yeah, why do you love him so much?" asked Jonah, putting the iron away.

"He never hurt anyone, for one thing." Emily remembered watching *A Night at the Opera* for the first time. She was little, and she followed Harpo's madcap antics like it was the only thing that mattered in the world. When the credits rolled, she felt like she'd been changed. Sure, she was quiet. But maybe that didn't mean what the adults always said. Maybe she wasn't deficient. Maybe she could be supercharged and hilarious and adorable, and maybe from that moment on, being quiet could just mean that she got away with things more. And her life had changed. Just like that. She wasn't awkward and wrong-headed anymore. She had her own little world happening, and people watching her had wanted in. People had started paying attention. "Even when he was acting mischievous, he was really cute. Who could stay mad at him?"

"I could get a wig," said Jonah.

"What?"

"It wasn't his real hair, you know."

"I knew that."

But Jonah was rifling through the clothes in a hamper. "I saw this raincoat, exactly like the one he used to wear."

"Raincoat?"

"I think I might be missing the point though."

"Some people know exactly what to do," said Emily, "and did you know that he never felt sorry for himself?" Emily always felt sorry for herself. She wanted to be as confident, as good, as the man her great-grandmother used to tell her stories about. "I love Harpo."

"That's why I bought his coat." Then Jonah put on a funny old raincoat. He raised his hands, and he looked just like Jonah in a ruined old trench coat. Emily started to back away, but he rushed forward and took her in his arms and hoisted her up just like Harpo had done in the dream.

"Dance?" he said.

"What?"

But Jonah was already spinning her, just like Harpo used to do to pretty girls in all the movies, a weird kind of waltz. He spun her more and more wildly, and Emily laughed out loud. She tripped over the ironing board and it fell with a clatter, but Jonah just held her tighter. And he was laughing too, breathlessly. She'd never seen him laugh like this, all lit up and sweaty.

"Jonah!" She could hardly see the room anymore, it was all swirling by so fast. She felt like they were standing still and the whole world was spinning around them.

They slowed, then stopped.

"Hey," said Jonah, when they'd both caught their breath again. "Do you want to go for a walk?"

"Can I invite my grandmother?" said Emily, because Harpo's wife, Susan Fleming, had said something like that when they were dating. He'd written about it in his autobiography.

"What?" said Jonah.

"Never mind."

Emily heard footsteps on the stairs above her head. It was probably Blima, running down to see what was happening down here. They'd been making a lot of noise, she suspected. So she squirmed free of Jonah's arms and ran out of the room, onto the deck, and down onto the grass. She turned. Jonah was tearing after her, just like she'd wanted him to do. She led him down to the broken-down dock.

Emily didn't think before she threw herself into the water, just felt a rush of air and then she was swimming. She looked back and saw Jonah swimming behind her, his arms moving crisp and fast, gaining on her.

Then he caught up, and she put her hands on his shoulders, and they were slick, and hard like a house. And then they were treading water together, and, just as suddenly, he'd grabbed her, and she was hugging him, and she could feel the muscles of his back working. There was a rumble of distant thunder and a strong arm around Emily's torso, and a kiss. She wasn't even kicking anymore. She wasn't afraid of going under, Jonah held her so tightly. She wasn't even afraid of what the dark clouds might bring, even though they were gathering above them like a fist.

Then he disengaged. Jonah crawled up onto the dock and helped her, hoisted her up by the arms, making her overbalance, right on top of him, her body a tent over his bigger one. Then she collapsed and felt him oof, then felt him laugh, and then she was shaking up and down, up and down, as his chest rose and fell. She sat up again, straddling him, and pressed her hands on top of his hands. She could fit both of hers inside one of his. Then she touched his arm. It was brown like toast, but all the little hairs on it were bleached white. He was beautiful.

She bent toward him, and watched her wet hair fall over his face. He blinked a bit. She bent farther, and touched her lips to his. He held his breath. Then she kissed him, a very chaste kiss like the kind a child gives, and his lips were soft and tasted like salt. She liked it. She licked them now, then kissed him again, then paused. She was reminded of Harpo again. She didn't know why. "Blima gave me a letter from Harpo Marx," she said. "She said it was a love letter. But it only had an L on it. The letter L and that was it."

"That's funny," said Jonah.

"What is?"

"L for love." Jonah reached an arm around her and pulled Emily on top of him again. "L is a love letter because it's the first letter of the word *love*."

"I get it," said Emily, and finally she did.

Jonah wrapped his arms around her.

THE LOVE LETTER

BLIMA, 1933

When Blima found Harpo again, he was at the dock, sitting quietly. She sat down beside him, carefully so that the package tucked in her pants didn't make a sound. She picked up some pebbles and sprinkled them into the water. The secret about having a secret was that you wanted to tell it, always. You wanted to talk about it so badly every second.

Harpo held up his pen. "I'm practising my letters."

"You can't fool me," said Blima. "You know how to write."

"Yeah."

"Is she pretty?"

"She's beautiful."

"Are you writing a love letter?"

"I'm trying," said Harpo.

Blima kicked at the water. She squirmed around, and pulled out the package, the love letter that she'd been hiding for so long, and silently passed it to Harpo. He put down his paper and pen, and took it.

Blima held her breath as Harpo silently pulled the book out of the envelope. Then he flipped the book open and pulled out the three crinkled sheets of paper with the faces on them, the faces of the family that her mother would rather have. That was her secret. For years, she'd kept it, but she couldn't know this fact by herself anymore. She felt tears on her cheeks. They were warm. Her mother loved another family more.

Harpo replaced the papers, and put down the book, and stared at her. His face was pale.

"My mother wants to trade me for another family," Blima whispered. "She wants to leave me and my dad and my sister. She already has her new family picked out. She asked me to post the letter, but I didn't want her to go."

"So you kept it." Harpo breathed. "Does anyone else know you have these?"

"Just me," said Blima.

"Let me take it away from you."

Blima snatched back the envelope and the book. "I need to keep them safe. The secret needs to be kept."

"Okay." Harpo nodded to himself. "Okay. Here's what we do. You put these back in their hiding place, but I need you to forget. If the secret needs to be kept, then I'll be the one to keep it. I want you to promise me that you'll lock this package away, and you'll never think about it again."

Blima stood, and tucked the envelope back into her pants.

Harpo picked up the paper again, but this time he wrote.

"You know what to write now?" asked Blima, craning her head to see.

"This is for you," said Harpo, folding the paper and handing it to her. "Not all love letters are bad. This is a love letter just for you."

Blima quickly unfolded the letter. In the middle of it, written big, was the letter *L*. "*L* for love."

"Hey," said Harpo. "You guessed it."

Acknowledgements

Many, many people helped me to write this book.

I'd like to thank my editor, Paul Vermeersch; the amazing team at Wolsak and Wynn and Hillary Rexe.

I'm also deeply grateful to all my teachers, including the entire faculty at the University of Guelph M.F.A. Program, particularly Linda Spalding, Thomas King and Catherine Bush, and Carolyn Smart at Queen's University. A special thank you to Connie Rooke. I have so much to thank her for.

I'd also like to thank readers (who helped with close readings, and inspired me with their work): my classmates at the University of Guelph M.F.A., particularly Jacob McArthur Mooney, Mia Grace Kim, Amina Farah, David James Brock, Abby Whidden, Melanie Mah, Kimberley Alcock, Jamie Forsythe, Kathy Friedman, Kathryn Husler; and my (very literary) friends, particularly Carolyn Black, Holly Kent, Amber McMillan and Katherine Arcus.

I'd also like to thank Anne Milyard for close reading, help, inspiration and mentorship.

Finally, I'd like to thank my family. Thank you to my parents, Andrea and Rainer, and to Kier, and Tai, for books, family, a boisterous childhood and adulthood. Thank you to Margaret and Ruth for telling me all the stories that inspired this novel, and who made me feel like I'd been to the Muskoka Lodge. Thank you to Jake and Oliver, who give me a place and a family to come home to.

Many, many books also helped me to write this book. This is a work of fiction, but it is informed by other people's work, including the following: *Harpo Speaks!* by Harpo Marx and Rowland Barber; *Groucho and Me, Memoirs of a Mangy Lover* and *The Groucho Letters* by Groucho Marx; *Growing up with Chico* by Maxine Marx; *My Life with Groucho* by Arthur Marx. I was also inspired by many works of fiction, but couldn't possibly list them all here.